TRAIL DRIVE

A McCabe novel

BRAD DENNISON

Author of *The Long Trail* and *Thunder*

THE McCABES
The Long Trail
One Man's Shadow
Return of the Gunhawk
Boom Town
Trail Drive
Preacher With A Gun
Johnny McCabe
Shoshone Valley
Thunder
Wandering Man
Going Home
Yesterday's Trail
Gunhawk Blood (Coming Soon)

OTHER BOOKS
Joe McCabe
Tennessee
McCabe County
Jericho
Early Trails

Editor: Donna Dennison

Copy Editor: Loretta Yike

Cover Design: Donna Dennison

To my father,
Ralph Dennison

He was instrumental in turning me toward writing. I always knew I wanted to be a storyteller but I didn't know what to do about it. He suggested I try writing a novel, and that started a path I'm still on, all these years later.

PART ONE

The Canyon

1

Johnny McCabe didn't need a clock to know it was about an hour before sunrise. He had set his mind to wake up at this time back in his days with the Texas Rangers. When you're on the trail, pursuing outlaws or renegade Comanches or Mexican border raiders, you want to be awake and already in motion by the time the eastern sky starts to lighten. His days in the Rangers were now long behind him, and he was now forty-five years old and sleeping in a warm, comfortable house with his wife beside him. But even still, old habits died hard. About an hour before sunrise, he would find himself awake, listening to the sounds around him. Ready to reach for his gun if he had to.

Jessica was buried to her shoulders in covers. Bed sheets and blankets, and a patchwork quilt. She was breathing in the slow and easy way she did when she was in a deep sleep.

Johnny sat up and swung his feet out and over to the floor. The bed creaked a little, but not enough to wake Jess up. The room was dark as Johnny wasn't one to sleep with a lamp burning low like a lot of folks did, and in the darkness he reached for his jeans where he had left them, draped over the foot of the bed.

He was in a long-handled union suit, and he slid his jeans on over it, then pulled on his boots and then folded his pant legs out and over the boots. He wore large-roweled Texas spurs and they were already strapped onto his boots. He usually just pulled his feet out of his boots at night, leaving the spurs in place.

He grabbed the range shirt he had taken off the night before, and shouldered into it. His gunbelt was draped over one corner of the foot of the bed.

In his early days with the Rangers, he had worn Paterson Colts. They were old and scratched up, but they worked. He had gotten them from an uncle who had ridden with the first incarnation of the Texas Rangers in the war with Mexico. Johnny was ten years old when his uncle returned to Pennsylvania. Those guns stayed with him when he grew up and went west, and he eventually replaced them with a pair of Remington forty-fours.

In those days, reloading a pistol took some time. If you were a man of the gun, you often carried two pistols. Or you carried spare cylinders on you. Johnny found switching cylinders to be more time-consuming than just carrying two guns, and when one gun was emptied, he pulled the loaded gun and kept on shooting.

A few years ago, Colt had come out with a revolver that could be loaded with metallic cartridges, just like a Winchester. One of these was what he now carried. This new revolver could be reloaded quickly, so his days of carrying two guns were behind him. After all, guns were heavy and cumbersome to carry around buckled around your middle.

He wrapped his gunbelt around his hips and fastened the buckle, and then tied the holster down to his leg so the holster would be held in place if he needed to pull his revolver fast.

He went out to the hallway, stepping lightly so he wouldn't wake anyone up. Though he was sure Dusty would be awake soon. Dusty had been raised on the trail by outlaws, and usually slept light and was out of bed early.

Johnny went downstairs and into the kitchen. A lamp on the table was burning low, so he turned it up enough to fill the kitchen with a pale, yellow light. Then he went to the full wood box waiting by the stove and built a fire.

Johnny's father had taught him and the boys years ago, back on the old farm in Pennsylvania, to keep the wood box full. The last thing you want is to wake up on a cold morning and have to go outside and start splitting wood while everyone is inside waiting for you.

Once a fire was burning in the stove, Johnny stepped outside the kitchen door for a taste of the morning air.

He had left his hat up in the bedroom. It was a battered old felt hat with a wide brim, and was a sort of neutral tan color. It could pretty much blend into any background. He had chosen the hat color specifically for that reason. Ginny referred to it as *desert neutral.* The jacket he wore was a similar color. Even the range shirt he was wearing.

Again, he thought about what Zack Johnson had said about him. He had been shot at once too often. Ginny had said once that he lived in a perpetual state of war.

Johnny had noticed Zack didn't really do this. His brother Matt didn't, either. Even Vic Falcone, who was now the marshal in town. Johnny's father hadn't lived this way. He hadn't chosen his clothes each day based on how well they could blend into a background.

Johnny had always been good with his guns. Even as a young boy, when his uncle gave him that first brace of Paterson Colts, Johnny had seemed to take to shooting like he was born to it. He would sometimes ride the family horse, the horse they used for plowing. He would ride bareback as they had no saddle. He would set up old tin cans on a fence and ride past them, shooting at them as the horse trotted along. Even at fourteen years old, he would hit the cans more times than not.

His uncle had shown him the border shift, and it wasn't long before he could do it better than his uncle could.

This worried his mother. She didn't want him to be one of those men who lived by the gun. Those men his uncle had ridden beside in the war with Mexico, and who had remained in the West while he returned to Pennsylvania.

And yet, here Johnny was. In a remote valley in the mountains of Montana. His ability with guns and to keep a steady hand even when bullets were flying about him had saved his life more than once.

He supposed he had become what his mother feared. Maybe she had been right to fear it. Being what he was came with a price. He had left a string of bodies that stretched back through the years, and sometimes they would come back to him in his dreams.

He couldn't guess at the number of men he had killed, but he remembered the first one. Many men he knew didn't count Indians among those they had killed, but Johnny did. The man had been a Comanche warrior. Johnny took him out of the saddle with one shot, and despite his skill with a pistol, he had done the shooting that day with a rifle. The old Colt revolving rifle that had been standard-issue among the Rangers, back in the day.

Part of the price was that he was forever on alert. He didn't seem to know how to shut off that part of his mind. When he heard a creak in the house at night, he was immediately awake, gun in hand. If Dusty or Josh got up to go downstairs and use the outhouse, they would rap a fist against Johnny's bedroom door and say, "Just me, Pa." It seemed to Johnny that sort of thing shouldn't be necessary. Yet in the McCabe household, it was.

Once he had a pot of coffee made, he crossed through the parlor and out to the front porch to stand in the cool morning air. He stood with steam rising from the coffee, and looked off into the darkness. The sun would be rising soon, and already the sky overhead was growing light enough that the stars were gone, but the ridges surrounding the valley were still just empty-looking dark voids.

He drew in a deep lungful of air. Nothing made him feel alive more than clean, mountain air.

He had spent a winter with a band of Shoshone a long time ago in this valley, and he took much of their philosophy to heart. After that winter, he had stopped cutting his hair. It was now what Ginny called *Shoshone long*. He usually tied it back with a length of rawhide, but at the moment it was hanging free about his shoulders, and as he stood outside the door, the mountain breeze caught it and moved it about.

One thing he did after that winter with the Shoshone was to keep his face clean-shaven. The Shoshone called a white man with a beard *dog face*. Even on the trail, if he had the opportunity, he would heat water and shave.

As he stood on the porch, he closed his eyes and inhaled deeply again. There was a taste of balsam on the air, and he could catch a scent of earth.

Then he was struck with a feeling, that unmistakable feeling, that he was being watched. That someone was out there somewhere in the darkness.

The eastern sky was now starting to show a little bit of gray. A hush had sort of fallen upon the land the way it often does right before dawn. As though the pine forest on the ridges that surround this valley, and all the life in that forest, were holding their collective breath to wait and see what the day would bring.

And yet, the feeling was there. That nagging feeling that someone was out there in the darkness.

Was it just that he had been shot at too many times? He wondered if he was going to turn into one of those crazy old men who saw enemies everywhere. He had seen them—men who had survived a war but continued to carry the war inside them.

He forced himself to turn away from the coming dawn, away from the feeling that someone was out there in the darkness, and stepped back into the house.

He went to the kitchen and set the cup down on the table, and then pulled out the chair he usually took at the head of the table and lowered himself into it. He didn't just drop into a chair. Never an uncontrolled movement.

He could hear Ginny's gentle footsteps making their way across the parlor floor, and she strolled into the kitchen. The woman never seemed to be hurrying. Always moving through life at a stroll, gracious and dignified, and yet always seemed to be where she needed to be.

She said, "Good morning, John."

She would refer to him as *Johnny* when she talked to someone else about him, but when she talked to the man directly, she always called him *John*.

"'Mornin'." He took a sip of coffee. "The water's hot for tea."

"Thank you."

She was in a robe, and her hair was in a long braid that fell over one shoulder and to her waist.

Ginny dumped some tea into a tea ball. Earl Grey, a blend she ordered all the way from England. She filled a small tea pot with hot water and then dumped the tea ball in to let it steep.

And all while, Johnny couldn't shake the feeling that someone had been out there in the darkness, watching the house.

2

The household gradually came to life. Ginny started breakfast going on the stove, and soon Temperance and Haley were downstairs to help her. Josh gave his father a good morning and went outside and grabbed an ax. You seldom saw Josh sit still for long. Not that there was any need at the moment to split wood, but with Josh around, there would always be a surplus.

Cora came bounding down the stairs with a delighted squeal of, "Daddy!"

Just hearing her call him that warmed his heart. He scooped her up and she wrapped her little arms around him.

Jessica stepped into the kitchen behind. She was fully dressed. She might lounge about in her nightgown and robe in the bedroom she and Johnny shared, but when she came downstairs, she was washed up and fully dressed and ready to start the day.

Johnny gave her a quick kiss, then he went upstairs to wash up and shave and grab some clean clothes.

Twenty minutes later, he was in a freshly laundered range shirt, a light gray in color. Again, it would blend well into any natural background. Desert neutral. He slid on a leather vest and tied his hair back. He checked in a mirror to look at a small nick his razor had given him on the side of his chin.

Johnny then saw his gunbelt, sprawled on the bed where he had dropped it when he came upstairs.

He picked it up and was about to buckle it back on, but then he had a thought, one he had been having almost every morning for the past couple of months. The thought of maybe leaving the gun here and just going downstairs without it. After all, Josh was outside splitting wood without a gun strapped to his leg. Last night, as they had sat in front of the fire in the parlor like they often did as a family, Josh and Dusty were both without their guns.

For years he had slept with the gun on a chair by the side of the bed and within reach. A few weeks ago, he had begun sleeping with his gun not on the chair, but in its holster slung over the foot of the bed. Should he really need the gun, he could get to it fast enough but he no longer wanted it within easy reach. He didn't know anyone else who slept that way.

The first night he had laid there in bed staring at the dark timbers overhead, aware of every sound about him. The wind outside. The crickets chirping. Dusty stepped out of his room and down the stairs to use the outhouse. He tapped the door with his hand and said, "Just me, Pa," and continued on. Johnny remained in bed and counted every step Dusty made to the back door.

The second night he had slept a little. But at one point he found himself instantly awake, thinking he had heard Cora calling for him. He snagged his gun from the gunbelt and bolted for the door.

He stopped in Cora's doorway. In the moonlight, he could see her in her bed, a tumble of covers pulled to her chin. Her eyes were closed and she was breathing easily.

Jessica came up behind him and laid a gentle hand on his arm.

He said, "I heard her calling out. Like she was afraid."

Jessica shook her head. "She's all right. She's sound asleep. Come back to bed."

They went back to their room, and Johnny sat on the edge of the bed and she sat beside him. She then did something he doubted he would allow anyone else in the world to do. He allowed her to gently take the pistol from his grasp and slide it back into the holster.

"It'll be all right," she said. "Give it time."

The third night, Johnny slept. In his dreams, he saw the faces. The men he had killed. A man in a border town, years ago. A wide brimmed hat and whiskers on his face. Grinning like an idiot as he reached for his gun. Whiskey had made him over-confident, but he must have come by his lack of brains naturally. Johnny couldn't talk him down. The man was determined to draw on him. Even then, Johnny's reputation as being too good with a gun was spreading, and this man wanted to be known as the one who had beaten him. The man's pistol cleared leather first, but it made little difference. Johnny was faster than he was. Johnny was faster than almost any man he had ever met. His pistol was cocked and pointed toward the man in half a second or less, and his gun was the only one to fire.

Then Johnny's dream shifted, and he saw ten Comanches riding down on him and Zack Johnson. Johnny was twenty years old, and Zack had taken an arrow to the leg and had fallen from his horse and hit his head on a rock.

So calmly he almost frightened himself, Johnny drew his right-hand gun and began cocking the hammer and firing. Like shooting cans from a fence. One warrior fell, then a second, and a third.

When the fifth fell, his gun was empty. In those days, they generally loaded only five cartridges, leaving an empty chamber in front of the hammer so if the gun got accidentally jarred, it wouldn't go off. With his pistol empty, he executed a border shift. The captain of the Texas Rangers whose command he was under had said he never saw a smoother one. With the fresh gun in his right hand, Johnny cocked back the hammer and was ready to fire, but the surviving Comanches had pulled their horses to a halt and were turning away.

Johnny had killed so easily. So calmly. He didn't

think about it much at the time because he had to get Zack back to the fort. Had to do so while they still had time to save his leg. But when he thought about it later, he realized he hadn't been afraid. When those Comanches had been riding down on him and firing their rifles at him, an almost unnatural calmness had come over him and he didn't even flinch as their bullets kicked up dirt at his feet.

It was this calmness that had helped him survive so many gunfights over the years. His skills at trick-shooting helped, but if you can't hold your gun hand steady when the bullets are flying, then trick-shooting won't do you a lick of good.

He had killed so many men over the years. So many bodies that stretched back and away, through his past. He had long since lost track of the number.

Last summer, Johnny had considered adding one more to the list. Aloysius Randall. Owner of the hotel in town and chair of the Town Council. Randall had tried to force his attentions onto Bree. Johnny had never killed a man who didn't need it, and he knew few who needed it more than Randall. But Bree had beaten the stuffing out of the man, so Johnny decided that would be good enough. He didn't want more blood on his hands.

To sleep without his gun within reach had been a big decision, but not as big as the one he was now considering. To go all the way downstairs without it.

He drew a deep breath. Just the thought of not having his gun with him set him on edge. But it was time. He had been living like he was in a perpetual state of war for too long.

He walked over to foot of the bed, buckled his gunbelt to itself and then hooked it around the post, and left it there.

He took a step back. He felt a little shaken, almost on the verge of panic. His stomach felt jittery. He found it a little hard to breathe.

He took another deep breath, and closed his eyes and focused on letting the air out slowly. The way the old Shoshone shaman had taught him to do when he needed to be calm. He drew in another breath, and did it again.

There was no gunman waiting outside the door to put a bullet in him. No sniper outside waiting to take a shot through the window. There were just the four walls about him, the mountain wind outside, and the family downstairs.

Johnny could hear them talking. He could hear Josh's booming laugh. Josh had apparently taken a break from the woodpile and come inside.

Johnny took another step back from the gunbelt, and then another. Then he turned and went out into the hall.

It occurred to him the last time he had stepped out of his bedroom without a gun tied down to his leg was...never. He realized he had never walked this house without his gun. Except for three summers ago, when he was recovering from being shot up so bad.

He went down the stairs to the parlor, and as he crossed the parlor floor and stepped into the kitchen, he found himself hoping no one would notice. He didn't want to have to comment about it. To share his inner battle with anyone. Jessica was aware of it—Johnny had known her only a year, and yet she seemed to somehow know everything about him. But he had never talked about it with anyone else. Not even to Ginny or Bree or the boys. Not to anyone.

The boys were at the table. Josh was cutting into his steak, and his eggs were already half gone. Josh charged into his food like it might be the last meal he would ever eat. He always had. He embraced his breakfast or dinner the way embraced life itself. Headfirst and without hesitation.

Dusty ate more calmly. Dusty seemed to do everything more calmly. As though the slightest motion was something he had given deep thought to. He cut a chunk of steak slowly, deliberately.

Ginny was at her usual spot, at the far end of the table. A muffin was on her plate and she was bringing a cup of tea to her lips.

"Well," Johnny said. "Breakfast sure smells good."

Bree sat across from the boys. She had scrambled eggs and a slice of steak on a plate in front of her. She charged into her food with an intensity that seemed halfway between Josh and Dusty. She looked at Johnny with a big smile and said, "Morning, Daddy."

"Mornin', Pumpkin."

Temperance was at the counter, placing some dishes into the sink.

Ginny said, "Temperance, won't you please come and eat?"

"I'll be there in a minute, Aunt Ginny."

Josh glanced over his shoulder at Temperance. "Come on, Sweetie. I'd like to spend a little time with you. Dusty and I'll be gone all day."

The back door opened and Fat Cole stepped in. *Charles* Cole, Johnny corrected himself. Bree wanted everyone to call him *Charles*. It was taking some getting used to.

The boy was long and thin, with bow-legs and a natural swagger to match. He pulled off his hat and said, "Mornin', everyone."

Charles seemed to Johnny like such a striking mass of contradictions. He was Josh's top hand on the ranch, aside from Dusty. More and more, Charles was becoming number three in the chain of command. Whether it was riding a cutting horse, handling a rope or a branding iron, or any of the other duties that fell onto a cowhand, Charles handled them with ease. But when it came to the social graces, his feet seemed too big and he became tongue-tied.

Though lately, he was starting to seem more relaxed. More at ease around people. Maybe a little less awkward.

"Morning, Charles," Bree said.

She was flashing him the kind of smile a woman reserved for the man she loved. The type of smile Jessica gave Johnny. This was most likely the reason for the new-found confidence in the boy.

"Morning, Bree," he said. He looked at her with the combination of deep joy and not a little wonder that a man has when he looks at the woman he loves.

It gave Charles a sort of sappy look. Johnny wondered if this was how he looked when he gazed at Jessica. He sure hoped not.

Johnny went to the counter and grabbed the tin range cup he had used earlier. Ginny had a set of ceramic coffee cups with matching saucers, but Johnny always preferred a range cup. The coffee pot was still about half full, so Johnny filled the cup and then took the chair at the head of the table, the chair that was waiting for him.

He took a sip of coffee and tried to look casual. He was waiting for the comments. *Pa, where's your gunbelt?* Or, *Pa, I don't think I've ever seen you without a gun.* But no one said a thing about it. Josh was talking about the job waiting for him and Dusty today. They would be working on the new house Josh was building for himself and Temperance. Bree was chatting about something with Charles, but she was speaking in low tones. Ginny was saying, "I wish that girl would just sit down and eat her breakfast." Temperance said, "Just a minute, Aunt Ginny."

But no one said a thing about Johnny's missing gun.

Jessica noticed, though. She knew him so well and never missed a thing. She said nothing, but her gaze met his and she had a sort of concerned look. He nodded and gave a little smile and she returned the smile, and that was all there was to it. An entire conversation between the two of them that no one else in the room was aware of.

"Pa," Temperance said. "Want your eggs same as usual?"

"That'd be nice, darlin'. Thank you."

Temperance had become like a daughter to him. Josh had brought her home three summers ago, and she was now a part of this family as though she had been born to it.

Ginny said, "Temperance, you need to sit down and eat your breakfast. I can fix the eggs."

Haley came through the door. Holding her hand and toddling along was little Jonathan.

Haley said, "Why don't you let me fix those eggs?"

Temperance didn't fully relinquish the stove. What happened was she and Haley started working together on the eggs and frying up some more toast. They were chattering away as they worked. Josh and Dusty were talking about working on the roof. Charles and Bree were discussing something—Johnny couldn't quite hear over the din. Cora climbed up onto his knee and Jessica was saying to her, "Come on over here and sit down, honey. You need to eat your breakfast."

Johnny looked at Ginny and said, "We do have a full house these days, don't we?"

Ginny said, "And you love every minute of it."

He found myself smiling. "Every single minute."

Johnny gave Cora a quick peck on the cheek and said, "You go on over to your Mama and eat your breakfast."

She climbed down and ran over to Jessica.

Ginny said, "Enjoy the noise while you can. It won't be long before Josh and Temperance are in their house. And Dusty and Haley will be building a house somewhere. This place will seem empty all too soon."

This reminded Johnny of something. He said, "Josh, what have you got planned for today?"

Josh swallowed a mouthful of eggs and reached for his coffee. "Dusty and I were going to work on the house. The roof is about done. We want it ready to move into by the big day."

Josh looked at Temperance and smiled. She returned the smile. *The big day*, Johnny thought. Twelve days away.

Johnny said, "I know you have a lot of work to do on the house, but I was hoping you might be able to spare Dusty for the day."

Charles had grabbed a plate of eggs and steak and sat beside Bree. There was little room, so his long knees had to be pushed over to the side.

He said, "I can come help you today, Josh. If Mister McCabe needs Dusty for somethin'."

Josh thought fast. In his head was an organizational plan for the ranch. What needed to be done today and tomorrow and next week, and what the goals were for the next year. Johnny had turned the reins over to him and he was handling it nicely. Like Johnny thought he would.

Charles said, "I was gonna scout the hills for some mustangin'. But that ought to be able to wait till tomorrow."

Josh nodded. "That it can. Okay, Charles. You'll be with me today. Dusty," he slapped his brother on the shoulder. "You've got the day off."

"All right," Dusty said. "Pa, what've you got planned?"

Johnny said, "You'll see."

3

Johnny and Dusty rode along the valley floor, heading down the stretch. It was spring and the nights were still cold, but the sun could warm the valley pleasantly during the day. The small river snaking its way along the valley floor was running high because of spring run-off.

"Pa," Dusty said as they rode. "We gonna check on Zack's ranch?"

"Maybe on the way back."

Dusty gave him a sidelong glance, "You know, you could give me a little hint as to where we're going."

Johnny grinned. Dusty wasn't as impatient as Josh, but if you worked him enough, his impatience could rise to the surface.

Johnny said, "Yeah, I could tell you."

Dusty waited. Johnny said nothing.

Dusty said, "But you're not, are you?"

Johnny grinned. "Now, what fun would that be?"

As they came to within reach of Zack's ranch house, Johnny cut east and away from the trail. Dusty followed. They cut a wide swath around Zack's, and aimed for a pine-covered ridge that began rising maybe a half mile away.

A few head of cattle were roaming about. In the distance there was a man on a horse. Johnny couldn't tell who it was, but the rider threw a hand in the air for a wave, so Johnny returned it and so did Dusty.

Johnny said, "Your eyes are probably better'n mine. Any idea who that is?"

Dusty said, "Never seen him before. Maybe someone new Ramon hired."

They rode on to the ridge and began to climb the slope. The summit was rounded and there was a grassy spot clear of trees. It was here they dismounted and loosened the cinches and let their horses breathe a bit.

Johnny stood in the green, springtime grass, enjoying the breeze. It was easier ten full degrees cooler up here than it had been down on Zack's range.

Dusty wore his buckskin shirt, and he flipped his hat off so the wind could catch his hair. His hat hung from a chinstrap and bounced against his back.

His hair had needed cutting when he first arrived here almost three years earlier. Since then he had let it grow long like Johnny's and Josh's.

Johnny's gun was in place now, tied down for a quick draw. He was in a faded gray jacket that he had cut off at the belt so it wouldn't hang down and be in the way if he had to reach for his gun.

"So," Dusty said. "We're a far piece from the house, now. Been doing some riding."

"That we have," Johnny said, but he offered nothing more.

He was looking off in the distance, back in the direction they had come. With his side vision, he noticed Dusty following his gaze. He could see a couple thin, distant tendrils of smoke rising up and bending around and spreading thin in the mountain wind. They were from the chimneys of the farmhouses toward the center of the valley. The Brewsters, the Fords, and Nina's family.

Thinking of Nina made Johnny think of Jack. So often gone and yet close to his heart.

Dusty was apparently thinking the same thing. He said, "Too bad Jack and Nina won't be here for the wedding."

Jack was attending law school back in Boston. He and Nina had had a quick wedding. They wouldn't be back until fall.

Johnny said, "Josh and Temperance understand."

"Pa," Dusty said, turning to face his father. "What are we doing out here?"

"Resting the horses."

Thunder was starting to graze. Dusty's horse Bucky apparently thought it was a good idea and was following suit.

"Pa."

Johnny chuckled. "All right. You know that canyon that's maybe a half mile north of here?"

Dusty nodded. It was a box canyon. Only one way in. The canyon floor was flat and grass grew, and a small spring provided a water source.

He said, "I know the one. It's where we saw that stallion, a couple summers ago. The one that ended up almost killing Josh."

Johnny nodded. "That's where we're going."

He said nothing more than that. He would explain everything to Dusty once they got there.

Johnny went to Thunder and lifted the canteen from where it was slung over the saddle horn and took a drink, then tightened the cinch. The *girth*, he usually called it. A term he had picked up in Texas, years ago. In his saddle boot was his Sharps fifty-caliber rifle.

"Let's ride," Johnny said.

4

They left the horses at the canyon floor and climbed one ridge. It was rocky and with uneven footing, and was covered mostly with smaller growth like junipers or short cedars. Gave it an untamed look, like God had just scooped away a layer of earth and left lots of broken rocks, and then trees and bushes started growing the best they could.

About half way up, one section flattened out for maybe the size of five acres. White pines grew here, staggered about the small plateau.

Johnny stood at the edge of the plateau and looked down at the canyon floor. Thunder and Bucky were grazing contentedly down there.

He had pulled off Thunder's saddle and left it at the edge of the clearing. He hadn't left his Sharps rifle with the saddle, though. It was in one hand now as he stood looking off at the small canyon. He didn't know if it was because he had been shot at one time too many, or just practical thinking. There were grizzlies in these mountains, and wild cats. He decided it was practical thinking. *Always best to be prepared*, his pa had said to him more than once.

"Quite a view," Johnny said.

Dusty's gaze was on the horses. "Aren't you afraid Thunder will run off and rejoin the mountain herd, where he's from?"

Johnny shook my head. "He'll come if I whistle. We have an understanding."

Dusty let his gaze travel along the far canyon wall. It was even more rugged than this one, and steeper. No flat edges at all. Climbing it might be possible, but just barely.

Dusty said, "This little canyon doesn't have a name, does it?"

"It does now. I've shown this place to Jessica. We've ridden out here a couple of times. We're thinking of calling it McCabe Canyon."

Johnny turned and walked into the pines. Not quite a forest but more than a stand. Dusty followed.

Johnny said, "She and I are going to put a house here."

This caught Dusty by surprise. He hadn't been expecting this.

He said, "A house?"

Johnny nodded.

"Not as big as the ranch house. Maybe one floor. It'll be made of logs. These trees here will provide some of them. We'll plant maples, maybe, for some shade. We had maples around the old farmhouse back in Pennsylvania. I've always been partial to 'em."

Dusty looked at his father. "I knew you were stepping back from running the ranch and letting Josh take the reins, but I didn't know you were stepping this far back."

"It's something I started thinking about over the winter. The things have been happening in town are part of what got me thinking."

Johnny drew a breath and looked up at the tall pines. "I hate to cut a tree. They're living things. They each have their own spirit. The Shoshone taught me that. But we need the logs for the cabin. The Shoshone believed you took from nature only what you needed, and you put back what you could. There are small saplings growing here, and I'll transplant them to other parts of the canyon. There's a small spring further back in the rocks, about the size of the one down on the canyon floor. We'll run a small line of piping from it and have running water in the kitchen."

Dusty stood watching his father.

Johnny said, "This seems to be a time of change, Dusty."

Dusty nodded. "After you left for California, Aunt Ginny was saying she felt change in the air."

"The little town of McCabe Gap turning into a boom town not three miles from our house is partly what got me to thinking about building out here. That town will have more than two thousand people by the end of the summer, and even more next summer. I've always found towns and cities to be a little restricting. They make me feel hemmed in. I've always been drawn to the more remote areas. The mountains, especially."

The realization was fully settling on Dusty. He said, "You're moving out here with Jessica and Cora."

Johnny nodded. "This will be our home. Jessica and I will raise Cora here. We'll have a couple of extra bedrooms. Bree might want to stay here sometimes. And you and Josh and Jack and your families will all be welcome. But I need some space between myself and civilization."

Dusty said, "This place must be something like what the valley felt like when you first moved the family here."

"It's somewhat close. But there are more reasons than that."

Dusty was listening.

"You and Haley have been married for six months, now. You need a place of your own. A place to raise Jonathan. And any other young'uns the Good Lord brings your way."

Dusty looked at Johnny like he didn't really know where he was going with this. Johnny had come to expect this when talking with people. He supposed he was just the sort who got to something when he got to it, and people talking with him just had to hang on for the ride.

He said, "I've talked this over with Josh already. I had to get his say-so before Jessica and I told anyone else. She's telling the women-folk back at the house right now."

Johnny drew in a breath of mountain air. It was strong with the scent of balsam. He said, "The house you and Josh have been working on, it's really for you and Haley. It's gonna be your house."

Dusty said, "But Josh said he always loved that little spot in the woods."

"He does, but when he heard my idea, he agreed it was best for everyone. He and Temperance are going to take the main house. That house is the headquarters for the ranch, and the ramrod should be there. Besides, Temperance has practically taken over the household management."

Dusty was speechless for a moment. Then he said, "This is a lot to take in."

"Sometimes change comes in little bits, here and there. Other times it descends on you all at once. I was thinking maybe I'd get started on the house after the trail drive."

Dusty nodded. Josh and Johnny had been talking throughout the winter about a cattle drive. The railroad would be in Montana in another year, they figured, but they didn't want to wait. They had already been too long without any major beef sales and the ranch's cash reserve was running low. Since Josh was now the ramrod, Johnny let him ride point on this. Josh contacted a buyer in Cheyenne who represented a firm back east. As soon as winter had passed and the trails cleared, Josh had taken the stage south to Cheyenne to meet with the man personally and negotiate a price.

"One thing," Dusty said. "*We'll* build it. McCabes stick together, right?"

Johnny clapped a hand to his shoulder. "That's right, son. We stick together."

That night at the dinner table, the talk was mainly about the house Jessica and Johnny planned to build. Jessica was aglow talking about how the master bedroom would have a window facing east and the morning sun would light it up.

And they would have a front porch that overlooked the canyon.

"That's as it should be," Ginny said and looked at Johnny. "You standing out there first thing in the morning and the last thing in the evening, having a cup of coffee or smoking your pipe."

Johnny was a little concerned about Ginny's place in all of this. Not so long ago, she had been the woman of the house. When Johnny had first brought her and the children to Montana, the arrangement they had struck was that he ran the ranch but she ran the household and helped raise the children. But now the children were grown, Johnny would be moving out, and Temperance seemed to taking over her duties of household management.

Johnny voiced these concerns later in the evening. The sun had set and he was standing on the front porch with a tin cup filled with trail coffee. He had very quietly left his gunbelt in the bedroom. If anyone had noticed, no one was saying anything.

Ginny came out onto the porch, a shawl draped around her shoulders. She was balancing a cup of tea on a saucer and making it look easy, like it was second nature. If Johnny had tried that, the tea would have been all over the floor or all over him.

He voiced his concerns, and she said, "I appreciate the concern, but there is no need. Things change, and this is as it should be."

"I just know what it feels like to have someone come in to territory that belongs to you. Like Temperance taking over the household."

She chuckled. "Oh, John. Thank you for the concern, but I'm fine. I always knew this day would come. I had at one time thought it might be Bree taking over the household, but as the years went by, I realized it wouldn't be. She's a girl who belongs on a horse, riding through the hills. Hunting alongside you and the boys. When I got her that pistol a couple of Christmases ago and saw how natural it looked on her, I realized she would never be the one to take over this household."

"Are you disappointed?"

She shook her head. "Not at all. I want each of these children to be who they need to be. A desire apparently neither of us had much success teaching Jack, at least in his early years. Temperance is a good girl. She's going to be a fine wife to Joshua, and a fine woman of the ranch."

"But what about you?"

She smiled. "I was here when I was needed. And maybe I needed to be here for myself, too. These children are my only link to my beloved Lura. But they are grown. It is my time to move on to my next step in life."

She took a sip of tea. "I have the saloon in town. I intend to take my half-ownership in that venture very seriously?"

Johnny couldn't help but smile. "You? A saloon keeper?"

"Hardly. But I don't see the saloon remaining as such for very long. The town is growing. The snows had only receded for maybe a week when wagon-loads of emigrants started filing in. Mister Franklin estimates that the town might double again in size this very summer. No, I don't see a rustic, *cowpoke* saloon as fitting the needs of this changing market. I've talked it over with Hunter, and what we see for the future of his venture is a restaurant with a saloon attached."

"You've talked this over with Hunter, already?"

"Indeed. Our plans are to keep the barroom very much like it is, but to expand the building, possibly doubling it in size. It'll be a fully functioning restaurant.

Johansen's is full to capacity almost every night. Sometimes there is a half-hour wait. On the weekends, it can be a full hour. And the meals at the hotel aren't enough to fill the need. We plan to call it the *Second Chance Restaurant and Saloon.*

"And of course," she hesitated a moment, taking another sip of tea and letting her gaze fall out toward the night, "I'll be waiting for Addison. He'll be returning one day."

Johnny nodded. "He will. Along with and Zack, and Joe."

They stood in silence for a while, then she headed into the house. It was getting cold out here. Dusty had built a fire in the hearth in the parlor. Johnny would be going in shortly, to sit by the fire with the family.

But for the moment, he stood on the porch and looked off into the darkness. And he again had the unmistakable feeling that someone was out there in the night, watching the ranch.

5

In the morning, he went out and fetched Thunder. Normally, you had to throw a loop on a horse, but when he talked to Dusty the day before about whistling and Thunder coming, he had been serious.

The morning was chilly and the springtime grass was already tall, and it was wet with dew. The remuda was frolicking about. Thirty-two horses. Johnny's eyes were on the coffee-brown stallion. The animal stood nearly seventeen hands and was easily the biggest animal in the herd. These were all mountain mustangs, and usually a mountain horse didn't grow to be much more than fifteen hands.

They had bays and there was an appaloosa among them. One horse that was almost jet black, and Bree called him *Midnight*. No paint horses, though. Johnny believed a paint horse was the result of some sort of inbreeding. He never allowed them in the remuda.

Thunder was trotting about in the morning air, his mane flying in the morning breeze. Then he saw Johnny and stopped and looked at him.

Johnny had never been the whistler his pa was. His pa could sit and strum a parlor guitar and whistle a song. But Johnny could make a call like a morning bird. He had learned it from that Shoshone shaman. He gave the call now, and Thunder left the herd and started walking toward him.

"Mornin,' old boy," Johnny said, and rubbed his nose. "Come on. We've got us a little riding to do."

Johnny started back toward the corral and Thunder fell into place beside him.

Johnny had already left his saddle across the top rail of the corral. He slid Thunder's bridle in place and was about to start on the saddle when Bree came walking out.

"Hey, Pa, where're you goin'?"

She was in a split skirt she used for riding, and black boots. Her pistol was riding at one hip. She was in a white shirt and a waist-length jacket that was a sort of neutral tan, and her dark hair was tied into a long braid. A wide-brimmed hat was pulled down tight.

"Just goin' for a little ride," he said.

"Want some company?"

They rode along at a leisurely pace. Thunder liked to move with a high-stepping sort of gate, so Johnny let him have his head. They were aiming toward the pine forest at the edge of the valley floor, moving sort of diagonally toward it from the house.

Bree was riding Midnight, and this was a smaller horse and had a sort of quick-stepping gate. Bree was letting him have his rein, too. Johnny had noticed over the years that a true horseman doesn't try to so much control his horse, as he moves with the horse. Almost like a team. Bree was as natural on a horse as any he had ever seen.

"So, Pa," she said. "Where are we going?"

"Just riding," he said. He tried to make it sound casual, but she wasn't buying it.

"Pa, you never are just riding. That's one thing I've learned about you. You're never just wandering. You're always going one place or another."

"All right," he said. "I suppose I should tell you."

And so he told her about how it was, being a man who had been shot at as much as he had. How he lived forever on edge.

"I'll admit," she said, "I've worried about you over the years. Having to sleep with that gun so close by your bed. When you wake up in the night at the slightest sound and have to check out the entire house before you can go back to sleep. When you're outside and you're always checking the trees, watching for snipers.

In fact, you're doing it right now."

Johnny realized he had let his gaze drift to a pine that stood a little apart from the others, and was noticing how long the branches were and how easy it would be to climb and to find a perch up there. You would have a clear view of the trail that cut across the valley. If you were going to take a shot at someone riding along that trail, this tree would be the perfect one.

He had been aware of this tree before today. He had watched it grow over the years. He was aware of every tree on this side of the valley that would be good for a sniper to use.

"I see your point," he said.

They reached the edge of the pine forest, and Johnny gave Thunder a nudge to their left, and the horse turned in that direction and began to move along at a walk. Johnny would swear this horse knew what he was thinking. He seemed to know when they were just riding with a destination in mind, and when they were scouting. And scouting was what they were doing now.

Johnny said to her, "Yesterday morning, when I first stepped outside, I had this feeling that I was being watched. That someone was out here watching the house. I had that feeling again last night when I was standing on the porch. I'm sure it's nothing. Just an old gunfighter feeling danger where there isn't any. But I just thought I should check it out. Just to put my mind to rest."

She said, "You know, Pa, we live in a land that's beautiful and wonderful, but you have to be careful. You've said that, yourself."

Johnny nodded. "True. But there are times when you can take it too far."

He gave Thunder's reins a slight tug to tell him to stop, but the horse was already stopping. Again, the horse seemed to know what Johnny wanted.

The morning was growing warm and Johnny thought he might take off his jacket. He thought Thunder could use a little breather and maybe a few minutes to graze. He swung out of the saddle and then loosened the girth. Bree was doing the same with Midnight.

Johnny said, "I suppose it's about balance. I want balance in my life. Right now, I feel like my life's not in the balance that I want it to be."

Bree was strolling ahead. Some wildflowers were standing tall. Some with long thin yellow petals that kind of opened up like a star. Ginny called them *glacier lilies*. Just beyond them were some pines that were the beginning of the forest that covered the ridges.

Johnny had seen more than one place where mountain slopes were covered with pines, but at the base of the mountain the forest just ended and a long grassy meadow began. That's the way it was here. The meadow covered the entire valley floor, and then the forest began again on the ridges at the far side of the valley.

Johnny looked off at the grass. It was spring and the grass was supple and green. Come August, there would be a lot of brown among it. Right now it stood about eighteen inches tall. His thoughts went briefly to how a man with a rifle could crawl through grass and sneak up on an enemy camp. It had been done more than once. But this grass wasn't quite tall enough for that, yet.

He said, "I made some major steps over the past couple of years in finding balance. Finding a way to finally put the death of your mother behind me. The guilt I felt, because of a bullet that was probably meant for me."

Bree said, "Aren't you always the one to say we pass on when it's our time? Isn't that what the Shoshone always said? It seems to me it was Ma's time or the bullet wouldn't have found her. If the bullet hadn't been there, it would have been some other thing that took her."

"It's often kind of hard to live by your own advice. You'll find that out as the years go by. But I'm trying to do that. To accept that it was your Ma's time and to let the guilt fade away. And I'm finding balance with Jessica and Cora."

Bree walked toward a grouping of three pines. One tall one and two shorter ones. Johnny thought quickly about snipers—the tall one would be difficult to climb because there were no branches close to the ground. A man would have to wrap his arms and legs around a tree and work his way up. And the branches, once you got to them, were thin and grew close together. Not the best place for a sniper to make his perch and wait. The other two pines were much smaller and wouldn't hold a man's weight well.

"Want some advice?" she said.

Johnny grinned. Bree was seventeen. She apparently felt old enough to be giving her old man advice.

He said, "Sure."

"I can see how you want to lay all of the edginess to rest. But don't stop trusting your instinct."

As she spoke, she was looking at the ground near the big pine. The springtime grass grew right up to the base of the trunk. He walked on over to see what she was looking at.

He saw two distinct boot prints, and a few others. Scattered about were some crimped butts of hand-rolled smokes.

"A man stood here," she said. "And from here..," she turned her back to the forest, "you get a pretty good view of the house. The tracks are recent. Maybe as recent as this morning."

Johnny stood beside her and looked at the house.

"Someone's been watching the house," she said.

He found himself grinning again as he realized maybe he wasn't too old to take advice from his daughter, after all.

"Come on," she said. "Let's go do some back-tracking."

6

Ginny stood in the parlor, facing so the hearth was in front of her and off to one side and the kitchen doorway was off to the other. To her far right were the stairs, and on the wall directly to her right was the door to her bedroom. The only bedroom on the first floor.

Josh came in from the kitchen with a cup of coffee in one hand. He and Charles had been off at the new house, putting on the finishing touches, and had come back to the main house for some lunch.

Josh said, "There's a lot to running a ranch. More than I ever realized, I guess. Negotiating a price with that buyer in Cheyenne. We've gotta get the herd ready to go. This means a second roundup to separate off the brood stock from the steers. I might have to hire a couple of more men."

He took a sip of coffee. "It'll sure be nice when the railroad runs a line up this way. Pa says it'll be coming soon, and he thinks this will be our last long overland trail drive. I think he's probably right. A trail drive is the kind of thing that's great to sit by the fire and tell stories about, but it sure is one long hardship when you're actually doing one."

Josh was walking across the room as he spoke and set his cup down on the desk. He was going to take a quick look at the ledgers before he and Charles went back to the new house. He then realized his aunt wasn't responding to anything he said, and he looked over at her and he saw she was just standing, letting her gaze travel over everything. From her rocker to the hearth to the stairs.

He walked over to her.

"Well, Joshua," she said. "This is your house, now. As soon as your father gets his new cabin built."

She looked at him. In her eyes was pride, and he thought he saw some tears forming.

She said, "You earned it. You're a fine young man, and you'll do good things with this ranch. I really believe running this place is what you were meant to do."

He put an arm around his aunt's shoulders. "Have I ever thanked you properly for everything you've done for us? Everything you gave up to move in with us and help Pa raise us?"

She nodded. "Every single day."

He gave her a curious glance.

She said, "Even without realizing it, just by being the fine young man you are, you're thanking me. Bree too, and Jack. Even Dusty, though he's been here only a short time. Just being the family you all are."

"I want you to know, you'll always have a place here. Your bedroom will always be right where it is. Even if you move off somewhere, your room will be right here waiting for you."

"That's very kind of you, Joshua."

"You did more than fill in for Ma. I want you to know you've made your own place in this family. And we're all grateful."

He gave her a kiss on the cheek.

She began blinking away tears. "Joshua, you're going to make an old woman cry."

7

It looked to Johnny like the man hadn't made any attempt to hide his trail. He had stood beneath a tree at the edge of the woods and watched the ranch, probably using binoculars or a spyglass. He had paced about sometimes, and rolled cigarettes and then thrown the butts on the ground. He had left a clear foot trail to where he left his horse, back a ways in the trees, and then left a clear trail as he rode away up the slope.

Some of the tracks he had made while standing or pacing about looked old and faded, and others were clearly defined. This told Johnny the man had been out here watching the ranch more than once.

As Johnny and Bree rode along, following the man's back trail, Johnny decided to trust his instincts and he pulled his rifle and rode with it across the saddle in front of him. Bree did the same.

The trail swung north and then down the side of a ridge, and came out in the mountain pass that led into the valley. The pass Johnny had started calling McCabe Gap when they first settled this valley.

The dirt on the trail was too hard packed to follow any particular set of tracks.

They rode along a ways, taking the trail out of the valley. Johnny didn't figure the man had ridden back into the valley, because he would have risked being seen. If he had wanted to be seen, then he wouldn't have been spying on the ranch from a distance.

They saw no tracks that might indicate a rider had left the trail, or come overland and then picked it up.

They reached a point where the trail forked. South would take them to Jubilee. North, the trail wound its way between ridges until it would come to the Willbury Ranch.

Johnny said, "He approached the valley by riding along the trail, then once he was in the pass, he cut up and over McCabe Mountain and then down to where he could watch the house."

Bree said, "Which direction do you think he came from?"

"I can't imagine Tom Willbury sending someone to the valley to spy on us. We have no beef with him. Must have been from town. Let's take a ride on in and see what we can find out."

Jubilee was growing every day. On the hills outside of town, hammering and sawing was going on, and frameworks of two-by-fours were being setup. Soon buildings would be there. Ginny was on the town council—even though she wasn't officially a resident of the town, she was a business owner—and according to her there was talk of zoning. Commercial zones and residential.

Give me a ranch house off in a remote valley, any day, Johnny thought. Or a cabin off in a remote canyon, since their little valley was now not so remote. He would build a house for Jessica, Cora and himself on that shelf in the canyon he had shown Dusty yesterday, and not have to worry about zoning or any of that. There would be no taxes. Their well-being wouldn't be subject to the political whims of town leaders.

It occurred to him as he and Bree rode along that with all of the building happening on the hills outside of town, those hills soon wouldn't be thought of as *outside of town*. They would soon be part of the town.

People Johnny had never seen before were riding along the street. A covered wagon was making its way along, with a middle-aged man and woman on the front seat. The man was not a cattleman, Johnny noted. He had a jacket and a short-brimmed hat like folks wore back East. Maybe he was a miner or a shop keeper.

People moved along the boardwalk. Some in ties and jackets, others in homespun shirts and pants and with suspenders over the shoulders. Some wore caps and others the wider-brimmed hats you normally saw in cattle country. Though, Johnny supposed, this was now mining country every bit as much as it was cattle country.

Jubilee had two main streets. One was actually called Main Street, and the other was Randall Street. Both converged on a small section that was starting to be called the town square. The *Second Chance* was on one side, and Randall's hotel was on the other.

A huge structure was being assembled immediately behind the hotel. It was two floors high and much longer than the hotel. When it was finished, it would replace the hotel, because the ramshackle structure Frank Shapleigh had originally built now looked almost comically out of place.

The town square at the convergence of Randall and Main was filled with people, and Johnny realized he didn't know any of them. A man in a buckskin shirt and a long beard that fell to his chest was riding along. There was silver in his beard—he was no spring chicken. But he wore his pistol high on his left side and turned around for a cross-draw. The only reason a man would do that would be if he knew how to use it. But he just rode along, not looking at anything in particular, and yet Johnny could see his eyes missed nothing.

There was another covered wagon, this one in front of Franklin's general store. A team of mules hitched to it looked tired and bored. A couple of young boys were bouncing a ball back and forth on the boardwalk in front of the store, but no adults were in sight. Probably in the store talking with Franklin.

"Let's head to Hunter's," Johnny said to Bree.

She was grinning. "In the mood for a cold beer? I don't see how that's gonna help us find the man we're looking for."

"Couldn't hurt."

She laughed.

A man maybe halfway through his thirties was riding along. His hair was shaggy and he had some whiskers on his face, but he had the look of a cowhand who was long between jobs, rather than a wandering saddle bum.

He rode up as Bree and Johnny were pulling rein in front of the *Second Chance*.

"Excuse me," he said. "I noticed the brand on your horse, Miss. Are you from the McCabe Ranch?"

Midnight had a circle M brand on his hip. Thunder bore no brand at all. It somehow didn't seem right to put a brand on an animal like this.

Johnny said to the rider, "I'm Johnny McCabe."

"The man hisself," he said.

"I tend to be."

He grinned. "Abe Taggart."

He leaned out over the saddle and held out his hand, and Johnny leaned forward and shook it.

He said, "I'm lookin' for a job. I was wondering if you might be hirin'."

"My son Josh does all the hiring, now. Just follow the road outside of town. Where it forks, take a right and it'll take you into the valley. Follow it south, and it'll lead you to the ranch house."

"Thank you kindly," and he was on his way.

Johnny and Bree stepped out of the saddle and went into Hunter's. It was now called the *Second Chance Saloon*, but those few who had been local before the gold strike still called it *Hunter's*. Johnny had Chen fetch him a cold beer from the root cellar, and Bree had herself a cold sarsaparilla.

They stood at the bar and told Hunter about what they had found. A man watching the ranch.

Partway through this, Vic Falcone came walking

in.

"Still wearing a tin star," Johnny said.

"Still the marshal," he said. "At least until the upcoming election."

Bree said, "You won't get my vote. Not that I can vote. Too young and not a town resident."

Johnny had to grin.

But to Falcone's credit, he said, "I don't deserve your vote, Miss."

The good marshal wasn't dressed in the dapper way he usually was. Not that Johnny got to town much. He never had before, and now that it was no longer the quiet, mountain community of McCabe Gap but the blossoming boom town of Jubilee, he had even less reason to come here. But he noticed Falcone was in a range shirt and jeans. He wore a dark, pinstriped vest that had one time gone with a formal suit but was now showing some wear.

"Slumming, Falcone?" Johnny said.

He shrugged. "The pay of a marshal isn't much. I make do."

Bree said, "Maybe you ought to raid a ranch or two. Might help your budget."

Johnny couldn't help but laugh. But as he laughed, he was watching Falcone for any sign of retaliation. Johnny was going to lay him out on the saloon floor if he gave the slightest provocation. Johnny have to admit, he was hoping he would.

But Falcone just nodded and said, "I have that coming. I totally deserve it."

She said, "You might think you're earning some sort of restitution, but—"

Johnny cut her off. "Okay, Bree. He's had enough."

She said, "No he ain't. I'm just getting started."

Falcone said, "Miss McCabe, I can't ask your forgiveness. I have no right. But believe me, I intend to do what I can for the citizens of Jubilee."

Hunter was behind the bar, and he said, "It's impossible to undo something that's been done, but maybe you can start over."

Johnny gave him a look. Hunter had been one of the most vocal critics of Falcone being hired as marshal.

Hunter said, "Been listenin' to that nephew of your'n. The preacher. He talks a lot about second chances."

Johnny continued talking about the man who had been watching their ranch. How he and Bree had trailed him here to town.

Bree said, "You have some experience with spying on our ranch, don't you, marshal?"

Falcone decided to ignore her. There was no way to win a fight with Bree, anyway.

He said to Johnny, "My jurisdiction ends outside the valley, but what I can do is keep my ears open."

Johnny nodded. "Much obliged."

When Falcone left, Johnny said to Bree, "You don't cut him much slack, do you?"

"He doesn't deserve any."

Hunter was giving a deep chuckle. He was a big man with a big voice that seemed to rumble from somewhere down inside his chest.

He said, "Bree, if you should ever square off against Falcone, I would put my money on you, anytime."

"Dang tootin'," she said, and took a sip of her sarsaparilla.

8

Johnny and Bree rubbed down their horses, and by the time they were walking back toward the house, the sun had dropped behind the ridge to the west and the sky was fading to a steel gray.

Johnny hurt as he walked. His lower back and hips. He hated to admit he was getting too old for being in the saddle as long as he had been today. He noticed this hadn't been the case before he was shot three summers ago. He had spent nearly two months out of the saddle, and when he went back to it, he felt like he had aged ten years. He was hoping he would regain what he had lost, but he never did seem to.

He didn't talk about to this to anyone. Except Jessica.

Bree skipped up the steps to the kitchen floor, as filled with energy as she had been before they had left this morning. Johnny took each step one at a time and winced a little as he did so.

He had been thrown by a horse ten years ago, and wrenched his knee in the process. Granny Tate had told him if he went easy on it for a week or so, he would be all right. And he was. But now he felt the old injury flaring up again. Part of age, he supposed.

The kitchen was a flurry of activity. Temperance was in charge, like she often was these days. Haley and Jessica were with her, and they were whipping up a meal. Porterhouse steaks. The smell made his mouth water.

Jessica scooted over to him and gave him a kiss, and said, "How was your day?"

He said, "Fine. Bree and I did some riding."

Johnny was amazed at what he and Jessica could say with just their eyes. And what they said beneath the words they used. Johnny could see in her eyes that she knew he was hurting and didn't want to tell anyone, and she knew there was a lot more to tell than just Johnny and Bree going riding. He would probably tell the family over dinner that they had found someone was watching the ranch. But he would tell only Jessica about the aches in his joints, and that talk would come once they were snuggled into their warm bed.

Johnny and Bree were both covered with dust and they knew Aunt Ginny would never allow them at the dinner table looking like this. Neither would Temperance. Bree never just walked but sort of bounded from one foot to another, and she did this as she went from the kitchen into the parlor, heading upstairs to make herself presentable for dinner. Johnny followed behind, trying not to hobble.

Josh and Dusty were in the parlor and Charles was with them, and they each had a glass of scotch in hand. Ginny was in her rocker and a goblet of white wine was on the stand beside her. Jonathan was in a playpen out in the middle of the wide-open parlor. A fire was roaring in the big stone hearth, and Cora was sitting on the sofa just enjoying the atmosphere of the whole family being together.

For many years, it had been just Jessica and Cora in their little canyon in California. Cora often looked at this bustling household with wonder.

Bree gave Charles a peck on the cheek and he said, "Where you been all day?"

She said, "Off riding with Pa."

And then she bounded up the stairs to get ready for dinner. Just watching her bound made Johnny feel tired.

Johnny needed to use a wash basin, too. Wash the dust off his face. Get on a clean shirt. Maybe unbuckle his gun belt and leave it upstairs. But his chair was calling to him and he decided to give in.

He dropped into the chair with maybe a little too

much of a groan, and Ginny said, "Joshua, go fetch your father a scotch."

He said, "Yes'm," and went to it.

She was looking at Johnny with a grin. She, too, understood the ache in his joints. But with Ginny, it wasn't that he had confided in her. She just knew from experience.

Johnny said to her, "I don't want to hear it."

She laughed.

Josh brought over a tumbler half-filled with scotch, and Johnny took a belt.

The chair he was sitting in was one he had built himself. He had used narrow pine logs for the frame, and upholstered it with cowhide. It wasn't very soft, like the cushions in the Ginny's rocker. She had brought the chair from 'Frisco. But he found it was just what the doctor ordered after a long day in the saddle.

Folks who don't drink whiskey wouldn't know this, but it has a way of warming you from the inside out. This was what was going on now, and he sat in his chair and let his aching joints have a reprieve. He sipped his whiskey and enjoyed the sound of the boys laughing and chatting about everything from the roof on the new house they were building to the price of cattle Josh hoped to get when they got the herd to Cheyenne.

Ginny said to Johnny, "We had two visitors this afternoon."

She spoke as though she were talking with some high-society folk. Like this was a mansion in a high-falutin' part of San Francisco and they had had callers, rather than just a ranch where folks rode up and said *howdy*.

Johnny said, "Do tell."

She said, "A young man by the name of Abe Taggart. He was seeking employment. However, Joshua was off with Dusty working on the new house."

Johnny nodded. "I met him town. Sent him out

this way."

"I told him to return tomorrow morning."

"Who else was out here?"

"Young Billy Mathers."

Billy was a kid in town. About ten years old. He had a mule he rode, and often ran errands.

Johnny said, "What did Billy want?"

"He was delivering a letter to you." She looked over to the boys. "Josh, where is that letter Billy Mathers brought out here for your father?"

"I'll get it." He went to the desk at the other side of the room and brought back an envelope.

It was time for Johnny to deal with another aspect of his diminishing capacities that he didn't want to talk about. He had noticed that it was getting harder and harder to see things up close clearly.

He opened the letter. The light in the room was getting dim because it was getting dark outside, so he sat forward and held the letter in the light of the fire. The message was written in ink and with a flowing hand, but he found he had to hold it back a bit so he could see it clearly.

"Funny thing," Ginny said, "how our arms grow shorter as we get older."

Johnny gave her a pained look and she laughed. She wore spectacles to handle the problem, but Johnny hadn't gotten to the point that he was ready to concede to them yet. Though he thought maybe he was getting mighty close to it, because even holding the letter out and away from him, the letters were still too fuzzy to read.

"Let me see it," she said.

He handed her the letter, and with her spectacles perched on her nose, she said, "Oh. It's from Bertram Reed. The new land speculator in town."

Johnny nodded. "Yeah, I know who he is. He introduced himself to me a few weeks ago."

Ginny said, "It seems he is requesting your presence tomorrow afternoon at Johansen's. He wishes to make you a business offer."

"A business offer?"

"Maybe he wants to buy some beef."

He said, "I'll bring Josh with me. After all, he's running the ranch, now."

They all sat for dinner. Johnny had managed to get himself upstairs and was now in a white boiled shirt, and he had left his gun slung over the foot of the bed. Talk ranged from Josh's and Temperance's upcoming nuptials to the trail drive Josh was planning. He talked about needing another hand or two, and Josh said he hoped this Taggart feller had some experience.

After dinner the house quieted down. Folks turned in to bed. Charles had joined them for dinner like he often did but then headed back to the bunkhouse. Jessica had gotten Cora to bed and was now sitting on the sofa in front of the fire. Ginny had gone to bed to read for a while. Josh was standing in front of the hearth with a scotch on his hand. Dusty and Haley had turned in.

Bree was in her aunt's rocker. She said, "I keep wondering about that man who has been watching the ranch."

"I have a plan for that," Johnny said. He was getting another glass of scotch from the small table where Ginny kept the decanter.

"What's that?"

But before he could answer, he heard the sound of a boot scuffing outside on the front porch.

Bree looked at him, but he held one finger up vertically to his lips to indicate for her to be quiet.

He said, as though he had heard nothing, "So, Josh, have you thought much about the route you'll be taking with the herd?"

As Johnny said this, he set his glass of scotch down on the arm of his chair and reached for his pistol.

Except his pistol wasn't there. It was upstairs in the bedroom. *Dang.*

He glanced across the room to the rifle rack. Three Winchesters stood there, along with a scattergun and his Sharps and the old Hawkin.

Josh said, "Been thinkin' about it. I got a couple of options."

Josh followed his father to the rifle rack.

Bree talked from where she sat, as though she was carrying on the conversation. "I would think one option might be just to follow the Bozeman trail all the way down. There should be water along the way, especially this time of year."

Jessica said, "The fire sure is nice tonight, don't you think?"

Bree said, "Sure is."

Johnny handed a Winchester to Josh. All of the rifles in the rack were loaded. One thing Johnny had learned over the years—a gun that's not loaded is of little use. Keep your guns loaded and treat them like they are loaded.

Johnny and Josh worked the action of their rifles carefully, slowly, to make as little sound as possible. Then with a round chambered and the hammer cocked, Josh pulled the door open and Johnny stepped out, rifle raised to shoot.

A man was standing there and Johnny could see his face in the orange glow from the hearth. Longish hair. A juniper bush of a beard. A floppy, dark hat.

It was his brother Josiah.

9

Johnny and Josiah grabbed each other in bear hugs. Josiah was the biggest of the McCabe boys and he lifted Johnny clear off the porch floor.

"You old grizzly bear," Johnny said. "Come on in."

Zack Johnson was with him. And Addison Travis.

Johnny said, "Bree, go get your Aunt Ginny."

Addison Travis was a man Johnny had met in California a year ago, but back then he had gone by the name Sam Middleton. When Johnny had known him, he had been well-groomed and moved with an air of sophistication. Now he looked like something that had ridden out of the mountains. His handlebar mustache had grown wild and whiskers decorated his jaw, and his hair flew every which way. But despite the dusty, worn clothes he stood in, it was with style and elegance that he watched Ginny emerge from her room.

Ginny was sixty-one and Addison had to be about the same age, but once they saw each other they were Bree's age again. Ginny ran to him and he took her in his arms and there was a kiss that made Johnny turn away. Wouldn't do for a gunhawk to blush.

"Addison," she said. "Oh, Addison."

There were tears streaming down her face. Johnny noticed tears were cutting rivulets through the dust on Addison's face, too.

"Is your name cleared?" she said.

He shook his head. "I just couldn't stay away from you any longer."

Jessica and Temperance got plates of food for them, and Josh filled glasses of scotch. The whole household was roused at the commotion, and the kitchen was filled with folks while Addison, Zack and Joe sat down to eat.

They talked about living on the run. Living in the

mountains and hunting their supper and living in a small lean-to they had made.

Joe said, "We tried looking for work using assumed names. Didn't work out too well. We looked like saddle bums. And the law was always hot on our trail."

Travis said, "That was my fault. Apparently the Mexican government has doubled the reward for me."

"Why?" Bree said. "So you had to kill a man. There are outright murderers out there who don't cause this much commotion."

"It's politics. I killed the son of a general. And now it's becoming a matter of political pride."

Zack said, "We stayed quite a long time with a band of Cheyenne living in the mountains, off the reservation. But we were runnin' the risk of bringing trouble to them, so we decided to light out. It was my idea to come back here. Poor old Travis, here, was just pinin' for you somethin' fierce," he looked at Ginny and she smiled. "And I figured if he goes by the name of Sam Middleton and no one asks questions, we might be able to hide him right here in plain sight."

The three slept the night wrapped in blankets on the parlor floor. The following morning, Zack rode out to check on his ranch. When Sam—his name was Addison but Johnny would always think of him as Sam—came downstairs, he was cleanly shaven except for his handlebar mustache. Ginny had cut his hair, and he was in a clean shirt of Johnny's. His formerly steel gray mustache was now nearly white, but otherwise he looked much like the Sam Middleton who had been fleecing miners at cards in that saloon back in Greenville, California, and who had come to the rescue when he was needed.

Breakfast was finished and Johnny was standing out back on the porch with a cup of coffee in his hand when Taggart came riding in.

"'Mornin," Johnny said, and called to Josh.

Josh came out and Taggart announced he was looking for work.

Josh said, "Look like you been on the trail a while."

"I have," he said. "Been doing some traveling."

"You look like you've done some work on a ranch, before."

"Yessir. I've pretty much done it all. Line boss, hay waddy, hasher, cow prod, jingler. You name it. I've done it."

Joe came walking out from the parlor. Where Sam was now once again his sophisticated-looking self, Joe still looked like he had just come from the mountains, chasing the wind and howling at the moon.

Joe said, "Taggart."

Taggart looked at him a moment and blinked with surprise, and said, "Joe Smith."

Johnny looked at them both.

Joe said, "Smith is what I'm known by, down Texas way."

Johnny said, "You two know each other?"

Joe nodded. "He's an old friend. Done me a real good turn, a while back. If not for him, I'd prob'ly be in the ground. The marshal I work for down there, too. Give him the job, if you can."

"Well," Josh said, looking at Taggart. "That's about as good a recommendation as a man can have. We're planning a trail drive."

Taggart said, "You don't hire drovers? You do it yourself?"

"That we do. You up to it?"

Taggart nodded. "Yes, sir."

"Then head on down to the bunkhouse. Tell Charles that I done hired you."

After breakfast, Johnny saddled up Thunder and rode out. He headed to the back trail that would take him out behind Hunter's. Nothing that would seem unusual to anyone watching the ranch.

But then, about two hundred feet into the wooded pass out beyond the valley floor, he turned north and cut up and over one ridge, and then up and onto the ridge they called McCabe Mountain.

He left Thunder ground-hitched partway up the mountain. Johnny knew the horse wouldn't wander far, and would come when he whistled.

Johnny pulled his buckskin moccasin boots from his saddlebags. His riding boots were tight and didn't want to come off, but he tugged for a bit and they gave up the ghost, and then he slipped on the buckskin boots and pulled them up to where they tied just below the knee. Now he could walk in almost complete silence.

With his Sharps in one hand, he started down the mountain. He took his time, stepping lightly on the pine straw and making sure to avoid any dried sticks. There were many of those, as they fell from the pine boughs overhead.

He walked the way a Shoshone hunter had shown him, years ago. How to walk silently. You don't tip-toe along, the way a lot of folks would think. You step down slowly, in a controlled motion, heel first. Then you let your foot roll forward and your toe is the last thing to touch the ground.

Johnny found the man who had been watching the ranch was back in place, by the large pine at the edge of the valley floor.

The man didn't strike Johnny as an outlaw or gunfighter type. He was in a gray Sunday-go-to-meetin' suit and a short-brimmed bowler. Johnny could tell by the way the right side of his jacket was wrinkling up that he probably had a gun under there.

The man was holding binoculars up to his face

and aiming them toward the ranch house, and that's where his full attention was.

Johnny came up behind him, and the man had no idea Johnny was even there until he felt the cold steel of Johnny's Colt pushing into his neck, and heard the hammer cock back.

"Mornin'," Johnny said.

10

Josh and Johnny headed to town for the meeting at Johansen's, as requested in the letter from Bertram Reed. Johnny was in a white shirt and put on a string tie. But otherwise, he was dressed the way he usually was. Jeans and boots, and was wearing his gun. Josh was dressed the same.

They walked into Johansen's, and walking in front of them was the man who had been spying on the ranch. They hadn't roughed him up, but had scared him a bit and they now had his hands tied behind him.

Reed was at a corner table and saw them come in. They marched their prisoner over to him.

Reed said, "I'm so glad you could be here."

People had stared at Johnny and Josh as they rode down the street with a man whose hands were tied behind him. Out of the corner of Johnny's eye he could see Marshal Falcone on the boardwalk. Falcone followed them into the restaurant and stood in the doorway, watching.

Reed looked at the man. "Chandler, what are you doing here?"

Johnny said, "I caught him watching our ranch from a distance, with a pair of binoculars."

Reed was a man of about forty. He had a hairline that had receded about as far as it could go, and brown sideburns that wrapped their way around to the front of his face to meet his mustache. He was in a three-piece-suit and had a gold chain stretched from his vest pocket to his jacket.

He said, "It's quite all right. Mister Chandler works for me. He meant no harm."

Johnny said, "No, it ain't all right. In this country, that sort of behavior can get a man shot. We'll let him go, this time. Next man you send out to spy on our ranch, we'll be bringing him to town draped over a saddle."

Josh pulled a bowie knife from a sheath at his belt. Its blade was about eight inches long. Reed's eyes went wide when he saw it. With the knife, Josh sliced the rawhide strip that was holding Chandler's hands together.

Josh said, "You're free to go. If we ever see you on our land again, we'll leave you hanging from a tree."

Chandler swallowed hard. He said nothing, but looked at his boss.

Reed said, "It's okay, Chandler. You can go, now."

Chandler didn't waste any time getting across the restaurant floor and out the door.

Falcone grinned and left.

Johnny said, "I wasn't joking. He's lucky to be alive."

Josh said, "What reason could you possibly have for having a man spy on us?"

"Not you," Reed said. "Your ranch."

"Same thing."

"Not really. Please sit down."

Josh looked at Johnny. Johnny gave a nod of his head, and they sat.

"Coffee?" Reed said.

Josh said, "Long as you're payin'."

Reed chuckled. Johnny had the feeling Reed was probably more accustomed to business meetings in places like St. Louis or Chicago, with men who did their business with a ledger rather than a gun.

Reed said, "But of course," and waved the waitress over.

He said, "Gentlemen, I would like to make you an offer. How much acreage would you say you own?"

Josh glanced at his father again, and then said, "About five thousand."

"Not more? Mister Chandler has been scoping out

your ranch for a few days, and from what he has seen, you have perhaps fifty thousand acres out beyond the valley."

Josh shook his head. "That's open range. What we actually own is in our end of the valley, only."

"I would estimate your end of the valley is closer to fifty-five hundred acres."

Johnny shrugged. He had never been good at estimating such things. When they filed their claim years ago, he had estimated the acreage at five thousand.

Before either of the McCabe men could say another word, Reed said, "I invited you here today, gentlemen, because I would like to buy your ranch."

"It's not for sale," Josh said.

"A dollar an acre would be a fair price. I'm willing to go a dollar twenty-five. And also a fair price for your herd. And another ten thousand for the ranch house itself. That will make you all very rich."

Johnny was about to say something, to explain there are different ways of looking at value. But before he could, Josh said, "We're already rich, Mister Reed. Rich in the ways that really count."

"As I understand it, the ranch ownership is actually divided by a number of people. Do you both speak for them all?"

Josh looked at Johnny. They both knew that they did not.

Reed said, "I'll go a dollar thirty an acre, and not a penny more. Mister Chandler estimates your herd at nearly four thousand head, including breeding stock. I'll offer two dollars a head for the whole herd. Including breed stock."

"Two dollars?" Josh said. "We'd get more than that in Cheyenne."

"But you're not in Cheyenne. If I am to make any profit from them, I would have to get them there. The cost of doing business reduces what I could offer per head. But add ten thousand for the house, and I believe we're looking at more than twenty-five thousand dollars."

Josh looked at Johnny again.

Reed said, "Take the offer home. Discuss it with everyone who has a stake in the ranch. I'll be here. I have a room at the hotel. I'll be awaiting your answer."

11

Temperance was at the stove, pouring some hot tea into two porcelain cups.

She said, "I'm still taken aback about that offer for the ranch. Twenty-five thousand is more than most cowhands see in a lifetime. "

Haley was at the table. Little Jonathan was in a wooden high chair, and she was holding a spoon in front of him.

Haley said, "Even so, we all said no pretty fast, didn't we?"

Haley brought the spoon to Jonathan, and made a whooshing, whispering sound with her mouth. Jonathan broke into laughter and she slid the spoon in.

Temperance set the cups onto saucers and brought them over to the table. When she had first come to this family three years earlier, she had never been able to balance a cup on a saucer without spilling half of the tea. But after three years of training at Aunt Ginny's hand, it was as though she had been doing this all of her life.

"What makes me wonder," she said, setting a cup of tea in front of Haley, "is why a land developer would want a cattle ranch like this. You look at Mister Reed, he doesn't know which end of horse is which. He'll have to hire someone to run the ranch for him."

"Maybe he wants the land for something else. Dusty and I were talking about that last night."

Temperance sat down. "Like what?"

"Like maybe selling it all off as farmland. With irrigation becoming more and more common, Reed could have potentially five thousand acres of corn fields, or whatever he wants to grow."

Temperance's thoughts were not really of land, though. Her and Josh's big day was coming up, and it was never long before her thoughts strayed back to it.

She said, "Do you wish you and Dusty had a big wedding?"

Haley's and Dusty's wedding had been in a small grove of maples that grew out behind the house, at the edge of the clearing. It had been mid-September, and the leaves of the maples were alive with the red of autumn.

Three weeks had passed since Dusty had convinced her not to take little Jonathan back east. The wedding had been put together quickly.

Josh served as Dusty's best man. Dusty had to admit to himself that as often as he poked fun at Josh, and even though Josh sometimes aggravated him to distraction, Josh was not only his brother but, aside from Haley, the closest friend Dusty had ever had.

Dusty had bought a broadcloth suit for the ceremony and left his gun at the house.

He had told Haley he was going to do this. Not wear a gun with his suit.

"A McCabe?" she said. "Without a gun?"

"I'm not like Pa," he said. "I don't have to wear a gun every waking moment."

Josh had a broadcloth suit, though he hadn't worn it in a while. Three years, in fact. It had been hanging in his closet but somehow was still rumpled, and Temperance ironed it flat for him and put a crease in it.

He had watched her do it and said, "I don't see how you do that without burning a big black patch in the cloth."

She shrugged. "I don't see how you boys handle a gun the way you do without shooting yourself in the foot."

Their cousin Tom officiated at the ceremony. Dusty stood waiting for his bride with his preacher cousin at one side and Josh at the other.

A small crowd had shown up for the ceremony. Granny Tate stood leaning on her cane and all bent at the shoulders. Her grandson Henry and his family were with her. Hunter was there, and Chen. Tom's wife Lettie and their daughter Mercy. And of course, Pa was there with Jessica and Cora. Aunt Ginny stood with them, wiping away tears. Bree stood beside her, beaming a big smile.

Bree had consented to wearing a civilized dress for the ceremony, and her hair was done up in some sort of fashion Aunt Ginny had seen in a magazine from New York.

Jack was there with Nina. They were to be married within a few weeks and then would be on their way to Cheyenne to catch an east-bound train. Jack was to begin Harvard's eighteen-month law school program in January.

Also in the crowd were Matt and Peddie. They had been married by Tom in a private ceremony a few weeks earlier. Only Johnny and Jessica had been on hand.

The men from the ranch were there, too. Charles was standing with Bree. He had no fine suit of clothes, but he wore a clean shirt buttoned at the neck and a string tie Josh loaned him. Old Ches was there, and the mysterious man known only as Kennedy.

The farmers from down in the center of the valley had come. The Brewsters. The Fords. Harland Carter was there, now known as Carter Harding. The former raider, probably still wanted by the law in several states. His wife was standing with him.

Vic Falcone had come out from town and brought Flossie. They hung back from the crowd a little, looking like they weren't sure if they should really be there or not. But Tom had been doing a lot of talking with everyone about second chances. Hunter had even used the concept as a new name for his and Aunt Ginny's saloon. In the spirit of second chances, Dusty stepped away from Josh for a moment and walked over to Vic and Flossie. Dusty extended his hand to Vic and said, "Glad you could make it."

After a short wait, the crowd parted. Pa had slipped away through the crowd and now he stood there with Haley. Her father was gone and there was no one to deliver her. Pa had said a fine gal like Haley needed someone to walk down the aisle with her. Pa had a dark broad cloth suit on and a string tie at his neck.

Haley hadn't asked, but she was sure he had a pistol tucked into his jacket.

Old Ches pulled out a harmonica and to everyone's surprise, he was right good with it. He played the wedding march, and Haley took Pa's arm and they walked in.

Little Jonathan was with Bree and Aunt Ginny, and Bree hoisted him up on her shoulder so he could see his mother.

"Mama," he called out, and the crowd laughed.

Pa gave Dusty a warm grip with his hand on Dusty's shoulder, saying it all with a gaze—he loved his son, and regretted that he hadn't been there when Dusty was growing up. And Dusty said it all with his gaze—none of that mattered, because he was here now.

Pa stepped back and Haley took her place at Dusty's side.

There was an old joke about frontier weddings. The preacher says, "Take her?" The groom says, "Yes." The preacher says, "Take him?" The girl says, "Sure." Then the preacher says, "Done. One dollar."

Dusty told Haley he had actually seen a couple weddings done that way. Once in a saloon and once outside the bunkhouse at the Cantrell ranch, down in Arizona.

Tom McCabe didn't do this, though. He conducted an actual wedding ceremony. He spoke of the bond that forms between a man and a woman. He spoke about the love of a man and a woman being the manifestation of God in this world. He spoke about how a man and a woman come together as two parts to create a whole.

Tom then recited the vows, with first Dusty repeating after him, and then Haley doing the same. They promised to love one another, and to have and to hold. Haley hadn't wanted *till death do us part,* because she believed the spirit was eternal. So they used the term, *forever and ever unto eternity.*

Tom then asked what symbol was going to be used.

"A ring," Dusty said.

Dusty looked to Josh. Josh hesitated, and had to suppress a grin.

Part of Josh's job was to hold onto the ring until the right time.

A few days earlier in the kitchen, Josh had said to Dusty, "I hope I don't lose it."

That had led to a round of horseplay, which ended up with Josh's coffee spilling to the floor.

Aunt Ginny reprimanded them. "If you're going to cause this kind of ruckus, you can take it outside."

But she was having to repress a grin, herself.

So now, as Josh was being asked for the ring, he hesitated. He felt at one pocket like he was searching for it, and tried not to grin. But then he dug into his jacket pocket and pulled the ring out and handed it to Dusty.

Despite himself, Dusty found himself wanting to grin, too.

"With this ring, I do thee wed," Dusty said, and slipped the ring onto her finger.

Tom said, "I now pronounce you man and wife."

Dusty didn't have to be told to kiss his bride. And then the crowd erupted with cheers and hollers.

Then it was back to the house for a party. Hunter provided a keg of beer and some bottles of whiskey.

The men from both ranches, even Old Ches, were

whooping it up and pouring down the beer or gulping whiskey.

"Honestly, Hunter," Aunt Ginny said. "Did you really need to bring all that whiskey and beer?"

He shook his head. "You shouldn't complain about that, anymore. You own half of it."

She gave him a look. "Then maybe this gives me another reason to complain. That's money we're losing."

He chuckled. She couldn't hold back a grin.

The following day, Dusty and Haley departed to the mountains for a week-long honeymoon of camping and roaming about the wilderness. Bree had been coaching Haley on riding a horse for the past month. With Haley sitting in the saddle and knowing at least a little about what she was doing, and Dusty beside her on his horse Buckskin and a pack horse with them, they waved goodbye to everyone and headed away.

Little Jonathan had never been away from his mother, but he would be all right. A tent had been set up beside the house, and he, Cora and Mercy were going to go camping with Bree.

One thing about Bree, Haley had noted, she knew how to make a day fun for little kids.

This all ran through Haley's mind as she sat at the table with Temperance and sipped tea.

Temperance had asked if she wished she and Dusty had a big wedding.

"You know," Haley said. "I wouldn't have changed any of it for the world."

12

The men from the ranch were at Hunter's. It was evening, and the following morning, Josh and Temperance were to be married. Zack and Ramon and Coyote were there, too. So was Tom McCabe. Even though he was a preacher, he showed up in jeans and with a gun strapped to his leg.

"If a preacher can wear a gun," he said, "he can have a mug of beer once in a while."

Danny McCabe was there. He had worked for the McCabes for a while, but now lived in town and a deputy marshal's badge was pinned to his shirt.

Chen had a mug of beer and was laughing along with Old Ches. Johnny wasn't sure which of these two was the older.

Johnny stood with Hunter by the bar. Johnny had a glass of whiskey in his hand.

Hunter was gulping beer from a mug and talking about the election for town marshal, which had been held in town the day before.

He said, "If you had asked me six months ago what the chances were of Vic Falcone winning, I would have said next to nothing. But danged if he didn't pull it off."

Johnny was chuckling. "Wait till I get home and tell Bree the news."

"I wouldn't want to be in the room when she hears it."

Johnny took down a mouthful of whiskey and allowed himself to a moment to savor it.

He said, "It helped that you gave him your public endorsement."

Hunter shrugged. "It helped that his opponent was that wild man Ned Pruitt. A drunken slob most of the time, but he has murder in his eyes. I don't know how he possibly thought he could win that election."

Josh drifted over to them.

"Pa," he said, "I've been thinking. Once Temperance and I are back from our honeymoon, we'll have to start doing some serious talk about that trail drive. But one thing I wanted to say before that."

Johnny was listening.

Josh said, "I'd like you to be the trail boss. I've been along on a couple of cattle drives, but I've never been a trail boss."

Johnny nodded. "All right. But you'll be my *segundo*."

Josh blinked with surprise. "I figured that job would go to Zack. It always did, years ago."

"It did. But I think I'm going to want to use him as scout."

Josh nodded. "Makes sense. Dan Bodine used to be our scout."

"You'd be a good scout, and so would Dusty, but I want you both with the herd for the sake of leadership."

Matt walked on over. He had a cup of coffee in his hand.

Hunter said, "Remember our first trail drive? We hadn't even been here two years."

Johnny said to Matt, "The nearest railhead back then was Sedalia, Missouri."

Matt shook his head. "That must have been quite a haul."

"Josh was too young to come along on that one. It was me, Zack, Hunter and some men I hired."

Hunter nodded. "It was when Reno first started working with us. Josh had some trouble with him a couple of years ago. Haven't heard anything from him since then. And Dan Bodine. A good man. Haven't seen him in years, either. Wonder what ever became of him?"

Josh had noticed Charles coming up to the bar to refill a mug of beer.

Josh said, "Chuck, can I have a word with you?"

Johnny took another pull of whiskey and listened to Hunter telling Matt about the old trail drives, but he had an ear tuned toward Josh and Charles.

"Listen," Josh said. "I've got to ask you something, and you might not like it."

"Go ahead, Boss."

"I know you're an experienced drover, but I need to leave one man back at headquarters. Aside from Dusty, and Pa himself, there's no hand on the ranch I would trust more than you. I don't want to leave the women alone that whole time. And there'll still be a sizable part of the herd to keep an eye on. You'll be in charge while we're gone."

Charles nodded. Johnny could see in his eyes that he was disappointed. No man with a good work ethic wants to be left out of a major project, and for a ranch, a trail drive was about as major as it got.

But Charles said, "I won't let you down, Boss."

Josh grinned. "You never do, Chuck."

This was when Bertram Reed walked in. Johnny looked over at Josh to see that Josh had seen him, too.

Reed saw Johnny at the bar and came on over.

"Reed," Johnny said.

"McCabe. I got word you were in town. I made you an offer a few days ago, and was hoping to get a reply."

"We couldn't get to town sooner. Running a ranch is often a daylong proposition."

"Could we talk about the offer now?"

Josh had come over, so Johnny said, "My son Josh is running the place, now. You need to talk with him."

Josh said, "We would like to thank you kindly for your offer, but we're just not interested in selling."

Reed waited a moment, then said, "Well? No counter-offer?"

Josh shook his head. "None at all. We're just not

selling."

"All right. You drive a hard bargain. Then let me increase my offer. A dollar seventy-five per acre."

Josh said, "It's not for sale at any price, Mister Reed."

Reed said, with a little chuckle the way a person has when dealing with someone who is painfully young and just doesn't understand something that should be obvious, "Mister McCabe, *every*thing is for sale, if the price is right."

All right. Time for Johnny to speak up. He had dealt with men like Reed before.

Johnny said, "Reed, you're from Chicago, is that correct?"

"I don't see what bearing that has on this matter."

"You're a businessman and you're accustomed to conducting business in a certain way. But the business world you live in is much different than the world out here. When you look at our ranch, you see dollar potential. You see cost-of-doing business. You look at the pine standing tall on the ridges and see it in terms of board feet. You look at the valley floor and maybe see potential farmland. But to us, it's our home."

Reed smiled. "Mister McCabe, I'll go two dollars an acre, but not a penny more. Why, with that money, you could move your family anywhere you wanted. St. Louis. Chicago. New York, even. You could set up a comfortable life for your wife, your daughter. Even one day, your grandchildren."

Johnny was about to correct him and say *daughters*, because he fully considered Cora to be his own. But he decided not to get side-tracked from the issue at hand.

He said, "We are where we want to be, right now. You see, Reed, I brought the family here years ago because this is where I wanted to raise my children. We built our home here out of choice. This is where we choose to be."

Hunter said, "You can offer this man three dollars an acre. Four. Won't make no difference."

Reed looked at Johnny and shook his head. "An offer like this doesn't come along every day."

"Doesn't need to," Johnny said. "My son Josh is speaking for the entire family when he says the offer is refused. And so will all offers be."

Josh said, "Nothing personal, Mister Reed. It's just this is our home."

"With all due respect, Mister McCabe," Reed said to Josh, "With the money I'm offering, you could build a home anywhere you wanted."

It struck Johnny that not everyone understands what the word *home* means. To some it is a place where you lay your head at night, and nothing more. But to others, people like Johnny and Josh and the rest of the family, it was so much more.

Josh said, "Thanks, Mister Reed, but we're happy where we are. It's not that your offer's not high enough. It's really more than generous. It's just that we're not interested in selling."

Reed said, "Well, if that's the way it's going to be..."

Josh said, "It is."

It struck Johnny again, as Josh stood and watched Reed walk across the barroom floor toward the door, what a man Josh had become. A man to ride the river with.

Reed paused at the door and gave Johnny and Josh a final glance before he disappeared out into the night. Josh had turned back to Charles so he didn't see it. But Johnny did. A certain look in Reed's eye. A look of not quite anger, but hard determination. And a look of coldness.

Matt and Hunter were still standing there. Matt said, "I don't think we've heard the last of him, yet."

13

Fred Mitchum sat at a table with a beer in front of him. He was in a white shirt and suspenders, and an old, beaten-up hat was pushed back on his head. He had a mug of cold beer in front of him. But he wasn't really working on it. He was working on telling Johnny something that would be hard to say.

He saw Josh talking with Dusty and Chuck, and realized he probably should tell Josh. After all, Josh was now the ramrod.

No time like right now, Fred supposed, and got to his feet and strolled on over. He didn't walk with a hurry, after all, he was not in a hurry to say what he had to say.

He listened to the boys talk for a few minutes. Josh was thinking he might ask Aunt Ginny to cut his hair in the morning. Maybe cut it short as Jack's, so he would look civilized at his wedding. Dusty told him he would look like a chicken. Fred had heard them have this conversation before, but Chuck hadn't and was laughing hard. Chuck also maybe had a little too much whiskey in him, so things sounded funnier than they were.

Finally, Fred said, "Hey, Josh, can I have a word with you?"

"Sure," Josh said.

They walked over to a deserted side of the bar.

"I been thinkin' about this trail drive," Fred said.

As the wrangler, Fred's job on the trail would be to manage the remuda.

Fred said, "I hate to ask out of a job, Josh. I really do hate to. I've worked for your family for a lot of years. Been on every trail drive your pa and Zack made. But, it's just that I'm fifty-one years old, now. My joints, they crick in the morning. I hate to ask this, but I'd like to stay behind on this one."

Josh looked at him. This was catching him by surprise and he didn't know what to say at first.

Then he said, "Fred, don't feel bad. You've given a lot of years to this ranch. There's work that'll need to be done here even while we're gone. I'm leaving Chuck behind, but it would be nice to have a second man around, too."

Josh paused a second while the words came to him. "Fred, you'll be doing me a favor if you stay behind and help Chuck out."

Fred said, "I hate to think I might be leaving you in a lurch."

Josh shook his head. "Not at all. You're doing me a favor. We've got to cover a lot of miles. Not quite as far as the old days, when we went all the way to Dodge or Ogallala. But I'll need your help in picking out a man who can manage the remuda for us. I'll need your expertise with men and horses. Someone you would trust with the remuda."

"Absolutely."

Johnny had drifted over and heard most of it. When Fred went to get Hunter's attention and ask for a refill, Johnny slapped his son on the shoulder.

Johnny said, "You're a good man, son."

14

Ginny couldn't sleep. She never could before a wedding. A man would never understand just what a wedding meant to a woman. How it was the manifestation of her childhood dreams. A fairytale come to life.

Moonlight gave her bedroom a pale bluish illumination, and from her bed she could see the clock on the wall. Twenty past twelve. The men had come home from the Second Chance, and the household was asleep. Every aspect of it, except for Ginny.

Maybe a cup of tea was what she needed. Though to do this, she would have to fire up the stove in the kitchen and she didn't want to go to all that trouble.

Maybe a glass of wine, she thought.

She slid out of bed and pulled on her house coat. It was made of silk, with ruffled trim. Kind of elaborate for life on the frontier, but she had bought in back in San Francisco and wanted some of the luxuries of home.

She stepped out into the parlor and could see a pale lamplight glowing from the kitchen doorway. Apparently she wasn't the only one awake, after all.

She found Temperance sitting at the kitchen table.

"Temperance?" she said.

Temperance was also in a robe, though hers was a plaid flannel.

"Oh, Aunt Ginny," she said. "I hope I didn't wake you."

Ginny laid a hand on her shoulder. "Is everything all right? I would have thought you were sound asleep by now."

"I can't sleep. I tried. I laid in bed until I heard Josh step into his room. The groom can't see the bride until the church."

"Are you having jitters?"

Temperance shook her head with a big smile. "Nothing of the sort. I'm just so excited. I want to do cartwheels. Though I haven't been able to do them since I was a child and would probably break my fool neck."

"I know what you need."

Ginny went to a little rack of wine on the counter. She preferred white wine and usually took a bottle out to a small duck pond at the far edge of the woods to let it chill before dinner. She wasn't going to go walking out to the duck pond at this time of night, so she would have to tolerate a warm Riesling.

She got out a cork screw, and once the cork was out, she filled two glasses and set one down on the table in front of Temperance.

"This will help you sleep," Ginny said.

Ginny slid out a chair and sat.

"So," Ginny said. "Tomorrow you'll be officially in the family. Though I hope you know, we already consider you family."

Temperance nodded with a smile. "You can't imagine how grateful I am for that."

She took a sip of wine. Ginny did, too.

Temperance said, "It's like a dream, you know. All of this. All of you. And especially Josh. My life had become such a living hell. And then he came along, like some sort of knight out of a fairy tale, and pulled me out of it."

Ginny said, "That's what the men of this family are like. Knights. Johnny uses the term gunhawk, but essentially they are knights. Crusaders. Except I don't think they fully realize it. It's just what they are."

"I wrote Faith. Told her all about you all."

Ginny knew Temperance had a sister by the name of Faith, living in New England.

"You've never said much about your family."

Temperance nodded. "It was hard for me to talk

about them, for a while. My mother and father died very close to one another. I was left with nothing and was forced into the life I was leading when Josh found me. He never judged me for it, and neither have any of you."

"We do what we have to do in order to survive."

"My sister had married before our parents died."

"She's older, am I right?"

Temperance nodded and took a sip of wine. "She's older by eight years. I wrote her when Ma and Pa died. She wrote back and asked if I needed help, but I never wrote back. I knew she would try to send money, which she didn't have. They live on a small farm in Vermont and have very little money. I knew she might want me to move there to live with them, but they have four children and I knew they didn't have the room for me. I was determined to survive on my own, without being a burden. What a fool decision that was, but I was fifteen and thought I knew more than I did."

Ginny sighed. "So do most of us, at fifteen."

Ginny had another sip of wine. "This household is yours, Temperance. You are now the lady of the house, as of tomorrow. You've earned it."

"But, Aunt Ginny, I feel like I'm somehow stepping into your place."

"Nonsense, child. My time here is done. It's time for this house to be yours and Josh's. I'll be moving into town, to be with Addison. We haven't made any announcements yet because I didn't want to take anything away from the joy and excitement of your wedding. But in two weeks, Addison and I are going to have just a small ceremony right here. I've talked to Johnny about it. Tom will officiate."

"Oh, Aunt Ginny." Temperance put a hand on Ginny's. "I'm so happy for you."

"And I for you."

Both wine glasses were about empty.

"You know," Temperance said, "I think I can sleep

now."

"Me too. Let's turn in. Tomorrow will be the biggest day of your life."

She and Ginny walked through the parlor. At the foot of the staircase, Ginny said to her, "I want you to know something. You're like a daughter to me."

Temperance said, "Oh, Aunt Ginny," and they took each in a long hug.

Ginny said, "Now get upstairs. Josh will never forgive me if his bride is falling over tired at the church tomorrow."

Temperance giggled. "You're right. I'll see you in the morning."

Ginny stood and watched Temperance climb the stairs. Ginny looked at her own bedroom door but realized sleep was still a long way off. After all, she had so much going on in her life now. Her upcoming marriage to Addison, which was in itself like a fairytale come true. There was also the expansion of the Second Chance into a full-fledged restaurant as well as a saloon. And in the morning, she would be coordinating the preparation of the wedding party.

She let herself stroll past the large stone hearth, and then stopped at her rocker. She lowered herself into it and looked at the darkened fireplace, thinking of all the evenings a fire had blazed to life in there, and how the family had sat before it and talked and laughed. Now she was sitting in the rocker for the last time as the lady of the house.

After a time, she rose to her feet and with her memories warm in her heart, she went to her bedroom and let sleep take her.

15

The following day, the church in Jubilee was preparing for the wedding of Josh and Temperance. However, Bertram Reed wasn't staying around for the festivities. The stage now rolled through Jubilee every day, and he climbed onto this morning's stage with a carpet bag packed for one night.

As the stage driver shouted, "Giddyap!" and the stage started forward, Reed gave a glance out the window at the church. He saw some sort of lacey ribbon twirled around the railing that led to the front door.

Two girls stood by the railing, applying the finishing touches to the ribbon. Both were in formal-looking gowns. One, a light-haired girl, he knew was the young wife of one of Johnny McCabe's gunfighter sons. The other, a dark-haired girl, was McCabe's daughter. The one who had beaten the stuffing out of Aloysius Randall the summer before.

The stage moved on and the church was gone from his view. He settled in for the long, jouncy ride down to Bozeman. He pulled a newspaper from his jacket pocket and unfolded it.

A man sat beside him. Gray-haired and a little heavy-set.

"Bound for Bozeman, are you?" the man said.

Reed gave a little sigh of exasperation. He was not in the mood for conversation. But he said, "That I am. Business trip."

The polite thing would have been for Reed to ask the man about his trip. Was Bozeman his final destination, or was he bound for Cheyenne, or some other place back east or further west? But Reed didn't really care. He wanted a few moments of peace. Just him and his newspaper.

The man didn't take the hint. He said, "Me, I have family out in Carson City. Ever been there?"

Reed had been through Carson City on his way to San Francisco. Not much to see in that part of the country. Mountains and a huge lake. He had never been one to see the aesthetic beauty in a mountain. He looked at a mountain in terms of potential mineral rights, and like McCabe had said, he looked at trees in the terms of board feet. In a lake, he saw water rights.

Reed focused on his newspaper and the man finally left him in silence. The scenery rolled by out his window, and the stage hit ruts and rocks and bounced its way along.

When they pulled up in front of the stage depot in Bozeman, Reed found himself thinking the railroad couldn't get to Montana soon enough. It was more expensive than a stage but gave a much smoother ride.

Bag in hand, he didn't go to the hotel where he had reserved a room, but headed directly to a restaurant. The name of the place was *The Bozeman,* and it was the closest you could find to real fine dining between St. Louis and San Francisco. Which meant the food was more than just glorified home cooking and the wine was actually aged more than six months.

He found his employer at a corner table. He was working on a steak, and a goblet of red wine stood before him.

Not many people in Jubilee knew that Bertram Reed had an employer. In fact, Reed didn't think anyone knew. Even the men who worked for him didn't know.

His employer's name was Aloysius Randall.

Randall looked up as Reed crossed the room.

"Bertram," he said.

"I am sorry I'm late," Reed said. "The stage left Jubilee later than planned, and the road is still a little rough."

Randall waved his fork in the air, dismissing the notion. "It's to be expected. The trails in this backwater part of the world haven't been open that long from the winter snows. Sit. Please."

Reed sat and placed his hat in an empty chair. A waiter scooted over and Reed ordered a vodka.

In most saloons in the vast wasteland between St. Louis and San Francisco, if you ordered a vodka, the bartender would look at you blankly. But here, the waiter actually asked him which brand. Reed didn't know how far he could push his luck but he thought he might try.

"Do you have Absolut?" he asked. A fairly new brand, started up two years earlier in Sweden.

The waiter didn't bat an eye. He was in a tie and jacket and spoke with a hint of the aristocratic Boston. "But of course."

Reed smiled. "That would do nicely. Thank you."

The waiter crossed the dining room, moving as though with a purpose.

Randall said, "Vodka. You have European tastes."

"Indeed," Reed said. "This is one of the few places you can get it within a thousand miles."

The waiter returned and placed a drinking glass in front of him with two fingers of clear liquid in it. He also gave Reed a menu. It didn't take him long to order. The porter house that Randall was cutting into was making his mouth water.

When the waiter left with his order, Randall said, "Did you know Vodka actually originated in Arabia? It was introduced to Russia in the thirteen century."

Reed said, "No, I didn't know that."

Which meant, to anyone who knew Reed, that he actually had no interest but was being polite. After all, Randall was his employer and was paying him a good deal of money. This was partly how he was able to afford Vodka imported from Sweden.

Reed took a sip of his vodka. It didn't burn. Vodka that burns is a sign of inferiority. He expected nothing but the best from Absolut.

Randall said, "Strange thing about the world. Russian vodka actually comes from Arabia. The Texas longhorn, from Spain. Gunpowder, which we all identify as being American or European, was actually invented in China in the twelfth century."

Reed had read more than one source that dated gunpowder back to the ninth century, but he wasn't going to correct his employer. The last thing most people wanted was to be proven wrong.

Randall chewed on a piece of steak and washed it down with a very civilized sip of wine. He didn't chug it or slurp, like so many did on what Reed considered to be this God-forsaken frontier.

Randall said, "My point being, I suppose, that seldom something that is highly identified with a certain place is actually from that place. If you dig deeply enough into history, everything is from somewhere else. Like we Americans, for instance. We believe this land is ours to take. Manifest Destiny, and all of that. But the Indian was here first. And if you look at an Indian, if you actually *look* at him, you can see distinct Asian qualities in the face. I was speaking with an anthropologist from Oxford a while ago and he speculated that in ancient times, the Indians made their way across the Bering Strait from Russia to Alaska. Not that I've ever been to either place or have any desire to actually go, but he showed me a map and it's a surprisingly small body of ocean that separate Russia from Alaska."

Reed waited patiently. He took another sip of vodka. He had little interest in history or anthropology. His interests were in business law, and profits and losses. But Randall was his employer so he listened as though he had an interest.

Randall said, "Take the little town of Jubilee. For a long time, it was McCabe country. Even the little hamlet that preceded Jubilee was called *McCabe Gap*.

When people think of that part of the territory, they think of the McCabes. In fact, they think of Johnny McCabe in particular."

Reed couldn't help but think about the fact that Randall had been knocked almost unconscious by McCabe's daughter the previous summer, and she had left him bruised and banged-up. It was weeks before the man was fully recovered. It made Reed want to laugh, but he held back that laugh by taking another sip of vodka. It doesn't do you a lot of good to laugh at your employer. Randall was giving him the equivalent of a cowhand's yearly salary every week. That kind of money you didn't laugh at. You could listen to a lot of rambling if you were paid like that.

Randall said, "But my intention is that before long, the McCabes will be gone. And I, the newcomer, will be the one people associate with the town of Jubilee."

"With all due respect," Reed said, "I have to ask. Why Jubilee? It's a very small pond for a man who has a lot of financial and business interest elsewhere."

"Because they stopped me. They stood in my way. They challenged me and made me look small."

You made yourself look small, Reed thought. Randall made unwanted advances toward a young girl and refused to take no for an answer. But she didn't need to go get her father or brothers to give Randall the violent thrashing he needed—she did it herself. Such a thing could be expected from a McCabe girl. The fault was all Randall's. Reed didn't see how Randall could consider himself the wronged party.

Randall didn't even dare show his face in Jubilee. This was why Reed had to meet him in Bozeman. He was partially afraid McCabe or one of his sons might decide to settle their score the old-school, vigilante way. With a bullet. But Reed suspected Randall was also afraid of the girl.

But with the kind of money Reed was being paid, if Randall felt he had a bone to pick with the McCabes and wanted Reed to assist him, then so be it.

Reed told him about what had transpired in Jubilee and the adjoining valley occupied by the McCabes. Reed had been willing to offer as much as two dollars per acre, an obscenely high figure given the current price of real estate, but had been refused.

Randall let all of this roll itself around in his mind while he took another sip of wine.

He said, "They're taking a herd south to Cheyenne."

It was a statement more than a question.

Reed said, "That's the talk around town. I'm not sure when they're departing, but I believe it's soon."

"And Johnny McCabe and his sons will be taking the herd themselves. They're not hiring drovers."

"Apparently not."

"Bertram," Randall said, "you have an assignment. I don't want those steers to arrive in Cheyenne. I don't care what you have to do. You have *carte blanche*. Scatter the herd to the hills. Destroy it if you have to. And if none of the McCabes return alive, I won't be disappointed."

16

Johnny had walked Haley down the aisle, and now he was going to do the same with Temperance.

Johnny stood in a suit and tie, and he was clean shaven and his hair was tied back. He left his gun back at the ranch.

Johnny found Temperance made a beautiful bride. He hadn't been to many weddings in his life, but no bride stood ahead of her. The gown was white and lacey, designed by Ginny based on something she had seen in some sort of magazine out of Paris, and sewn together by her and Haley.

Bree had never been much help with a needle and thread. She was more at home dealing with livestock. Evaluating horseflesh. She couldn't thread a needle, but Johnny had seen her light a match with a rifle shot from three hundred feet away. Josh had stood a match in a crack in an old stump and they marched off what they estimated to be a hundred feet. Johnny stood and watched while his daughter jacked a cartridge into her rifle. The first two shots missed, but on the third shot, the bullet struck the top of the match and a little lick of flame flickered to life on it. Johnny thought it was some of the finest piece of rifle-shooting he had ever seen.

Bree looked at home with a stetson pulled down over her head and a pistol at her side, but she also could bring a gown to life, and she now looked elegant as she stood with Haley at the back of the church. She was in a mint green dress with white lace and a neckline that fell off the shoulder. She had a long, graceful neck, and those hands that could hold a Winchester like they were born to it were now in white gloves, and she looked every bit as natural this way. Her hair was pinned up and she looked like something out of a magazine from back East.

Ginny was with them. She was the wedding

coordinator and was busy with final touches of preening Temperance's hair, and making certain the bride's bouquet was put together just right.

Ginny said to Johnny, "I think we're about ready to start."

"All right. Let me take a quick walk up front to make sure everything's all right up there."

Johnny walked up the aisle. The pews on both sides were full. Josh was standing in front of the altar and Tom was him. Josh had decided against cutting his hair, and it fell long and to his shoulders.

"You ready?" Johnny said to his son.

Josh said, "More than ever, Pa. She's the woman for me."

Johnny nodded. "I know. You know how?"

Josh shook his head.

"Because you two look at each other the same way your Ma and I used to."

Josh was grinning wide. Johnny thought he saw his son's eyes sparkling a little.

Johnny held his hand out and his son shook it.

Johnny said, "You're a fine son and a good ramrod. You're going to make a great husband and father."

"Coming from you," Josh said, "that means the world."

Johnny gave a nod to Lettie, who was sitting at an upright piano. The church hadn't yet acquired an organ, but Tom had gotten the piano second-hand from a saloon down in Bozeman. Some of the parishioners objected to having a saloon piano in the church, but Tom had said, "Don't turn your nose up at the Lord's bounty. He works in mysterious ways. We should be thankful."

Johnny walked back down the aisle and then Lettie's fingers began working over the ivories, producing the Wedding March.

Cora walked down the aisle first. Johnny was now standing with Temperance, but he could hear the shuffle as everyone in the church rose to their feet. Cora held a basket in one hand, and her job was to toss red rose petals to the floor as she moved along. Josh had gotten the petals from a wild rose bush that grew on the valley floor.

Dusty was standing out back with Charles. Josh had needed a third man to stand with him, and had had chosen Charles. Both were in a tie and jacket. Dusty's hair fell freely about his shoulders, where Chuck's was short. When Johnny had first come West, many men had worn their hair long, and oftentimes with sweeping mustaches and full beards. Now, among the younger men, there were fewer beards and when there was a mustache, it was short and tidy, and hair was usually cut short. The result of the West becoming more civilized, Johnny figured.

Charles was one of the tallest boys Johnny had ever met and was built like a fence pole, but Ginny had gotten him a jacket and trousers and then found some way to adjust them so they fit him.

When Cora was halfway down the aisle, Charles began forward and Haley was beside him with her hand resting gently in the crook of his arm. Then when they were partway toward the altar, Dusty and Bree began down. Dusty was the best man and Bree the maid of honor.

Then, when they were halfway along the aisle, Johnny took his place alongside Temperance.

He said to her, "Are you ready?"

Her face was covered with a veil but he could see her beaming smile. "I am, Pa. I only wish my parents could see me now."

"They can, Sweetie. They can."

She stood, smiling.

He said, "You're like a daughter to me. I hope you

know that."

She said, her voice breaking a little, "I know, Pa. It means the world to me."

He nodded. "Come on. There's a boy waiting for you at the other end of the church."

She placed her hand in the crook of his arm, and they began down the aisle, one step at a time.

They didn't march, but walked slowly. Josh stood with Dusty now beside him and his face in a big smile.

Hunter was there in the crowd with a huge grin. Johnny's brother Joe was there. Kennedy stood in a range shirt but with the collar buttoned and a crooked string tie in place. The new man Josh had hired was there. Abe Taggart. Zack was in one of the pews, along with Ramon and a couple other men from his ranch. Harlan Carter stood in the fourth row, another of the tallest men Johnny had ever met. His wife was beside him, almost two feet shorter. Matt and Peddie were there, and pretty much everyone else. The place was full.

Temperance and Johnny got to the head of the aisle. Josh was looking at her like she was the most beautiful sight he had ever seen. The way a man in love looks at his bride.

And then Johnny stepped back, and Temperance stepped forward to stand at Josh's side.

Johnny slid into the front pew beside Jessica and Cora. Ginny was there, and Sam Middleton. The man Ginny called Addison. Ginny had a kerchief in her hand, and a tear was already decorating one cheek.

Johnny leaned over and whispered to her, "Starting early, aren't you?"

She said, "I'm entitled."

"I suppose you are."

Tom talked about love and marriage and commitment. How from the dawn of time a man and a woman have come together in matrimony, and so forth.

Johnny had never been one for sermons.

Then came the vows. Pretty much the same vows given at every wedding. And yet, every time they were said, it was as though it was the first.

Then came the slipping on of the ring, and Josh didn't wait to be told to kiss her. Dusty hadn't with Haley. Johnny hadn't with Jessica, and he hadn't all those years ago with Lura.

Tom addressed the congregation, "Let me introduce Mister and Mrs. Joshua McCabe."

And everyone got to their feet and broke out into a roaring ovation. There were cowhands present and they made it known with whoops and hollers.

Johnny glanced to the back of the church and saw Vic Falcone was standing there. He nodded at Johnny with a trace of a smile. Johnny thought about the idea of second chances. There had been a lot of talk like that going around these past few months. Johnny decided to nod back at him.

17

The reception was held at the *Second Chance*. Champagne was served. A fiddle and a banjo were providing the music. Ches joined in with his harmonica a couple of times.

Josh and Temperance had their first dance. Then it was time for Johnny to dance with the bride, and for Josh to dance with the bride's mother. Since Temperance's mother had died when she was younger than Bree, but Temperance had said more than once that Ginny had become like a mother to her, Ginny filled the role here and danced with Josh.

After a meal, some folks were standing and others were sitting, and the room was filled with that chattering buzz that comes from dozens of conversations going on at once. It reminded Johnny of a flock of wild birds in a tree.

Johnny saw Falcone at the doorway. Falcone motioned him over with a nod of his head. Johnny went on over.

"How's everything going?" Falcone said.

Johnny nodded. "Fine. Everyone seems to be having a good time."

"When're you boys leaving for the trail drive?"

"I'm estimating two weeks. Separating out the stock, final head counts, and the like. And Aunt Ginny and Sam Middleton are getting married. They don't want a lot of fuss, but I don't expect there'll be a lot of work done that day."

Falcone nodded. "I wanted to let you know, there's a group of men camped maybe five miles south of town. Off the trail a little. I sent Danny to scout them out yesterday and he told me their names. Trevor Jordan. Buck Peters. A couple of others. Those names mean anything to you?"

Johnny shook his head. "Not really."

"I've seen their names on reward posters. Cattle thieves. Wanted for rustling off Virginia City way. I can't do much about it because their camp is beyond the town line. Out of my jurisdiction. But while Danny was watching them from a distance, he saw a man ride into camp. Do you know the name of Cornelius Chandler?"

"The man who works for Bertram Reed?"

"The very. It might be nothing, but I thought I should bring it to your attention. There could be trouble afoot."

Johnny shook his head and felt exasperation wash over him. "Isn't there always?"

PART TWO

The Fire

18

Johnny wasn't sure how old Ches Harding was. Somewhere between seventy and eighty, he guessed, but even Ches wasn't sure. He had lost track over the years.

Old Ches was one of those old men who got older but never seemed to become frail. He might have lost a step over the years and his back hurt in the morning and his knees creaked when it was going to rain, but his hand was steady and he could still ride a horse as well as anyone Johnny had ever seen, and he could still drop a loop over a cow.

The thing that made Ches the most valuable, though, was his cooking. He had worked for Jessica for years, and before that, for her late first husband.

She had said to Johnny, "You haven't tasted anything until you've tasted his chili."

So when Johnny decided to go looking for a trail cook, someone to drive the chuck wagon and supply meals to the drovers, Ches was the first one he looked to.

Ches was outside the bunkhouse. He had rolled a smoke and was enjoying the early evening air. The sun had just set and the sky overhead was a steel gray. Here and there a bird would go swooping by, looking for a last meal before it got dark. A sort of hush was falling on the land, as though daytime was tucking itself into its blankets and nighttime was about to wake up.

"Trail cook, eh?" Ches said. "I been on a few trail drives over the years. I was with Charles Goodnight and Oliver Loving in their first big drive. Back in sixty-six. Or was it sixty-seven? Bernard Swan was there, too. We were drovers. That's where I met him. We went west after that together, and I helped him build his ranch. Never served as a trail cook, though. But I suppose there's a first time for everything."

Johnny had leather chaps strapped on over his

jeans. He had been on the range all day, and he and his chaps were covered with a layer of dust that made his clothing look gray in color. He didn't tie his gun down over the chaps, and since he didn't want it to bounce around while he rode, he tightened his belt so his pistol was riding high on his hip.

He said, "Had me a trail cook by the name of Sanborn. We made a number of drives south to the railheads. But he married one of Alicia Summers' girls, a girl young enough to be his daughter, and they lit out to Oregon."

Ches chuckled. "Trail cooks. They are an eccentric lot."

He shrugged. "Don't know how eccentric I am. But I'm too old to work as a drover anymore. These old bones couldn't take that many hours in the saddle, anymore. So if you want me to give bein' a trail cook a try, I will."

"Much appreciated."

"Just don't call me Cookie. A lot of trail cooks are called that. I had a dog called that when I was growin' up. Just wouldn't seem right."

Johnny chuckled. "All right. I'll resist the urge."

When Sanborn had lit out for Oregon, he left the chuck wagon behind. The wagon had sat at Zack's ranch since the last cattle drive. Johnny explained this to Ches.

Johnny said, "We've done some minor cattle drives since then. To Fort Logan a couple times. And the gold fields in Alder Gulch. But those were only maybe a hundred head at a time. Nothing a small handful of drovers couldn't handle. The last major cattle drive was to buyers we met in Dodge City the summer before I got all shot up when Falcone and his men attacked this place."

Ches chuckled. "Falcone is a marshal who prob'ly should arrest hisself. Not the first one I met, though.

Most lawmen rode the other side of the law for a while before they put on a badge. Maybe in the mornin' I'll ride on out to Zack's ranch and see what kind of shape the chuck wagon is in."

"We need you out at the roundup. We'll be staying the night tomorrow night, and probably the next one too."

"I'll be there late tomorrow. Day after at the latest."

Johnny knew a man like Ches was as good as his word. And his word was as good as gold. No matter what condition the chuck wagon was in, Ches would find some way to have it ready and stocked, and out at the round up and ready for service.

19

A longhorn was long-legged and could run like a horse, and after a winter of roaming about and searching for good grass, a herd the size of the McCabes' could spread out over many square miles of rangeland. Hence, in the spring, there was a roundup or what they sometimes called a gather. The stock would be tallied, which would include any new calves.

The range used by the McCabes was all open range, like they had told Bertram Reed. But Johnny was thinking it might be a good idea to lay claim to some of it because as more and more folks moved into the area and laid claims of their own, the open range they used might become not so open anymore.

Zack and Johnny had never been all that particular about grazing rights. Cows from one herd tended to mingle with the other. During the round up, Josh kept a tally of the Circle M and Swan cattle, as well as the Circle T cows that had mingled in. Zack did the same and he and Josh compared notes to get an accurate count, but never bothered to separate the herds.

Spring roundup had ended a few weeks ago, but now they were conducting another gather, specifically to separate the road stock from the breeding stock.

Johnny and the men planned to work right up until sunset. The valley was an hour's ride away by daylight, a ride Johnny didn't intend to make after dark. Too many rocks to ding up a horse's leg, or holes for a horse to step into. So they brought their bedrolls along.

A campfire was built, and Johnny dumped some beans from a can into a skillet and heated them over the flames. As he was eating, scooping the beans with a fork directly from the skillet, Zack came riding up and swung out of the saddle.

Zack needed to take some cattle to market too, so

he and Johnny had decided to combine both herds. Zack had eight hundred head ready, and going along with the larger outfit made good business sense to him. They had done this on their last trail drive, four summers earlier, and it had worked out well.

Zack walked over to Johnny like his back and legs were stiff, and said, "I'm getting too old for this."

Johnny nodded. "You're not the only one."

Johnny was sitting on the ground. He had taken off his gunbelt but it was within reach.

Johnny said, "I sent Ches over to your place to check out the chuck wagon. I hope he's here by tomorrow."

"Me too," Zack said. "Ain't right for cowpokes to have to feed themselves."

Zack fished a skillet out of his saddle bags and a can of beans.

Johnny had set a coffee pot in the flames and it was boiling over. Third boil. The coffee was ready. He used a bandana to grab the pot with, and filled a tin cup. Zack held out a cup and Johnny filled it, too.

Johnny said, "I want you to be our scout. I know it's partly your herd, but with Bodine gone, I can't think of anyone better suited for the job. Josh could do it, but since he's the ramrod of my place, I'd like him to be on hand as my segundo. It'll help him establish leadership among the men. Dusty's a good scout, but he doesn't know the terrain like you do."

Zack nodded. "Most of the cows are yours. Makes sense."

He took a sip of the coffee, and spit out some grounds. "Think we have enough men?"

Johnny nodded. "It's the largest herd we've ever taken to market. But I think we have enough. We'll have to mix the horses for one large remuda. Maybe use two wranglers."

"I'll use Ramon for that. He'll work well with

Fred."

Johnny chewed and swallowed a mouthful of beans. "Fred ain't coming."

Zack looked at him.

Johnny said, "He asked to stay behind. He's got too many years on him to sit in the saddle all day for five or six weeks. Gotta find a new wrangler for the drive. I'm thinking on asking Dusty. You won't find anyone who knows more about horseflesh than he does."

Zack nodded.

A horse walking like it was tired approached the campfire. The sky was nearly dark, but Johnny could see a man swinging out of the saddle. He approached the fire, long and tall and covered with dust.

"Chuck," Johnny said. "Grab some coffee."

Chuck nodded. He had left his cup at their makeshift camp earlier in the day. He didn't even bother to shake any dirt out of the cup. He just snatched it from where he had dropped it in the grass and filled it with coffee.

He said, "We gonna give these critters a road brand?"

Johnny shook his head. "Don't see the need to. Everything should have either a Circle M or a Circle T or the Swan brand."

Charles dropped to the grass to sit cross-legged, his elbows resting on his knees. Nothing like a round up to make you weary to the bone.

He said, "I worked as a drover for two herds comin' up from Texas. But none this big. We must have close to four thousand head, all total."

Zack nodded. "We'll handle 'em, though."

"Think we'll have enough men?"

Johnny said, "We were just talking about that. Every man we have is an experienced hand. And Josh should be back from his honeymoon in a couple of days."

Charles took a sip of coffee and spit out the grounds.

Johnny said, "Look, Chuck, I hope you don't feel bad about staying behind. But I need a man I can trust to watch over the ranch while we're gone. Sam Middleton will be there, but he doesn't work for the ranch. Fred's a good man, but he's the wrangler. I need a man who can keep a watch over the whole operation."

Charles said, "I'm all right. I appreciate the confidence you have in me."

"Well, you've earned it."

Zack said, "He just doesn't want to be away from Bree that long."

Charles tried not to blush, but wasn't quite up to the job.

Dusty came riding in. Even though Fred wouldn't be coming along on the trail drive with them, he was out here at the round up serving as wrangler. Dusty swung out of the saddle and handed the reins to Fred.

"Thanks, Fred," he said.

Dusty walked up to the fire. He was in leather, batwing chaps that flapped as he walked. Like Johnny, he had tightened his gunbelt so his gun rode high on his hip. He was in a shirt that had been a faded blue at the start of the day but was now gray with trail dust.

He sat on the ground and flipped back his hat so it hung onto his back, and then rubbed his hands through his hair.

He said, "Any coffee left?"

"Help yourself," Johnny said.

"Got me a question."

They were all listening.

He said, "Those men Falcone mentioned to you. The cattle thieves camping outside of town. Have you given them any more thought?"

"I've been focusing on the round up and preparing

for the trail drive, but I've kept what Falcone told me in the back of my mind. Why do you ask?" Johnny said.

"Because there's a campfire off in the distance."

Johnny climbed to his feet, despite the protest he got from his aching joints. He buckled on his gunbelt and he and Zack followed Dusty out into the darkness. Once they were beyond the edge of the firelight, Johnny could see it off in the distance—a pinpoint of light.

"There it is," Dusty said.

Johnny nodded. "A campfire."

Zack said, "Could be nothing. Just someone traveling through."

"Could be," Johnny said. "But remember our old Texas Ranger captain? What he said?"

"Hope for the best, but prepare for the worst. What you get'll usually be somewhere in between."

Johnny said, "Dusty, in the morning I want you to ride back to the valley. Catch up with Ches. Tell him to load the chuck wagon with rifles. I want one for every man. And bring along my Sharps. Zack, in the morning you and I are going to ride out there and have a look. See just who's camping out there."

20

Johnny and Zack were awake before sunrise, saddling their horses. Johnny had left Thunder back at the ranch headquarters, because even though the horse was strong and had good stamina and was his first choice if he was traveling overland, Thunder horse was a half-broken stallion and of little use when it came to working cattle. Johnny saddled a mustang they had caught a couple of years earlier, a roan that stood almost fifteen hands.

Johnny had been trying to discourage Bree from naming the horses. They weren't pets. But she had taken it upon herself to start calling this horse Gray, even though it didn't strike Johnny as looking all that gray. Bree tended to get what she wanted, and now the horse was called Gray. Just like Fat was now called Charles.

"We got no rifles," Zack said, as he tightened the cinch on a bay he had taken from the remuda. "The chuck wagon won't be here with 'em until afternoon, at the earliest."

"We shouldn't need 'em," Johnny said. "This is a scouting mission, only."

Even still, Johnny drew his revolver. A campfire was burning which they had used to heat some coffee before they got going, and in the firelight, Johnny checked the loads.

He and Zack started out. But they didn't do so by swinging into the saddle. It was still fully dark and a horse could step into a hole. Also, they didn't want to spook the cows that had been rounded up. Johnny estimated they had over fifteen hundred head on hand that would be taken to market. If they stampeded, it would take the boys days to round them up again. The idea was to get them to market while the grass was still springtime green, and the streams were running high with runoff.

Johnny and Zack walked along. Johnny had the rein in his left hand and kept his right free. Old habits. Zack was doing the same.

Ahead of them they could see the small pinpoint of light. The campfire in the distance was still burning.

Zack spoke, keeping his voice low so it wouldn't travel with the distance. "Kind'a reminds me of three years ago. Seeing a campfire in the distance."

Johnny said, "Like you said, could be nothing at all."

"Let's hope."

They kept walking.

The cows were down for the night, and spread out. Longhorns tended not to bunch together, if given their druthers. Johnny and Joe walked along through and their horses loped along behind them.

After maybe half a mile the sky started to lighten. First stars began dropping out of sight, then the sky became a sort of dark gray. Then it grew to a steel gray and the terrain about them started coming to life. Junipers and an occasional short, fat pine, spread out with sometimes hundreds of feet of grass between them. The land rose and fell in gentle hills.

They could now see where the land rose into little humps that could trip a horse, or fell away into small, grassy ravines. Time to mount up.

Johnny and Zack rode along easily. Turned out the camp was only about three miles away. Johnny and Zack covered the distance in a little over an hour. They found it deserted.

At the center of the camp were the blackened remains of the campfire. Handfuls of dirt had been dropped on it to extinguish it. They could see where five men had bedded down for the night. They found cigarette butts and a couple empty cans of beans. The horses had been picketed back a ways.

Johnny said, "A string of fifteen horses."

Zack nodded. "That's five to a man."

"A lot of horses for a small group of men just passing through."

The tracks headed away south. Hoof prints were in the grass, and in some places the hooves had torn up small divots.

Johnny said, "Maybe we ought to follow 'em a while."

The riders headed south for a while, but then started swinging east.

Johnny said, "There's no reason for them to circle east from here. All the ranches in the area are to the west. So's Jubilee."

Zack nodded. "Bozeman's southwest, and Helena's to the northwest. There's no reason for them to turn east at all, unless they're trying to circle around the herd."

They continued along. At one point, they estimated the riders to have an hour's lead on them.

Johnny reined up where it looked like the riders had stopped to let their horses blow. As good a spot as any for Johnny and Zack to do the same.

"Think they know they're being followed?" Zack said.

Johnny nodded. "If they're worth their salt, they do."

"I'm thinking they have to be those horse thieves Falcone told you about."

"I can't imagine who else they might be."

After a short time, they continued along. Johnny pulled a length of jerked beef from his vest pocket and began chewing. Zack did the same.

About mid afternoon, Zack looked back over his shoulder and said, "Riders comin'."

They stopped and waited. They didn't have to wait

long, because the riders were coming at a good clip.

Johnny grinned when he saw who it was. Josh and Dusty.

The boys reined up.

Dusty said, "You two make good time. We were starting to think we wouldn't catch up to you before nightfall."

Johnny said to Josh, "You look well-rested, for a man coming back from his honeymoon."

Zack was grinning. "I wouldn't think a newly-married man would be getting much sleep."

Dusty said, "He ain't stopped blushing since he rode into camp."

Josh gave an impatient nod. "All right, all right. Leave me alone."

Josh had a Winchester in one hand and Dusty was carrying Johnny's Sharps. They each had another tucked into a saddle boot.

Dusty said, "We thought you might need these," and tossed the Sharps to Johnny.

Johnny said, "You boys made really good time catching up to us. But now, we're gonna take things a little slower. I don't want to catch up to them until after dark. Give them time to build a fire. It'll give us the chance to go in and get a look at 'em."

The men posted one guard. A man to stand outside the camp, beyond the circle of firelight. He had a rifle in his hands, and he paced about in the bored way a night sentry sometimes does. He had a cigarette in his mouth.

His hard-soled riding boots occasionally scuffed on the gravel underfoot. The leather of his gunbelt would creak a bit from time to time. He heard a wolf calling from somewhere off in the distance. He was experienced enough to know it was nowhere close. What he didn't hear was Dusty coming up behind him.

He felt the cold steel of the blade of a bowie knife against his throat.

Dusty said, "Don't say a word, or I'll cut you a new smile from ear to ear."

Dusty left the man about a mile from the riders' camp. Dusty used his own lariat to tie him hand-and-foot, so all the man could do was wiggle around a little in the grass.

The man said, "You can't leave me like this. There's wolves out there."

"We won't be gone that long. You'll be all right."

Dusty rejoined the others. They were waiting just outside the circle of firelight, upwind so the string of horses wouldn't catch their scent.

The moon hadn't yet risen, but the sky was clear and the stars were creating a sort of faint, gray lighting. Between that and residual firelight that reached them, Dusty could barely see his father.

Dusty held both hands in front of his chest. Then he touched the fingertips of both hands together, the wrists apart, roughly forming the letter A. Indian sign-language for *tie-up* or *tied-up*. Johnny nodded. He got the idea.

Four men were in the camp, milling about the fire. One was standing and he had a coffee cup in one hand. Another was kneeling by the fire. They had apparently gathered some wood from the pines scattered about. The fire smelled smoky, so Johnny figured they were burning green wood. One man was stretched out on his soogan, his hat over his eyes. A fourth was sitting, sticking a twig in the fire and then pulling it out and watching the small flame dance on the end of it. There was light conversation, but Dusty and the others were too far out to catch the words.

Johnny motioned toward one side of the camp, then pointed toward Dusty and Josh. They nodded and started away in the direction Johnny had indicated. Johnny then motioned to Zack, who headed off toward the other side.

They had discussed this plan before they approached the fire. Dusty and Josh knew just what to do.

They moved along slowly through the grass on their hands and knees. It was soft and slippery, and made no sound as they crawled along.

They stopped at a point that put them at three o'clock to the fire, with Pa at six o'clock. To go much further would put them in risk of falling downwind of the horses.

Dusty pulled his pistol but didn't cock it. A sound like that would carry in the night. Josh did the same.

The plan had been for Johnny to wait fifteen minutes for Dusty, Josh and Zack to take their places. By Dusty's reckoning, it had been about fifteen minutes.

Johnny called out, "Hello, the camp!"

The three men who were down scrambled to their feet. One of them grabbed a rifle and the other three pulled pistols.

One of them called out, "Come on in, nice and easy."

Johnny came in, hands in the air.

The one who had spoken said, "Not that we don't mean to be friendly, mister. We just gotta be careful."

"I don't blame you," Johnny said. "You been doggin' my herd for at least a day. I gotta ask why."

The men looked at each other. Apparently they hadn't been expecting this.

The one who had spoken said, "We don't know what you're talking about. We're just passing through."

Johnny shook his head. "If you were just passing through, you would have continued on south. Or turned west. Right now, you're about three miles from our herd, the same distance you were last night."

Johnny was letting his hands drift downward as he spoke.

One of them said, "Hold it, mister. We'll shoot. I mean it."

Johnny said, "I would drop those guns. You're surrounded."

That was the cue, Dusty figured. He cocked his gun. Josh did the same. Zack had taken a Winchester with him, and he jacked in a round. The sound of all of this carried well in the night, and the four men were looking off at the darkness around them.

"Zeke!" one of them called out. "You out there?"

Johnny said, "Zeke's down and out for a little while. He won't be any good to you. Throw down those guns."

The first man who had spoken raised his pistol and aimed it at Johnny. He called out, "You all come in and throw down your guns, or I'll put a bullet in this man!"

Dusty could see the position of the hammer of the man's gun. He hadn't thought to haul back the hammer first. These men were cattle thieves but not experienced gunfighters.

Dusty called out to him, "You gotta cock the gun if you want it to work!"

That was when Johnny's gun hand shot down and then came up with his own gun. The man cocked his but Johnny fired first. The others were cocking and bringing their guns up, but the three surrounding the camp unloaded on them. Dusty got three shots off and so did Josh. Dusty thought he counted four from Zack's rifle, maybe five. One of the men at the campfire spun around like he was doing a little dance, then dropped to the ground. The head of another man snapped back like he had taken a punch, and then fell over. The third started running but got only thirty feet from the fire before he fell over from the bullet he had taken. The string of horses all bolted into the night.

Dusty and Josh got to their feet and came on in. Zack was doing the same.

The three at the fire were dead. The one who had spun around had three bullets in his chest and two more in the side of his ribs. One had a bullet dead center in his forehead.

Zack said, "That was my shot. I was aiming at him."

One had taken two more bullets to the chest. The one who had run a bit had a bullet in his chest and one in his shoulder.

Johnny dumped out his empty cartridge, and thumbed in a new one.

Dusty said, "I'll go get the one I tied up."

Josh went with him. A quarter moon was peeking into view over the horizon as they approached the spot where Dusty had left him. They could see for a fair distance now, and the man was gone. His ropes had been cut.

Josh said, "Looks like he had a knife on him."

"Dang," Dusty said. "I didn't see any knife sheathed on his belt or in his boot or anywhere, but he must have had a jackknife tucked into a pocket. I should have searched him more thoroughly."

"Well, he's gone. Nothing can be done about it now." Josh slid his gun into his holster.

"Now we won't be able to find out if these men are the ones Bertram Reed's man rode out to see." Dusty holstered his own gun. "And it means I've lost a good lariat."

21

Ches had two shovels in his chuckwagon, and the men grabbed them and buried the four dead men in unmarked graves.

Johnny stood, looking down at the humps of grass.

Ches said, "We buried 'em as close to six feet down as we could. Maybe discourage the wolves from getting to 'em."

Johnny supposed it would seem a little cold to a man from civilized parts to just leave the bodies out here. But the nearest incorporated municipality was Jubilee, and it would have taken half a day to haul the bodies all the way there. And even then, Marshal Falcone's jurisdiction ended at the town line. A rider would have to be sent to Bozeman, where he would wire the territorial marshal. If the marshal was out in the field, it could be days or even weeks before someone brought the telegram to him.

Someday, Johnny thought, Montana would probably have statehood, and the territory would all be divided up into counties and there would be laws and such. But at the moment, this was just open land, open and wild as it had ever been. The only law was the law of a man's gun. And the night before, the law had spoken. These men had drawn guns on Johnny, and you don't draw a gun on a man if you're not prepared to receive the consequences.

Zack was standing beside Johnny. "What do you suppose would be Reed's motivation for sending these men out here? Small-time horse thieves and cattle rustlers. They might be able to cut a few head at night, but it wouldn't cause us any real problem. All it would do is get them killed if they were caught."

"We'll probably never know," Johnny said. "They may not even be the same men."

Zack nodded.

"Come on," Johnny said. "Let's mount up. We've got a job to do."

Every trail drive has at least one lead steer. A steer the others would follow. For Johnny and the trail drives he had made down to the railheads, that steer was Old Blue. Some longhorns were various shades of brown or gray, and others tended to be spotted with brown and white. Old Blue was a sort of light gray around the neck and body, more of a charcoal gray around the snout and down along the legs and tail. The light gray struck Johnny as having a little bluish hue in the dimmer light of early morning, and so he had taken to calling the animal Old Blue.

This was the only steer that returned to the ranch with Johnny and the boys after a trail drive. Old Blue was just too effective a leader to part with. Johnny had received offers from drovers to buy Old Blue, but had always turned them down.

Old Blue was larger and more heavily muscled than most. Johnny remembered years ago seeing the man called Bodine drop a loop around Old Blue's horns and then as he tried to tie off on his saddle horn, Old Blue pulled and one of Bodine's fingers got caught between the rope and the saddle horn, and the finger was popped off. A painful way to lose a finger.

They had been on the trail, a few day's ride to the nearest settlement. Sanborn had been with them as the trail cook in those days, and he heated a knife until it glowed red and sealed off the wound.

Johnny had seen more than one cowhand lose a finger that way. Kennedy had a missing finger on his left hand, and Johnny hadn't asked but wouldn't have been surprised if he had lost it to an ornery steer.

Old Blue was nearly twelve years old. Johnny didn't figure he would have many trail drives left in him, but with the coming railroad, this would be the last long-distance drive the old boy would have to make.

Johnny was sitting in his saddle watching Old Blue chew on some springtime grass when Josh came riding up.

"Got 'em tallied at twenty nine hundred and three with our brand or the Swan brand, and eight hundred and forty-one with Zack's."

"You satisfied with the count?"

Josh nodded. "About as accurate as we're gonna get."

"All right. Then in the morning, we start 'em moving."

Josh looked over at the old steer.

"What're we gonna do with Old Blue afterward?"

"I was thinking maybe we retire him. Let him graze. He's earned the right to have a life of leisure for his last few years."

Chuck Cole was still with them. Even though he would be staying behind at the ranch, he was an experienced drover and Josh found him a big help during the roundup.

The sky was growing dark and Ches had a big campfire going. A few of the hands were out riding night herd, but most were sitting in the grass with a bowl of beef stew.

Johnny came riding in, and Fred took the reins from him as he swung out of the saddle.

Johnny grabbed a bowl of stew and went over to where Chuck was sitting. Zack was there, and Josh.

Johnny said, "We're gonna start 'em moving in the morning. Chuck, you and Fred can ride back to the ranch at first light."

Chuck nodded.

Johnny said, "There's something I want you to do. Go into town and see if Reed's man Chandler is still around. And see Falcone and ask if he's seen anything interesting. Reed left town the day of Josh's wedding, but I'd feel better if Chandler was gone, too. And I'd like to know what any other men who might be working for Reed have been up to. There's something about Reed I don't trust."

Ches was standing nearby, a leather apron tied on over his jeans and the butt of his revolver sticking out from the side.

He said, "That's what they call good judgment. That man is a snake. I feel it in my bones."

Johnny said to Chuck, "We won't be far down the trail. I don't expect to make many miles the first few days. Ride on out and tell me what you find."

"Yessir."

Johnny took a spoonful of stew. "Ches, I have to say, this is some of the best stew I've ever tasted."

Ches was smiling. "Butchered me a steer yesterday. Brought the potatoes from Zack's root cellar."

Dusty came riding in. He swung out of the saddle. "I could smell that stew a couple hundred yards out," he said. "A man could just follow the smell on in."

He grabbed a bowl and joined them.

Johnny said, "I'll be riding point. I want you there with me, Josh. I was thinking Kennedy can ride right swing, and Coyote left swing."

Josh nodded. "Sounds good."

Johnny looked to Dusty. "Son, I've been giving this a lot of thought. I want you to serve as the wrangler, along with Ramon. We need good men watching over the remuda, and there ain't two better when it comes to working with horses."

Dusty nodded. "I can do that."

After they ate, Josh asked Fred to fetch him another horse. Josh thought it might be good for the segundo to go out and do a little night herd duty. It was good for the men to see one of their leaders pitching in with the less-desirable duties.

The rest of the men bedded down. By the time the moon was up, the camp was quiet. The men were asleep. The horses were still, and the wind was blowing with that easy feel a night wind often has.

Johnny strolled out to the edge of the camp and looked off into the night. Just to make sure there were no campfires off in the distance. There were none.

He had a tin cup of coffee in one hand. His back porch wasn't available at the moment, so he stood at the edge of camp and looked off at the darkness, and at the stars overhead.

He would be riding point in the morning. Josh would be riding as a sort of second point, as his segundo. This would allow one of them to ride back occasionally and check on things while the other maintained position. Kennedy would be right swing, and Coyote left. Patterson and Palmer would be right and left flank. Palmer was one of Zack's men and Johnny didn't know him, but Zack said he was a stand-up man. Good enough for Johnny. Riding drag would be Searcy and Moffit and Abe Taggart, as the newest members of the crew. Matt and Joe would be off to the side, riding along. But they would be pulling their fair share. They would be riding night herd, and filling in if someone became injured.

With most trail drivers, the new men rode drag. Drag meant riding behind the herd, to keep the stragglers in motion. Drag was the least desirable job because it meant eating the dust of the herd, and a herd could kick a sizable amount of dust. Men riding drag wore bandanas over their faces like highwaymen.

Johnny's feeling on this was a little different from most trail bosses. He felt the men should all share the duties, so while the positions for the first day would be based on seniority, they would rotate beginning the second day.

There were two stark differences for Johnny between this trail drive and the ones that had come before. One was that this was going to be the last long trail drive. By the time they had grown the herd enough to be taking it to market again, the railroad would be here. At least as close as Bozeman. A cattle drive to Bozeman would take no more than four days. But the big difference was there was a woman waiting at home for him, a woman who brightened his days and warmed his heart. A woman he missed when he wasn't with her.

His coffee cup was empty, so he turned back toward camp. He unrolled his soogan and then pulled his boots off and climbed into the covers. Time to get some sleep, he figured. Tomorrow was going to come all too soon.

He set his gunbelt on the ground within reach, but he left his pistol in the holster. Something he had never done in camp, before. He had always kept it drawn and no more than two feet from his pillow.

I'm making progress, he thought.

22

The morning sun was resting just above the eastern horizon and Ches had the chuck wagon loaded and was already in motion, off a bit south of the path the herd would take. Zack Johnson had saddled up and was somewhere ahead, scouting the trail. Chuck and Fred had headed back to the ranch.

Dusty and Ramon already had the remuda moving, and they were also off to the south and were almost out of sight. They wouldn't roam too far ahead, because when a drover needed to change a horse he didn't want to have to ride too far to do it. But the remuda needed to be off and away. Removed from any dust, and if the herd should start running, you didn't want the horses to get hurt.

The herd was gathered together, covering an area of about a quarter square mile. By Josh's count, three thousand seven hundred and forty-four of the critters. Many were standing and grazing lightly, and a few were still down.

Johnny sat on Midnight and gave the herd a look-over. The countryside was black with cows. Kind of reminded Johnny of the old buffalo herds, from years back.

Old Blue was up at the front. He was standing and looking at Johnny, as though he knew what was required of him.

Johnny nudged Midnight forward a little, moving at an easy walk. Johnny's revolver was on his hips, leather batwing chaps were strapped over his jeans, and a large bandana was hanging over the front of his shirt like a bib. His rifle was in the chuck wagon and he had left his vest there, too. Kennedy was in position as right swing, and Coyote as left. Further back were Patterson and Palmer and Searcy and the others.

Josh came riding up. He had been riding the perimeter of the herd and checking on the men, making sure everything was in order. He kept his horse to a walk. No need to spook the herd and start them running. A stampede wouldn't be a good way to begin the first day.

Josh nodded to Johnny, then Johnny nudged his horse forward until he was maybe fifty feet from Old Blue. The steer raised his mighty rack and looked at Johnny.

Johnny said to him, "All right, old friend. Let's start 'em goin'."

In years past, when Blue was younger, Johnny would ride behind him and urge him on. The first trail drive Johnny and Zack made, back in '68, Johnny had done this. The second one he did the same. But on the third one, all he had to do was look at Blue and the steer knew it was time to get the herd moving.

Johnny turned Midnight south and started along. Old Blue had pulled some grass and was chewing it. He chewed for a moment more, then began walking along behind Johnny.

Coyote and Kennedy began urging the steers along, one at a time. Josh went to assist. The first day, it was a slow process. After a day or two, the critters would be more accustomed to the rhythm of life on the trail.

Johnny looked back over his shoulder. Eight or ten of them were following Blue. One decided he wasn't of a mind to and cut away from Josh, and Josh went galloping after him, twirling a loop overhead. Kennedy got three moving, then four. Then one tried to cut away from him, but Kennedy turned his horse into the steer's path and blocked him.

Matt and Joe were joining in. Johnny could hear the drag riders calling out. "Get a-movin'!" or "Hiyaa!" One of them—he wasn't sure which—let loose with something that sounded like the old rebel yell.

By mid-morning, the herd was moving. Old Blue was leading the way and the herd was following. They were moving at a walking pace. Some were bunched together and others were walking alone.

Some trail bosses rode ahead and scouted for camping spots, or streams where the herd could get some water, or to see if any streams they might have to cross would be running deep and present a problem. And the cook drove the chuck wagon ahead of the herd. Johnny preferred to be with the herd should problems arise, and so had a scout ride on ahead, and Ches had said he didn't want to drive the wagon ahead of the herd in case of stampede.

He said, "I seen a chuck wagon reduced to splinters once when there was a clap of thunder and the herd started runnin'."

Josh rode up to his father. "Looks like things are progressin' nicely."

Johnny nodded. "You ride point. I'm gonna ride ahead a bit and see if I can find Zack."

Not that Johnny needed to find Zack, but it gave Josh an opportunity to ride point and be in charge while Johnny was gone.

Chandler was not a man of the outdoors. He had been raised in Chicago and he preferred cobblestones underfoot. When he rode, he preferred to be in a carriage or even on a train. Horseback was not something his backside liked, and he vowed to himself that once he was safely back in Chicago, he would never sit in another saddle.

His horse moved along at a pace between a walk and a light run. Every time the horse took a step, Chandler bounced in the saddle. The first couple of times, his teeth had clacked together, so he had learned to keep his mouth shut and his jaw tightened.

The man riding with him moved like he and the horse were one. In some manner Chandler couldn't possibly figure out, when the horse stepped along, the man just rode up and down with the saddle. Like he had applied glue to the seat of his pants.

The man's name was Jenkins and he wore jeans and he wore a gun like he knew how to use it. He had a beard that was more from a lack of shaving than a fashion statement, and smelled like he hadn't bathed since the last time it rained. But Mister Reed had hired Jenkins for the job.

Mister Reed had said Jenkins had the necessary qualifications. From what Chandler could see, Jenkins was a killer and a horse thief. He didn't know what qualifications he really needed, other than the fact that he had managed to avoid the noose so far.

Chandler had been there when Reed hired him. Reed had said to him, "So, Mister Jenkins...is Jenkins your actual name?"

Jenkins said, "It is when it has to be."

Reed had nodded. Apparently he liked that answer. Chandler did not.

Reed and Jenkins discussed money and then shook hands.

Jenkins' job was to make sure the McCabe herd didn't reach Cheyenne. Or, at the very least, very little of it did.

"Your background is in banking," Reed said to Chandler over a glass of whiskey after Jenkins had left the room.

Chandler nodded. He said nothing. How he had gone from banking to the business he was now in was a long and tangled road. The more Chandler thought about it, the more whiskey he wanted to drink.

Reed said, "This is the situation. In a town like this, everyone subsides on credit. The ranchers purchase their supplies with credit. As such, the merchants in town have no capital on hand so everything they purchase must also be on credit. When a herd is sold, the rancher then has cash and can repay debts, so there is an exchange of cash that goes through the entire town. Then the whole process starts over again."

Chandler nodded. "I was raised in a farming town in Ohio. It's about the same situation there. All debts are paid at harvest time, then the whole process begins anew."

Reed smiled. "Exactly. So the McCabe ranch has been living on debt for almost three years. They have made small sales to the army and even to restauranteurs here in town and in Bozeman, but those have been limited. This cattle drive will repay whatever outstanding debts they have. If the herd fails to arrive in Cheyenne, then there will be no sale. If much of the herd is destroyed in the process, so much the better. That's where Mister Jenkins comes into play. Instead of stealing cattle, which he is experienced at, he is simply to make certain the McCabes make no money from the herd."

Chandler nodded. "It'll take them two or three years to rebuild the herd with the brood stock they have."

"Indeed. And by then, any credit they might have with merchants in town will be lost. Some might be forced to go to court and sue, to avoid bankruptcy. In effect, the McCabes will be forced to sell. And that's where my employer comes into play. He wishes to purchase the ranch."

"Why would he want to do that?"

Reed shrugged. "I haven't asked. It's not my business. He's hired me for a job, and I have hired you and Jenkins for a job."

"So, by the way you say that, I take it my services are still needed out here?"

"Sorry, Chandler. I know you'd like to get back to Chicago, but I need you to ride along with Mister Jenkins. Sort of as my representative on the trail."

Chandler drained the rest of his glass and reached for the bottle.

He thought about it all as he bounced along in the saddle.

There was a third man with them. He had skin the color of buckskin, and long black hair. He wore a wide-brimmed hat that was a faded gray and a buckskin shirt. Strapped to his back was a buckskin sheath that carried something long and narrow. A flap covered the top end of the sheath but the only thing Chandler could figure that might be in there would be a rifle.

Jenkins had said they were following tracks but Chandler couldn't see any. They were riding through grass that was green with a springtime suppleness but Chandler didn't see any tracks. He couldn't figure how anyone could on ground like this.

They came to a section of land where it looked like someone had taken the blade of a shovel and cut out some rectangular sections of sod and then set them back in place. Each one looked to be about six feet long and three feet wide. The sod was mounded up a little. It then occurred to Chandler they were looking at graves.

Jenkins spat out a load of tobacco juice, and said, "Well, now we know what happened to them men your boss sent out."

Chandler said, "There was a fifth man. I wonder what became of him."

Jenkins shrugged. "Prob'ly run off. Some men just want to run when the shootin' starts."

The other man—Chandler hadn't heard his name—said, "That was stupid, sendin' these rustlers out here to deal with men like this. Johnny McCabe. Zack Johnson. You need more'n second-rate cattle thieves to deal with men like that."

Chandler said to Jenkins, "Excuse me, but Mister Reed said you are a cattle thief. If these men couldn't stand up against McCabe and Johnson..."

Jenkins said, "I've helped myself to some beeves at one time or another. But I've been a bounty hunter. I rode with Quantrill's raiders before that. And my partner here spent some time with the Apache, and some time in a Mexican prison. That satisfy you?"

The other man said, "I've ridden with men who would skin alive a city-slicker like you just to hear you squeal like a pig."

Chandler swallowed hard. He thought it best to say nothing.

Jenkins grinned and led the way off to where the herd had been.

They found the remains of a large campfire.

"This is where the cook fire was," Jenkins said. "Chuck wagon was right there."

He indicated with his eyes a point a few yards away from the fire. Even Chandler could see matted-down grass where it looked like two sets of wagon wheels had rested.

The other man said, "Looks like they pulled out this mornin'. They got maybe a three-hour lead on us."

Jenkins said, "Which is just about how we want it."

He spit another wad of tobacco juice to the grass.

The other man had a bowie knife sheathed to the left side of his gunbelt. He slid the knife out and began picking his teeth with the tip.

Chandler said, "Excuse me, but aren't you going to bring any other men?"

"Don't need no others. Lawson and me will handle it fine."

"How is that possible? You're dealing with Johnny McCabe."

Lawson looked at Jenkins. "Asks a lot of

questions, don't he?"

Jenkins nodded.

Lawson said, "He might be kind of loud out on the trail. And he might slow us down. An operation like this, we gotta be able to move quiet and fast. In and out. Strike hard and pull back fast."

Jenkins nodded again. He said, "Go ahead. Do it."

Chandler was about to ask what Jenkins meant, when Lawson raised his knife and threw it.

It landed in Chandler's chest. It went in sideways, sliding in between two ribs and buried itself almost to the hilt.

Chandler wanted to ask why. He wanted to ask how they thought they would explain this to Mister Reed. He wanted to ask all sorts of questions, but he was sitting in the saddle with a knife buried deep in his chest and he found he couldn't breathe.

Strange, he thought. He had always figured it would hurt more than it did. It didn't really hurt at all. He just felt numb all over.

Then his eyes rolled up in his head and he fell out of the saddle.

Lawson swung out of the saddle. He said, "Good place to let the horses rest a bit."

Jenkins nodded and dismounted. He lit up a cigarette while Lawson strolled over to the body of Chandler and pulled the knife out. He wiped the blood off in the grass and then slid the blade back into the sheath.

Jenkins said, "Shame about Chandler. Got hisself killed by McCabe."

Lawson grinned. "That's the risk you take when you ride with the big boys."

23

Charles Cole rode into town. He took the back trail from the ranch, the trail that came out behind the Second Chance. It was morning and way too early for a beer, but he thought Hunter might still have the coffee pot on.

He turned the horse through the alley between the saloon and the building next to it. It had been abandoned over the winter and now a land office was setting up. It would be another month before it was open, and then no one would have to ride all the way to Bozeman to file a claim, anymore.

He rode around to the front of the saloon. One wagon was working its way down the street. A buckboard being driven by two men Charles had never seen before but he thought they looked like farmers. A conestoga wagon was further down the street. Settlers moving in. A man with a long, drooping mustache and a ten gallon hat and big rowels on his spurs was riding by. A man and a woman were walking along the boardwalk across the street, most likely heading toward the hotel. He was in a jacket and tie and a top hat and she had a fancy feathery hat pinned to her head and was carrying a parasol. A man was sitting in a rocking chair to one side of the hotel's front door. A long white beard and a miner's cap pulled down to his brow. Charles recognized him as Alton, a prospector who had moved in. Alton was trying to locate a claim, and Charles saw him at the Second Chance sometimes on a Saturday night. A man he didn't know was sitting on a bench at the other side of the hotel door.

Charles was wearing his gun on his hip and his jeans were tucked into his riding boots and spurs were strapped to his feet.

He had conflicting feelings about being where he was. He wanted to be out there with the herd, sharing the work. And yet, he would have been away from Bree for weeks and would have missed her something awful.

His job was to find out if Bertram Reed's man Chandler was still here, and to see if there was any other information Falcone might have about the men he had seen Chandler visiting outside of town. But first, Charles was going to enjoy a cup of trail coffee at the Second Chance.

He swung out of the saddle and left his horse at the hitching rail, and went into the saloon.

What he didn't notice was that the man sitting on the bench had watched him ride around to the front of the saloon. He was in a black hat that had taken on a charcoal grayish color because of trail dust, and he wore his gun low and tied down. A long knife was sheathed at his left side. A cigar was clenched in his teeth. He had watched Charles swing out of the saddle and then walk into the saloon.

The man said, "That him? That tall galoot?"

Alton nodded. "Yessir. Thet's him, all right. Stayin' at the McCabe ranch while all the rest of the men are off on a trail drive."

"Jehosaphat Cole."

The old man nodded. "Goes by the name Fat, though. Some folks are takin' to callin' him Charles. What you lookin' for him for? He owe you money?"

The first man shook his head. "Been hired to find him, that's all."

He got to his feet and walked into the hotel. He didn't stride, he strolled. Like he had all the time in the world, and if the world didn't like it, the world would just have to wait.

He walked up the stairs the same way, taking them one at a time. At the second floor, he stopped at room 3, and knocked on the door.

He had to knock only once. It was opened by a man with graying hair and a matching mustache that turned a corner at either side of his mouth and made its way down to his chin. He had soft hands and a round, soft belly. The look of a man who did his work behind a desk. He was in a vest that belonged to a three-piece suit, but he had taken off the jacket and the tie.

"Mister Wellington," he said. "I think I found him."

"So, he is here, then."

The man nodded. "Appears to be. Just walked into the saloon. A long tall kid. Looks like a cowhand."

"A cowhand?" Wellington shook his head. "That can't be right. Must be the wrong man."

"It's been eight years. A feller can change a lot in eight years. And one of the locals gave the name. Fat Cole."

Wellington nodded thoughtfully. "That's what we were told they were calling him in Texas."

"So, you want me to go put a bullet in him?"

"No, no," Wellington said quickly, and gave a glance up and down the corridor to make sure they were alone, that no one had overheard. "We don't want him dead. We want to find him, and present his brother's offer to him."

The man took a draw on the cigar. "What if he don't take the offer."

"Well, then I suppose we *will* have to kill him."

24

Zack Johnson found a stream that Johnny and Josh had found earlier when they were scouting the area. A stream that was fed by spring run-off, and that by August would be nothing but a dry bed with sprouting weeds.

This was where they bedded the herd down for the first night. The stream wasn't very wide or deep, and the beeves drank it dry.

Ches got a fire started and heated up some beans and coffee. As Johnny stood with a plate in one hand and a tin cup filled with coffee balancing on one of the wagon wheels, he saw a rider approaching.

Josh walked up to him, a plate in his own hand. "Looks like Chuck coming."

Johnny nodded.

The rider was Charles, and he swung out of the saddle and handed the reins to Ramon.

He got a cup of coffee, then walked over to Johnny and Josh. "I talked to Hunter and then to Marshal Falcone. They said Chandler rode out this morning with two men. Hunter and Falcone both said they looked like gunfighters."

"They say which direction they rode in?"

"Out toward the Gap. But that's all. I rode back out to the valley to see if anyone had seen 'em. That's why I was late getting out here. I stopped at Carter Harding's place. He doesn't miss much that goes on around him, but he said he hadn't seen any riders all day. I rode out to the ranch and told Fred and he said he'd watch for 'em."

"It's getting dark. You gonna bed down here for the night?"

He shook his head. "No, sir. I told Bree I'd be back."

Josh grinned. "Well, if you told her something,

you'd better be true to it."

He nodded. "Absolutely. She'd never let me forget it."

Dusty came strolling over, a cup of coffee in one hand.

They chatted a bit about trail conditions, and how the first day had gone.

"Six miles," Josh said. "Not bad at all."

"Not at all," Charles said. "I've seen some trail drives where they didn't get more'n four miles the first day."

Charles saddled a fresh mount and headed back toward the valley.

Josh said, "Here he is, riding back at this late hour because he told Bree he would. She tells us to call him Charles, and we all start doing it just because she says so. Why is it everyone thinks I'm the demanding one?"

Dusty said, "You're louder."

Night passed easily. The first couple of nights on the trail were always a little tenuous, because the herd was accustomed to grazing lazily on almost countless acres of grass. Being pushed along for miles could make them jumpy, and a jumpy herd could start running at the slightest provocation.

Matt and Joe rode night herd. Matt had been a fair hand with a harmonica when they were growing up, and as Johnny sat against a wagon wheel with the fire blazing a few yards away and a cup of coffee in one hand, he heard the harmonica in the distance and it made him smile.

Come morning, Zack was gone again before first light. The drovers got the herd moving as they had the day before. They started with Old Blue, and then the others behind him. It didn't take as long this time. Within an hour the herd was fully in motion.

The sky overhead was clear and blue. They were now a little east of the foothills. In some places the grass was thick and other places the ground was gravelly and the grass sparse. They crossed a small stream bed that was fed by spring runoff but it was late spring and the stream had been reduced to a trickle.

They made six miles the second day, which Johnny thought wasn't bad. By the third day, he expected the herd to be fully into the rhythm of the drive, and they were. By nightfall of the third day, he estimated they had put nine more miles behind them.

The fourth day began with a few clouds on the southern horizon.

"Could be rain comin'," Ches said.

"Maybe so," Johnny said. "But as long as the wind keeps coming from the northwest, we should be all right."

The wind was strong like it usually was here in the more open lands east of the foothills. The fire was flapping and snapping in the wind as Johnny finished a cup of coffee. Josh was standing with him, a cup in his hand.

When the coffee was finished, Ches had the team hitched to the chuckwagon.

"All right," Johnny said to Josh. "Let's move 'em out."

He and Josh mounted up and rode out to the herd. Ches put a few shovel-fulls of dirt onto the fire to fully smother it, then tossed the shovel into the back of the wagon and climbed up onto the seat and grabbed the reins.

The sun climbed into the sky, and the clouds to the south drifted away. The day turned off hot like Johnny expected it to be. His mid-morning his canteen was already half empty, and he knew the water barrel in the chuck wagon was in about the same condition.

There was a ranch maybe twelve miles south of

the previous night's camping spot. It was run by a man named Bingum, and he had a supply of water. When Johnny and Josh had been scouting earlier, they visited the place. The man had dug a well and hit a gusher, and now had enough to water a herd. Johnny had worked out a deal for water. Two cents a head.

Johnny said to Josh, "I figure we'll hit the Bingum ranch sometime tomorrow morning. Probably late morning."

Josh nodded. "Would have been nice to be there tonight. There won't be any water for these critters between here and there."

Zack came riding in around noon. He rode directly for the chuck wagon. Ches pulled the team to a stop and hopped down, and Zack filled a tin cup from the water barrel.

Johnny rode over.

Zack said, "I found a likely spot to spend the night. About four miles ahead. It's a hollow in the ground that's not quite a ravine but more than just a low area. I marked it with a stick and my bandana."

Zack had been wearing a red bandana and Johnny noticed it was missing.

Johnny said, "Four more miles will make for a good second day."

Ches was standing with them. "Takes a good two days to get a herd used to the trail. Should be making eight, ten miles a day after this. Barring anything going wrong."

Johnny looked at Zack with a grin. "Ever see a trail drive where nothing went wrong?"

Zack nodded. "Once. In my dreams."

The three men laughed.

Zack said, "I'm gonna fill my canteen and then flag down Dusty or Ramon and have one of them fetch me a fresh horse."

Johnny gave the order for the herd to push on.

The men had rotated. The drag riders from the previous day were now riding swing. The rotation wasn't quite even because there had been three riding drag, but it worked out that one rider would ride flank two days in a row.

Matt and Joe were assisting here and there. Sort of floating from Swing to Flank to Drag. They would also have the first two-hour shift of night herd every night.

It was late in the afternoon and Johnny was riding a little ahead of the herd. For the previous mile they had been in country where the grass was good. A dark ridge loomed off to the west, and Johnny knew the ridge was dark because of tree growth. Tall pines that reached to the sky.

At one time, forests of tall pines had covered the east coast, from Georgia to Maine and on into Canada. The first settlers from Europe had cut the trees, needing wood for cabins and fires, and needing to clear the land for cattle and for planting crops.

Johnny had grown up in Pennsylvania, and much of the land had been clear and open. There were fields of corn and other crops. Corn, wheat, potatoes. Johnny's father had been a farmer, and he and Matt and Joe had grown up tending the crops alongside him. Some of the hills behind the house had been wooded, but they were maples and oaks and birches and alders. What their father had called *new growth*. The old pine forest had been cleared away generations earlier, and now hard wood trees were growing in its place.

When Johnny rode through the ridges of Montana and Wyoming, riding among the tall pines with trunks straight as arrows, he wondered if the feeling was similar to what the first explorers had experienced on the east coast.

They found the marker Zack had left, his bandana tied to a branch stuck in the ground and flapping in the wind. It was here that they bedded the herd down for the night.

Ches got a fire blazing and started working on a beef stew. He had pulled some wild onions and was adding them in for flavoring.

He said to Johnny, "We only got enough wood in the possum belly for another couple of fires. In the old days we could just grab buffalo chips, but there ain't many buffalo left."

Johnny nodded. He said, "When Josh and I met with that rancher ahead, he said there was a source of firewood. A ridge a few miles west of his place. The land isn't claimed and he said there was firewood. Maybe you can ride out and fill the possum belly there and I'll send Joe and Matt along."

Johnny had a cup of coffee in one hand when Zack came riding in.

Zack went for the coffee and then said to Johnny, "I met with that rancher Bingum, this afternoon. He knows we're coming. He has a cord of firewood on hand and I worked out a deal so we can fill the possum belly. Ches told me this morning we were running low on wood."

Ches was grinning. "You're a good man to have along."

Johnny bedded down once dinner was done. His joints were hurting and he felt tired deep down to his very soul. He heard the sad sound of Matt's harmonica in the distance, and his thoughts were that he never would have felt this tired before he was shot, and those were the last thoughts he had until Ches woke him by clanking pots together at the morning fire. Ches was frying up some smoked bacon and boiling some coffee. The eastern horizon was beginning to lighten from black to a dull gray.

"Hope you boys like the bacon," Ches said, "because this is last of it. Starting tomorrow, it's grits and hominy, without the hominy."

The men ate their breakfast the way hungry, working men do. Without dallying and with little conversation.

Then they saddled up. Josh swung up and onto a bay, and the horse started bucking and jumping. These mustangs were often only half-broke. Hardly the riding stock an equestrian back east would prefer. Josh held onto the saddle while the horse spun a couple of times, then arched its back and jumped hard, landing on all four hoofs. Then it reared up and then bucked a couple of times more.

Kennedy and Patterson were there, cheering on Josh. Zack was laughing and yelling, "Ride 'em!"

Johnny was grinning, a cup of coffee in hand.

The horse then gave a couple of angry snorts and decided to give up the battle.

By the time the sun was fully above the horizon, the men had the herd moving.

Josh rode point, and Johnny rode a little ahead and Zack was with him. Not much scouting to do this morning. They would be making Bingum's place sometime mid-morning. They would let the herd have water, then after that they would continue on and Zack scout out a good place to spend the night.

Zack's red bandana was once again tied around his neck. He wore it with the large triangle section hanging behind his back, like a cavalry rider.

He said, "There's something about open land like this, and moving a herd along. The hardest job on Earth, but there's a peace to it."

Johnny nodded. "For us, this is the last one. My aching bones won't miss it at all. I'm getting a little too old for this kind of thing. But my heart'll miss it."

"When the railroad comes, it'll bring more civilization. Jubilee will grow. The railroad'll most likely hit Bozeman first, then Jubilee."

Johnny thought about how life had changed in the years since he and Zack had brought Ginny and the children to Montana. If you had wanted to mail a letter in those days, you had to ride clear to Bozeman, and if you wanted to do so in the winter, you were plumb out of luck. The trail from the valley to Bozeman was often impassible from November to April. The Cheyenne and the Lakota roamed free back in those days, mostly on the grassy plains east of the mountains, and the Shoshone were to the south. Buffalo herds drifted about in massive herds, chewing on the wild grass and drinking from mountain springs and rivers.

Nowadays, the Indians had been rounded up and were on reservations. The government had put a bounty on buffalo hides and the hunters had come in and all but decimated the herds. The town of Jubilee stood just beyond the valley and a telegraph line was being strung. The stagecoach came through almost daily, and Johnny figured Zack was right about the railroad. It was only a matter of time before a line of tracks were laid all the way to Jubilee.

He thought about the little remote canyon where he was going to build a home, where he and Jessica would raise Cora. He wondered if the canyon would be so remote by the time Cora was marrying-age. He wondered how much longer he could retreat into the mountains to escape the oncoming civilization. He wondered if he would eventually grow too old to run anymore, and would just settle in on a front porch with a cup of coffee while civilization sprung up about him like a field of weeds.

They had been on the trail a couple of hours when Johnny noticed a thin tendril of dark smoke to the south.

Zack had lifted his canteen for a drink, tipping his head back. When he put the cork back in, Johnny said, "What do you suppose that is?"

Zack followed his gaze. "Looks like smoke."

Johnny nodded. "But it's the wrong time of day for a camp fire."

"A campfire wouldn't be black like that, either."

The tendril disappeared. Then it was back, and it grew into a black cloud that stood stark against the bright blueness of the sky.

Zack said, "Want me to ride ahead and see what it is?"

Johnny nodded. "I'll go along with you. Let's ride back to the wagon first and get some rifles. I have a bad feeling about this."

They rode back. Zack got a Winchester long rifle, .44-40 caliber and it took eighteen rounds. Johnny grabbed his Sharps. His vest was in the back of the wagon, so he grabbed ten cartridges from a box of ammunition and dropped them into a shirt pocket.

Johnny said to Josh, "Keep the herd coming. If there's any kind of trouble, one of us will ride back and let you know. But keep your eyes open."

Josh nodded.

Josh watched Johnny and Zack ride out, then pulled his pistol and checked the loads.

Ches was on the ground. He had stopped the wagon so he could dig the rifles out of the back.

Josh said, "Ches, grab me a Winchester, would you? And keep one close at hand yourself."

25

Johnny and Joe reined up at the top of a low grassy rise and stepped out of the saddle to let the horses blow. Stopping on a rise would make them visible, but would also allow them to see further. A trade off.

Normally you loosen the cinch so the horse could breathe a little easier, but this time they didn't. They wanted to be able to mount and ride at a moment's notice.

Johnny set his rifle in the grass and then drew his revolver and checked the loads. Zack was doing the same.

Zack said, "The source of that smoke is only about a half mile ahead. It has to be the Bingum ranch."

Johnny nodded. "That's what I was thinking. Josh and I rode this land about a month ago. There's nothing for miles of the Bingum place in any direction."

They said nothing more. Johnny picked up his rifle and opened the action to check the load. A fifty caliber cartridge. This rifle could drop a buffalo at two hundred yards. He had once taken a man out of the saddle at a greater distance than that. He hoped there would be no gunplay, but he had a feeling that before this played out, he would be firing one of his guns. Maybe both.

"Let's ride," he said, and swung into the saddle.

He and Zack had seen enough homes burned by Comanches during their years with the Texas Rangers to know what to expect. Boards and timbers burn differently than firewood. The smoke is often darker. Johnny was hoping to be wrong, but he didn't figure he would be.

When he and Zack topped a low rocky ridge that rimmed a small basin where Bingum had built his ranch house, Johnny found what he had expected. The house and barn and stable had all been reduced to a tumble of blackened boards. Smoke was still pouring out of the barn, but was only drifting from the house and stable.

Bodies were scattered about the ranch yard. A couple of horses, too.

Johnny started down the ridge with Zack following. He doubted whoever had done this would still be nearby, but he hadn't lived this long by being careless so he held his rifle in his right hand, finger on the trigger and ready to shoot.

He pulled his horse to a stop at the edge of the ranch yard and didn't have to pull the rein too hard. The horse was more than willing to stop. Most horses Johnny had known weren't fond of fire.

He swung out of the saddle and held his rifle with both hands, ready to fire from the hip. Zack did the same, jacking a round into the chamber.

A man was face-down in the dirt. Johnny knelt down and placed a hand on his shoulder and rolled him over. It was Bingum. Not overly tall, with the weathered face that comes with a life of facing into the wind and sun. Johnny had figured him to be somewhere between fifty-five and sixty when he met him last month.

There was a bullet hole in his chest and it was ringed with blood. Dead men don't bleed, which meant he had lived a few minutes after being shot.

The top section of his scalp had been cut away and tossed to the dirt a few yards away.

Zack was checking the other bodies. "They're all dead. Scalped."

Johnny rose to his feet. "I doubt it was Indians. They take a scalp as a war trophy. They don't toss it aside."

Zack shook his head. "This was done for pure mean-spirited fun."

They looked about. Bingum had stacked three cord of firewood, and all of it was burning. There was little left to salvage. The horses had been driven off.

They scouted about for tracks and found a trail of two horses that had approached the basin from the southwest.

"They rode in here," Zack said. "About sun-up, I would reckon."

Johnny nodded. He walked up to the front of what had been the ranch house. "Hard to tell the details of what happened next. Tracks are all scattered. But Bingum fell here. Took a bullet to the chest and crawled a few yards off to the side."

Zack said, "The other men came running at the sound of the gunshot and were shot down."

"Josh and I met these men. They were cowhands, not gunfighters. They didn't stand a chance."

"Senseless slaughter," Zack said.

"They wanted to make sure we couldn't use the firewood, and they drove off any horses so we couldn't replenish the remuda if we needed to. They killed the men just for the sake of doing it."

"There's still the water."

"I wonder. Is there?"

Off to the side of the ranch yard was a well house. An iron pump was mounted on a long wooden trough. It was designed to water a dozen horses or head of cattle at a time. Johnny cranked the handle and water gushed. A tin ladle was resting at the side of the trough, so Johnny grabbed it and dipped some of the water.

He spit it out. "It's been salted. Someone likely dropped a bag of salt down the well."

Zack nodded. "They thought of everything."

They found the tracks of two horses that led the basin, heading northeast.

Zack said, "Wanna trail 'em? Let 'em know we ain't very pleased about what they did?"

Johnny shook his head. "They did this because of us. Trying to make life harder for us. I don't know who sent 'em or why they're doing it, but I think we'd best get directly back to the herd. If they're capable of this kind of killing, there's nothing to stop them from attacking our men."

They mounted up.

26

Johnny and Zack found the herd was making good time, moving along at a fast walk. The beeves were acclimating to life on the trail well.

Johnny and Zack headed for the chuck wagon and Josh rode over to meet them. They told Josh what they had found.

Ches said, "What'll we do for water?"

"There's a small stream maybe ten miles south of the ranch," Josh said. "Not a very big one, but maybe enough for the herd to get a little drink."

"Maybe I should take a man or two and head to that ridge over yonder and cut us some firewood."

Johnny shook his head. "It looks like someone is trying to stop us. I don't want anyone riding out alone like that. Even you, Zack. I want a man with you when you're scouting. Take Dusty. Joe or Matt will have to work with Ramon."

Johnny knew Ches had two shovels in the wagon. He said, "We'll make early camp near the ranch. Those men deserve to be buried proper."

It was mid-morning when Johnny gave the signal to stop. Josh turned Old Blue, and the steers behind him followed suit. This caused a chain reaction where other animals behind them began to stop.

Ahead of them was the gravelly ridge that rimmed the Bingum ranch headquarters.

"Without water," Johnny said to Josh, "we're not going to be able to push the herd as hard."

Josh said, "How far do you reckon we are from that big stream?"

When they had scouted the area, they found a stream that fed into a pond.

"Fifteen, maybe eighteen miles."

"That pool should be too big for anyone to salt.

Eighteen miles, we'll be there in two days."

Zack and Dusty came riding out. Dusty had taken a Winchester from the chuck wagon and was riding with it across the saddle in front of him.

Dusty said, "We haven't seen a sign of anyone. Doesn't mean they're not out there, though."

The herd milled restlessly for a bit. The ground got gravelly near the ridge, but the grass was good this far away. It was common for a rancher to build his headquarters on the worst section of land he claimed and to keep the best grass available for grazing. After a few minutes, the herd settled down to grazing.

"Well," Ches said, "there's a job to do."

He took Patterson and Palmer and Taggart with him and they headed for what was left of the Bingum ranch buildings. They had both shovels. Zack and Dusty went along too, to stand guard.

Jenkins and Lawson stood knee-deep in the grass. It was nearly dark, and the first stars were starting to come to life. Jenkins reached into his vest and pulled out the makings, and started rolling a cigarette. Their horses were picketed a short ways behind them.

The wind was blowing from the west and was strong at their backs.

Jenkins said, "I figure we're maybe two miles off from the herd."

"We approach 'em from this direction, they'll smell us long a'fore we're there."

"What do you figure we ought to do once we're there?"

Lawson shrugged. "Cause some trouble. Maybe flap a blanket and see if we can start a stampede."

"Trouble is, they ain't ordinary cowpunchers. Not like that ranch we torched this morning. These boys is gunfighters. At least, most of 'em are. We ride in and we're taking a risk of catching some lead."

Lawson shrugged again. "Goes with the job."

"Now, there you go, not thinkin' like a businessman. See, that's your trouble. You gotta minimize yer cost of doin' business. And cost can be measured in a lot of ways. One of 'em is risk."

He struck a match and brought his cigarette to life and then shook the match out and tossed it away.

He said, "They got some mighty fine dance hall girls down in Dodge City. We're gettin' paid real good for this job, and I'd kind'a like to live long enough to get to Dodge and spend some of that money."

"What do you have in mind?"

Jenkins struck another match. He said, "This wind is blowin' straight at the herd. And it looks like it's gonna be a mighty windy night."

"You do like fire, don't you?"

"I like whatever gets the job done the easiest, with the least amount of risk to myself."

Jenkins tossed the match to the grass. It wasn't as dry as it would be come August, but it was dry enough to burn. One blade of grass caught fire, and then the flame spread to three more. Within thirty seconds, a section maybe a foot in diameter was burning. The wind was already catching it and stretching the flames toward more grass in front of it.

Jenkins said, "Ever see a herd run from a grass fire? It ain't like no ordinary stampede."

Johnny had just filled his belly with a can of cold beans. He had told Ches to use the firewood only to boil coffee. The men could eat their beans cold.

He asked Ramon to fetch him a mount. He was going to ride out and check the night riders himself. He was also going to visit the guards. He didn't think he would be getting a lot of sleep tonight, now that he knew there was trouble out there somewhere in the dark.

He had experienced cattle thieves taking a steer or two on previous cattle drives, and more than once Indians had stolen a few animals. But what he had seen at the Bingum ranch went beyond just cattle thievery. It takes a certain level of cold-heartedness to just ride up to a man and gun him down and then burn his house. He had seen this kind of thing in Texas when the Rangers were fighting the Comanche, and he had heard of it being done in Missouri and Kansas during the late War Betwixt the States.

He supposed what bothered him the most was he couldn't figure the motivation. Generally when there is a killing, you can figure why. The why of it at the Bingum ranch was apparently because someone was investing time and probably money in holding up this trail drive. But who could gain from it?

Johnny had no further time to think about it, because as he swung into the saddle he saw an orange glow off to the west. He knew immediately what it was.

"Fire!" he called out.

Ches came running. Josh was there, and Dusty and Taggart.

There was little that could be done. The wind was strong and the fire was coming right at them.

There was a sudden snorting and bawling from the herd, and Johnny knew they were on their feet. He knew what was coming even before it started.

The ground began to rumble. The beeves were running and they would be running wildly.

Ches had positioned the chuck wagon a little to the south of the herd and the cows would be running directly away from the fire, which meant they would be going east. The wagon should be safe.

Men were leaping into the saddles.

"Stay with the herd!" Johnny shouted, but he doubted they could hear him over the roar of the stampede.

The ground was shaking and black shapes were charging toward him. His horse reared. The last thing he wanted was to be thrown because to be afoot in the middle of a stampede was to invite death. Johnny had seen a man survive once when he was thrown and the beeves ran around and past him. But he had seen more than one man trampled to death. He held to the saddle and got control of the horse and spun him around and spurred him into a gallop.

In a stampede, sometimes you could turn the lead steers and the rest of the herd would follow and you could sort of coil them up and they would stop running. But with a grass fire coming at them, such a plan couldn't even be considered. He hoped to just stay with the herd.

Then it happened. What Johnny dreaded. His horse's right front hoof stepped into a hole. The horse and Johnny went down hard.

Johnny threw himself away from the horse, and the animal hit the ground and rolled and Johnny tumbled in the grass. His hat was gone and he didn't have time to even check to see if his gun was still in his holster. He scrambled to his feet and began to run.

He headed directly south. He hoped to avoid the steers. He had been riding at the periphery of the herd and he hoped they wouldn't be spreading out, but would instead be running directly east to get away from the fire.

His smooth boot soles slipped in the grass and he almost went down, but he managed to keep his footing and continued on.

The ground was uneven and he almost stumbled twice more. A dark mass of pounding hooves came charging and shot past, behind him. Another ran by ahead of him.

Most of the rumbling was now behind him as the herd was pulling away, so he stopped to catch his breath. The fire was now a large orange glow and he could smell the smoke. It was coming on fast.

The fire could kill every bit as fast as being trampled. But he realized he was not even a quarter mile from the gravelly ridge that was just beyond the Bingum ranch house. The question he had was, how fast could he cover a quarter mile?

27

The night sky had been clear and dotted with stars when Johnny had first seen the grass fire. As he stood on the ridge looking off in the direction from which the fire had approached, he noticed there were no more stars. At first he had thought it was because of the smoke. A grass fire throws off more smoke than you might realize. After a while, he realized it wasn't the smoke, but a cloud cover that had developed as the night wore on.

The fire dissipated somehow off toward the east. He didn't really know why, but it just seemed to have stopped. By midnight, the air was filled with the smell of burning grass, but the fire was gone and the stampede had long since stopped.

Johnny had left his horse behind. When the horse stepped in the hole and took a tumble, Johnny had scrambled free and run for this ledge. He had only the clothes he was wearing, including the gun at his hip.

He waited out the night. He found a place by the ashen remains of the barn, where part of a blackened wall was still standing. The wind was strong and cold, but the wall provided shelter from it.

He dozed, but he didn't fall into a deep sleep. Whoever had started the fire was out there, and he wanted to be ready should they happen upon him.

He was awake before first light, and as the eastern sky began to lighten and push back the darkness, he found the land beyond the basin to be a blackened ruin of the grassland it had been. Smoke still rose from sections of it.

He checked the water trough by the well house, and it still had a little water from the last time Bingum had worked the hand pump, before the well had been salted. Johnny cupped his hands and dipped them in and brought the water to his mouth. The water had been sitting there a day and was a little harsh tasting, but it was wet.

Then he started out in the direction where the chuck wagon had been.

He walked along. The sun was hot overhead sky as he walked along the blackened remains of the grass, little puffs of smoke rising as he stepped down.

He saw movement ahead of him. His hat was gone so he held his hand over his brow like a visor and he thought he saw what looked like the chuck wagon.

He walked on and after maybe half a mile, he found he was right. It was indeed the chuck wagon. The land behind the wagon was blackened in places, but there were sections of green.

Ches had a small fire going and a pot of coffee was almost to a boil. Dusty was there also.

They looked up as Johnny came walking in. Soot had blackened his face and clothes.

"Pa," Dusty said, and ran to him.

Johnny pulled his son in for a hug.

Johnny said, "This has to be the worst stampede I've ever seen. I didn't know who I would find alive, if anyone. Not just from the stampede, but the fire."

Dusty said, "Kennedy was here with us. He lit out on foot maybe an hour ago to look for survivors. So far, it's just Ches, Kennedy and me. No horses. Ches cut the wagon team loose when the fire approached."

Ches said, "They would have bolted and taken the wagon with 'em."

The coffee was ready so Ches took the kettle away from the flames. But what Johnny wanted was water, so Ches filled him a tin cup from the barrel.

"Not much water left," Ches said. "We gotta go easy on it."

Johnny said, "How'd you all survive?"

"I called Dusty and Kennedy over, and we burned

a fire break. We were south of the herd, and the fire was burning straight across from west to east. It started somewhere west of the herd, from what I figure. It was working its way in this direction, but it didn't have the wind in its favor so it was moving slower. Gave us time to burn that break."

Dusty was looking off at the blackened countryside north of them. He said, "I've never seen anything like it. All we had is gone. The men. The cattle. The horses."

He turned to his father. "What'll this do to the ranch? How will we pay expenses? And Zack's ranch, too. We were all counting on this trail drive."

Johnny had just drained the tin cup. Walking in the soot with small wisps of smoke drifting up at him had dried his throat. He really wanted another cupful but he was mindful of what Ches had said. They were low on water, and he knew they could no longer count on the Bingum well.

Johnny said, "I'm more concerned about the men right now. I want to find out if any are still alive. We'll assess the financial damage later."

"Josh is still out there somewhere. And Zack."

Johnny went to the kettle and filled his cup with coffee. Not exactly what he wanted at the moment, but it was wet.

He said, "Dusty, I want you to stay here with Ches and the wagon. Keep a rifle within reach. This fire wasn't started by accident. The same men who butchered Bingum and his cowhands are probably the ones behind it. For whatever reason they did this, they're still out there. You see anyone you don't know approaching this wagon, don't worry about being courteous."

Dusty nodded. "Understood."

Ches said, "We're low on water, but you can't go out there without a canteen. There's miles to cover and that's a lot to do on foot. And breathing the smoke can dry you out."

Ches filled a canteen and handed it to him. He also gave Johnny a couple strips of jerky.

Johnny took off his chaps. They were leather and could be hot to wear, especially if you were on foot. With the chaps out of the way, he loosened his gunbelt so his holster was now once again riding low at his right side, and he tied it down.

Ches reached into the chuck wagon and pulled out a black slicker and tossed it to Johnny. "There's a feel of rain on the air. This will keep your powder dry."

Johnny rolled up the slicker and tucked it under one arm. He said, "I plan to be back no later than sunset."

Dusty watched his father start off across the blackened plain.

He said to Ches, "At least it's cloudy. If he had to walk in the hot sun, he'd dry out even faster."

"Tell you what," Ches said. "Help me get the water barrel down and we'll take the lid off. Try to catch any rainwater we can."

Johnny walked along. He headed east, because that was the direction in which the herd had been running.

After a half mile or so, a rain drop fell, followed by another. He unrolled the slicker and pulled it on over his shoulders. A few more drops came down, one splattering against the top of his head, another landing on his shoulder. Then it started driving down fast and hard, like God had lifted a flood gate. It flattened down his hair and if it hadn't been for the slicker, his shirt would have been soaked as though he had jumped in a lake. But at least the stopped the little wisps of smoke that had been drifting from the charred grass, and it cleared the air. Washed away the scent of smoke that was so deeply imbedded in Johnny's nose that he thought he would never be free of it, and brought the clean water smell of water that a good rain brings.

Then the rain lightened up and within moments was gone. The clouds overhead were heavy and dark and he could see what looked like a patch of haze drifting from one distant cloud to the earth, and he knew it was raining over there. But where Johnny was, at least for the moment, the rain had stopped.

Johnny opened his slicker and let it fall open behind him like a cape. The wind caught it and flapped like a bedsheet on a clothes line.

He saw a blackened lump on the ground ahead of him and figured he had found the first casualty. It was a horse, and as he got closer, he realized it was his horse. He could tell by the odd angle at which one of the front legs was twisted. The leg had been fully broken when the horse stepped into a hole. He found the hole a few yards away, partially filled with soot and ash. The fur on the horse was charred black but he didn't think the fire had killed it. Probably the smoke.

He walked on. The land was barren, like a blackened desert. He uncorked the canteen and took a pull from it.

He hadn't walked far beyond the horse when he saw an object bouncing along in the wind. He chased it down and found it was his hat. It was the color of soot, but had somehow managed not to be consumed by the fire. He was able to brush off some of the soot and then pulled it down over his head.

He walked on for an hour more, and then the sun broke through the clouds. He took another drink from the canteen.

The blackened land rose to a small ridge up ahead, and he saw a rider atop it. The slicker had fallen over his right arm, so he flicked it back so he could have access to his revolver. But the rider saw him and started down the ridge toward him, and he recognized him by the set of his shoulders and the way he rode with the horse. Every rider has a way of riding that's as distinctive as the way he walks. This rider's hat was gone and his shirt has stained with soot, but Johnny knew it was his brother Matt.

Matt reined up. "Johnny." He said with relief.

Johnny nodded and said, "Matt," the same way.

He stepped out of the saddle to give his horse a rest. His canteen was empty so Johnny handed him his.

Matt's face was streaked with blackness, like Johnny had seen with coal miners. Matt's mustache was normally almost white, but was now as black as Falcone's.

"The fire gave the beeves reason to keep running longer than they normally would have," Matt said. "Some ran themselves out. I came across about fifteen carcasses on my way back here. There's a dry crick bed about fifteen miles east of here, and that's where the fire ended. Most of the herd got that far, and they spread out. I saw a couple head roaming about looking for grass."

"You see any riders?"

He nodded. "I saw Josh and Coyote. They were heading south thinking they might find some water, and were trying to round up some of the stock. The grass is good beyond that crick bed, so Josh was thinking they might do a gather there."

Johnny said, "I'm gonna continue on. Maybe you should ride on back to the chuck wagon. It's about three miles behind me."

"On foot?"

Johnny nodded. "That horse of yours is about done in. Take your time on the way to the wagon. I plan to be back there by nightfall. Maybe I can find some of the others."

Matt headed out, on foot and leading his horse.

Johnny continued on.

He knew he wouldn't make the dry creek bed and then all the way back to the chuck wagon by nightfall. He was out here mainly to get a feel for the situation. How many beeves had died in the fire. Maybe see if he could find any more of the men.

Since Matt had come directly from the east, Johnny thought he would turn northwest. See what he could find.

He put another mile behind him when he saw a riderless horse. It was a roan and a saddle was still strapped to its back.

Johnny started toward it, and the horse gave him a look like it was ready to run in the other direction. Johnny was sure it was probably frightened. Johnny began talking gently, "Here, boy. Come on. It's all right. Nothing to be scared of."

The horse stood and looked at him, his mane waving in the breeze. Johnny walked up to him, holding out his hand and then rubbed the horse's nose. He saw the Circle T brand on the rump.

"Easy, boy," Johnny said.

He loosened the cinch so the horse could breathe a little easier, but kept hold of the rein as he did so. The horse was bound to be a little skittish, having survived a fire and a stampede all at the same time.

There was nothing for grazing. The grass had been burned clear to the roots. But Johnny thought the animal looked strong enough for riding.

He tightened the cinch and then stepped into the saddle. "Come on, boy," he said. "Let's see what we can find."

The sun had dropped behind the horizon when Johnny made it back to the wagon. Matt was there, and his horse was grazing on some grass behind the firebreak. Johnny pulled the saddle from the roan and

Ches filled a pan of water from the barrel and let the horse drink.

The following day, Johnny and Dusty rode out to meet up with Josh and the others. Beyond the dry creek bed, they found about thirty head of cattle grazing. Josh was there, and he greeted his father and brother with hearty handshakes.

He said, "I was afraid you were both dead."

"Could easily have been," Johnny said.

Josh looked over at the thirty steers and said, "That's all we've found so far. Coyote's scouting ahead. Searcy's dead, we found his body."

Johnny said, "I'd like to find the team for the chuck wagon, so we can bring the wagon over to this side of the creek."

Turned out Josh had seen them. The two horses were sticking together, probably because they were used to each other's company. He had brought them in, and also rounded up four horses that belonged to the remuda, so Johnny changed saddles with one of them and brought the team back to the chuck wagon. The following day, Ches was setting up shop on the green side of the creek bed.

Zack and Joe both came in on foot. Joe was a little shaken up from a fall he had taken, but he seemed all right. More horses were being located, so they could mount up and help with rounding up the herd. One horse had a saddle strapped to it, and Ches had a spare saddle in the chuck wagon for the other horse.

Johnny found Taggart and Patterson. Both were afoot. Patterson's foot had been caught in the stirrup and the horse ran a few steps before Patterson's foot came free. It had been enough to twist the ankle badly. When Johnny found them, Taggart had his arm around Patterson's back and was helping him limp along. Ches thought the ankle might be broken. He took a spare axe handle from the wagon and improvised a crude splint.

That evening, Palmer came riding into camp. He had seen Ches's campfire from a distance. The following morning, Johnny found the remains of Moffit a few of miles to the north.

On the fourth day after the stampede, Ches took the chuckwagon to the remains of the Bingum ranch and raided it for what he could find. Johnny didn't like the idea of stealing and neither did Ches, but these were desparate times. Johnny sent Kennedy and Taggart with Ches. Kennedy was a good cowhand and a capable drover, and the man carried himself like one who had been in a few gun battles. Possibly military, or maybe even a gunfighter. It wasn't the way of the West to pry into a man's background, and Kennedy was a good hand and struck Johnny as honest. And Taggart wore his gun like he knew how to use it, and Joe said Taggart was a good man to have with you in a fight. Johnny figured the two of them could stand guard while Ches had a look about the remains of the Bingum ranch.

Turned out the firewood hadn't all burned. At the bottom of the ashen remains, Ches found enough good wood to account for almost half a cord, and loaded it into the possum belly.

With about half of the remuda recovered, the men were able to start gathering the herd, but it was slow going. They had roamed far and spread out over miles. Twelve head were found in a creek bed that looked like it probably ran a couple feet deep at the height of spring runoff but was now little more than a trickle. Occasionally a steer was found in bushes and had to be driven out. Scattered head were found in the open, grazing contentedly.

Johnny saw Old Blue standing among a small grouping of eighteen head. Blue saw Johnny and came walking toward him.

Johnny said to him, "Glad you made it old friend."

They were hindered a bit by more rain on the

sixth day, but Ches took advantage of it to fill the water barrel.

At the end of the seventh day, with the sky mostly clear and a couple of clouds hanging overhead and glowing red from the sunset, Josh was having a cup of coffee when Johnny came riding in.

Josh said, "We're losing too much time. It's been six days and we only have eight hundred head rounded up. That's way less than half the herd. The buyers are expecting us the second week of July. They know to wait a while because you can't predict exactly when a herd will arrive, but how long will they wait?"

Johnny understood the buyers had come out by train from Chicago. In the days of the big herds coming up from Texas, buyers tended to be on hand at the railheads. But those days were largely gone.

Josh said, "If we show up with what we have, it won't be enough to cover the ranch's bills. But if we stay here and keep the roundup going, we might miss the buyers altogether."

Zack was there and had wandered over. Johnny looked at him and then at Josh. Johnny said, "There's no telegraph station between here and Cheyenne. But maybe we could send a rider down to Cheyenne and have him leave a letter for the buyers for when they get there."

Josh nodded. "I'll write up a letter and we can send someone down tomorrow."

Zack volunteered to go. He said, "If I make good time, I should be there in maybe five days. Maybe six."

"I think maybe we should send Joe," Johnny said. "We need you and Josh both here for leadership. I've got some business to attend to, and I might be gone a few days."

Josh said, "Huh?"

But Zack had ridden with Johnny enough to have an idea as to what Johnny meant.

Zack said, "You're gonna go hunting for those men who started that fire, and killed Bingum and his men."

Johnny nodded. "I'm riding out in the morning."

Josh didn't like this idea at all. He said, "Pa, you can't go off and do this alone."

"Sometimes one man can get a job done where a group can't."

Zack said, "I hate to admit it, but your Pa is right. Besides, we can't spare too many men from the gather."

Johnny said, "I'll be riding out before sun-up. In case this camp is being watched, I want to be on my way while it's still dark."

Before first light, Johnny was rolling up his soogan and dropping it into the chuck wagon. He grabbed his Sharps and dropped a box of ammunition into his saddle bags. He filled a canteen and then saddled a bay gelding.

Zack was awake and stood by the chuck wagon as Johnny started off into the darkness. Johnny was walking, leading his horse. He would do this until the sky began to lighten enough for him to feel it was safe to ride.

Josh and Dusty came up behind Zack.

Zack said to them, "If he finds them, then God help them."

28

Johnny headed south. He was two miles from camp by the time the sun began to peek over the horizon.

He now regretted leaving Thunder back at the ranch. For the job he was now doing, there was no better horse than Thunder. But the mustang he was riding would have to suffice.

He dismounted and loosened the cinch so the horse could breathe easier, then left the rein trailing. The horse was in a low area between a low rise and a small hump of grassy earth. Johnny held his Sharps ready, and he climbed the hump.

At the summit, he looked about. He was watching not for any riders specifically because the human eye doesn't pick up detail as well as you might think. He was watching for any sign of motion. While he did this, he stood still so that he himself wasn't creating any motion that anyone out there might detect.

When he was a young man with the Texas Rangers, one of the senior Rangers had told him oftentimes the best way to anticipate what your enemy might be doing is to figure what you would do in their place. Johnny had done some of this figuring the night before while he was wrapped in his blankets. In their place, he would have gotten away from the fire-damaged range because his horse wouldn't have been able to graze. Since the wind was currently from the northwest, he would have headed to the south or east. From one of these directions he would be able to approach the camp without being concerned about one of the horses in the remuda catching his scent. A horse is as good as a watch dog.

When he felt the horse was rested enough, he climbed down from hump of earth and tightened the cinch and swung back in the saddle. Time to cut for sign.

He rode in a rough perimeter, maintaining a distance of two miles from camp. As he rode, he saw two steers roaming about. He let them be. He was not out here to round up strays. He was on a manhunt.

The sun was three hours in the sky when he found the trail of a shod horse. The trail seemed to meander about. It could have been made by one of their own drovers the day before, but he decided to follow it for a bit.

The trail led him further away from camp. After a time, he saw the tracks of a steer. The rider had found a stray but was leading it away from camp. Johnny figured the rider wasn't one of theirs.

He followed along. The rider seemed to find another steer, and was leading both of them.

Johnny followed them for another mile. Then he heard what sounded like a rifle shot. It was muffled, but sometimes sound can be like that when the wind is blowing against it. It came from somewhere further ahead, so he continued along.

He decided not to follow the rider's tracks directly, but to swing wide. Just in case the rider was watching his back trail.

He came to a basin that was similar to the one where the Bingum ranch headquarters had been built, but it was not quite as wide or deep. There was also no grass. It was gravelly and there were sections of flat rock.

He saw carcasses of steers lying in the basin. Maybe thirty head. He saw no riders, so he rode down into the basin and dismounted by a steer.

There was a bullet hole, right behind the ear. Someone had shot the animal. The wound was fresh, within the past hour, so he figured the shot he had heard was this one. Which meant the rider was nearby.

The brand on the steer was the Circle M.

Strange, he thought. Someone was rounding up strays and leading them in here, and then shooting them. He couldn't imagine what the reason could be.

The wall at one end of the basin was sharp and broken and there were small alders growing. Johnny mounted up and rode on over. It looked almost like God had carved a notch in the wall, and small thin alders were growing.

Johnny dismounted and walked in. At the edge of a rocky section of wall was a pool of water maybe five feet across. He cupped his hands and brought some of it to his mouth. It was cool and clear, with that almost sweet taste of fresh water from a spring.

This wasn't just a reservoir of rain water from the previous day's storm. This was fresh water running from a small break in the rock wall.

Just beyond the notch were the remains of a campfire. Looked like whoever was shooting cattle had camped here the night before. Johnny and Josh hadn't found this place when they scouted the trail earlier because it was more than fifteen miles east of the route they had planned for the trail drive.

The ground around the remains of the campfire was covered with tracks, but Johnny saw they all seemed to belong to only two pair of boots. This meant the rider had a partner.

Johnny was not a gambling man, but it was a safe bet these were the same men who had killed Bingum and his men, and who had started the grass fire.

They would be back. Only a fool would abandon a source of fresh water, and this basin was a good place to use as a sort of natural corral.

Johnny let the horse drink a little, then loosened the cinch and let the horse graze. Some grass grew in among the alders, and the horse would be hidden from view until a rider was fully at the floor of the basin.

Johnny found a chunk of rock just inside the tree line. Looked like bedrock. He sat on it, his rifle across his lap, and waited.

He didn't have to wait long. He saw motion at the edge of the basin by a low point in the wall, and a rider came into view. He was leading a steer. Johnny watched as the rider called out with "yeehaw" a couple of times and waved his hat at the steer. It seemed to Johnny this man had some experience at cattle work, but not a lot.

Johnny watched as the man rode down to the floor of the basin. He waited should the second rider arrive, but it became clear this rider was alone at the moment.

Johnny wasn't here for a fight. He was here to stop these two men, and find out who they were working for. He intended to let the man come closer, and then get the drop on him.

He brought the Sharps to his shoulder where he sat on the rock. He hauled back the hammer. His horse looked up from where it grazed.

Johnny said, "Easy, boy. Don't make any sound. Don't give us away."

The horse went back to grazing and Johnny sighted in on the rider. What he didn't see was the snake that was lounging in the small shade provided by a juniper out on the basin floor. The rider's horse did, though. The snake coiled and began shaking its rattle, and the horse reared up. Caught Johnny by surprise, and the rider even moreso. The rider slid back and out of the saddle and landed hard. The horse and the steer took off at a run.

The man was on his back, maybe three hundred feet from the alders. Johnny eased the hammer off, and then set the rifle down and drew his pistol. He advanced on the man, pistol ready. The man seemed to be awake, but was thrashing about like he had been injured.

When Johnny was thirty feet away, the man saw him and drew his pistol, but because he was hurt his motions were sluggish. Johnny ran the remaining distance and kicked the gun out of his hand before the man could fire.

"Don't shoot," the man said. "Don't shoot. I think my leg's broke."

Sure was, Johnny thought. Looked like the man's thigh bone had a joint in it, the way it was bent at an angle.

Johnny said, "I'm not gonna shoot you. But I'm gonna leave you here unless you tell me what I need to know. The sun's gonna be hot, for a man laying there with a broken leg."

"Can you at least fetch me my canteen?"

"Could. But I'm not going to. I want your name and the name of your partner. And I want to know who you're working for."

The man gave a long, weary sigh. He knew the game was over and he had lost.

He said, "My name's Lawson. The man I'm riding for is named Jenkins."

"Stu Jenkins?"

He nodded fast. "Yeah. You heard of him?"

"I've heard the name. A second-rate gunfighter and horse thief."

The man named Lawson smiled. "You know what? You're just about to meet him."

Johnny heard the sound of a horse thundering down onto him. He turned to see the second rider at the floor of the basin and galloping straight toward him, not two hundred feet away. There must be a second entrance to this basin, one Johnny hadn't seen, but he didn't have time to think about it now. The rider had a pistol in one hand and was charging at Johnny and firing. Johnny felt the wind of a bullet as it passed his left ear.

Johnny brought his arm out to full extension and fired, and the bullet caught the rider in the chest. The man fell backward and rolled out of the saddle. At the saddle suddenly becoming empty, the horse turned and reared and started running off across the basin floor.

Johnny then heard the sound of a hammer clicking from the man with the broken leg. No time to question how he had gotten a gun. Johnny leaped forward, landing in a head-first roll as the man's gun went off and the bullet cut through the air where Johnny had been standing. Johnny rolled to a flat-out, face-down position, cocking his gun as he moved, and fired and his bullet caught Lawson in the forehead. Lawson's head snapped back and he laid out flat in the dirt.

Johnny cocked his gun again, in case either man was still alive and able to get off a shot. He climbed to his feet and found both men were dead.

Johnny hadn't been afraid or even tensed-up, the way men get during a gun battle. He had felt a strange calm overtake him. The same strange sense of calm that always seemed to take him when bullets were flying.

He thought about what he had done. The maneuver he had pulled off. He hadn't planned it, he had just done it. He was glad there were no witnesses, or men would be talking about it in cattle camps and saloons for years. Johnny was getting tired of his exploits becoming the stuff of gossip.

A writer from New York had sent him a letter over the winter wanting to interview him. Trying to turn him into a legend. Johnny had ignored the letter. If he let these people have their way, they would turn him into a legend, and he didn't want to be a legend. He just wanted to a be a man, living his life.

He dropped the two empties out of his gun and loaded in fresh cartridges and then slid the gun back into its holster.

He looked at the two dead men. One who had ridden down on him in what Johnny considered a foolish maneuver. To get an accurate shot like that from a galloping horse was difficult. Johnny had seen trick shooters do it, and he had done some similar trick shooting himself in his younger years, but to try it when the target is shooting back was to invite death. The man called Lawson still had his gun in his hand. A short-barreled Smith & Wesson he had apparently pulled from his vest. Johnny had failed to check the man for hide-away guns. A foolish mistake of his own that almost cost his own life.

Now that both of these men were dead, they couldn't tell Johnny who had hired them. He searched them for papers or letters or anything that might indicate who was paying them to stop the trail drive. He found nothing. Whoever it was, these men took the knowledge with them.

He didn't like to kill, but he had long ago taken the stance that if you drew your gun on a man, you had better be prepared to die. These men brought death on themselves. Though he knew there were now two more in the long trail of bodies he was leaving behind him as he moved through life. Two more faces he would see in his sleep.

Zack was at the chuck wagon eating a plate of beans when Johnny came riding in. Johnny was leading a horse, and two bodies were draped across the back of it.

"They the ones?" Zack said.

Johnny nodded and swung out of the saddle. "I'm hungry as a bear and those beans look good."

Ches was trying to conserve water by not washing the plates. He scrubbed them off with dirt, and Johnny figured he would probably have a grain or two of sand mixed in with the beans, but he was hungry enough not to care.

Johnny told them what had happened, leaving out the part about the acrobatic maneuver he had done.

He said, "Those men weren't trying to steal cattle, they were shooting them."

"Shootin' 'em?" Ches said. "What in tarnation for?"

Zack said, "Any idea who they were working for?"

"None at all."

Ches poured himself a cup of coffee. "Maybe we can figure it out. Who do you know who might have reason enough to cause this kind of trouble? Anyone who might benefit from this herd not reaching Cheyenne, and who can afford to hire two men?"

Johnny put some thought into it while he chewed on the beans.

He said, "My nephew Hiram, maybe. Out in California."

Zack nodded. "I wouldn't put it past him."

Ches said, "I suppose he'd benefit from revenge."

Zack said, "What's your gut tell you?"

Johnny thought about it while he chewed on some more beans.

He said, "My gut says if Hiram was going to strike, he would have done so by now."

Ches nodded. "Then, who?"

One name came to mind. Not for any rational reason, just that Johnny hadn't liked the look in the man's eyes. He said, "Bertram Reed."

Zack let that roll around in his head for a moment. "You think so?"

Johnny said, "He had that man Chandler watching the ranch. He made an offer which we refused, and he wasn't happy about it. His man was meeting with men Falcone said were known cattle rustlers."

"Probably the men we dealt with a couple of nights before we started moving the herd."

Johnny nodded. "And there was the look in his eye. I've seen it before. He might not be a gunfighter, but he's capable of killing."

Ches said, "You mean, like shooting a man in the back?"

Johnny shook his head. "There's more than one way to kill a man. Once we get this herd to Cheyenne, I think I'm going to pay a visit to Mister Reed. See what he has to say about all of this."

29

While Johnny had been off hunting Lawson and Jenkins, Josh and the men had been searching for the cattle. The number recovered was now over nine hundred head.

The following day, Johnny joined them. He found a steer grazing by itself, and the animal saw him coming and decided to be contrary. It broke into a run and Johnny spurred his horse into a full gallop, and pulled his rope and got a loop going and dropped the loop over the horns.

The horse pulled the rope tight and the steer gave a pull and the horse gave a pull, but the horse had been through this before and the steer decided to throw in the towel.

Johnny led the steer back to the growing herd. He then rode out and found three more. With the other men having about the same rate of success, the herd was now numbering near eleven hundred.

That night over the camp fire, Josh said, "Joe's been gone two days, now. I hope he make it to Cheyenne okay."

Zack said, "There ain't many more capable on a trail than your Uncle Joe. He'll be all right."

Johnny had a tin cup filled with coffee in one hand. "I figure Joe'll be there in maybe another two days. Then he'll be back in five or six days. That gives us seven or eight days more to round up strays. Then we'll have to make a decision."

Josh nodded. "Stay and continue with the round up, or take what we have and head to Cheyenne."

"We stay too long, and we run the risk of not finding water between here and Cheyenne. All the water sources we found were from spring runoff. That little spring I found where those men were shooting our cattle wouldn't be enough to water a herd this size. But if we go into Cheyenne with not enough of a herd, we won't make the money we need."

Taggart was there. He said, "Beggin' your pardon, but haven't you taken herds down this way before?"

Johnny shook his head. "Not along this route. We've taken 'em southeast to railheads like Dodge and Wichita, but never directly south to Cheyenne."

The following day, Johnny awoke to a sky that was again clouded over and before he finished his coffee, rain was coming down. Rounding up strays in the rain was a miserable job, but because they were pressed for time they didn't have the option of waiting for the weather to clear. Johnny rode with a slicker down over his clothes and water dripping from the brim of his hat. He found one steer only that day.

Over another supper of beans, he said to Josh and Dusty, "At least the rain washed all of the soot off of us."

The following day was cloudy but dry. Johnny found eight steers, but had to ride miles from camp to do so. The next day the sun was out and the heat of summer was on them. He rode with sweat soaking his shirt and dust clinging to his face, and found twelve more head.

Taggart was proving to be an able hand. He worked hard and didn't complain about conditions. Kennedy was the same. They were pulling in as many head as Johnny was. They were not only rounding up strays, but looking for stray horses, and brought in five to be added back to the remuda.

Joe returned seven days later. He had made good time.

He said to Johnny, "I left the letter with the front desk at the hotel."

At the campfire that night, Josh said, "We have almost two thousand head. That's still a whole lot unaccounted for. And we have most of the remuda now."

Dusty had a plate of beans in one hand. He said, "We've been covering the countryside for miles in every direction. They ran far and wide. I don't think we're gonna find many more of 'em."

Josh looked to Johnny. "You're the trail boss. What do you think?"

Ches said, "The longer we wait here, the more we're gonna eat into our supplies."

Johnny said, "All right. I say in the morning, we take what we have and light out for Cheyenne."

PART THREE

The Attack

30

Charles had started working for Johnny McCabe a couple of years ago, and he fell in love with Bree probably the first time he saw her. She was pretty, sure, but it was more than that. There was somehow magic in her eyes, her smile, the way she sort of cranked her mouth to one side in a crooked pout when she was trying to make a point. The first time he saw her, he couldn't take his eyes off her.

What he didn't count on was her falling in love with him. Proof to him that miracles did indeed happen.

His name was Jehosaphat Cole. They all called him Fat, and he was okay with it. Then Bree found out his name was Jehosaphat *Charles* Cole. She said she wanted to start calling him Charles. He liked that. But then she told everyone to start calling him Charles. When Bree said to do something, people generally started doing it. Folks thought Josh was the most demanding McCabe, but put her and Josh's tempers up against each other, and Cole would put his money on Bree any day.

Her demand that everyone call him Charles kind of embarrassed him a little. After all, one thing he didn't want was attract attention to himself. He never liked attention. He had always been a little more comfortable trying to blend into the background.

This was always a little tough for him, because he was taller than pretty much everyone else in the room, no matter which room he was in. Tall and thin.

What a lot of folks didn't know was that his name was actually Jehosaphat Charles Cole, *the Fourth*. The name would mean something to anyone from high society in New York City. His father owned a townhouse there. And a vacation home in the Adirondacks. His father was the son of an investment banker from England, and had begun his own career as a lawyer working for a Wall Street firm. By the time he was forty, he owned the firm. The Cole family had money coming out of its ears.

His father was an esteemed gentleman as far as the investors on Wall Street knew. He belonged to a local club. He had played polo when he was younger, and he told Charles and his older brother that they had to learn, too. Saturday afternoons were often spent at the Polo Grounds at Coogan Bluff in the City, rooting for one Polo team or another.

But Charles never had any interest in such things. His tastes were always more on the working class level. His brother Adolphus told him that he was an embarrassment to the family. But Charles found he would rather attend the baseball games that were played at the Polo Grounds, rooting for the local team. The New York Gothams.

What the fine folks of high society in New York didn't know was that his father also drank his brandy a little too much when he was home, and when he did, he became mean. When Charles told him that he had no interest in polo, he was met with a backhand across the face. His father told him once that he would take the fireplace poker to him if he ever dared embarrass him in public.

However, Charles was fifteen and already taller than his father. Charles had been seen associating with some boys whose fathers worked in a local factory, and his father told him this was going to end, and punctuated it with his usual backhand to the face while holding a brandy snifter in the other.

Charles decided it was time to reply to the backhands as a man would, and drove his fist into his father's face. The old man was knocked back and into his velvet upholstered parlor chair. The brandy wound up soaking his smoking jacket.

"Jehosaphat!" Mother screamed.

Charles looked at her. Adolphus was standing there, three years older than Charles and with a brandy snifter in his own hand. Charles looked at him but said nothing, then turned and strode out of the house.

Adolphus followed him out onto the street. He called out, "Jehosaphat!"

Charles kept on going. He came from a family of tall men, but he was the tallest and his strides covered a lot of ground. Adolphus ran after him.

"Jehosaphat!" He grabbed Charles by the arm and spun him around.

Charles was ready to punch Adolphus, too, if he dared to raise his fists. But he didn't.

"Jehosaphat," he said. "You have to come back. You have to apologize to father."

"I'm not speaking to him again. Ever."

"Well, how do you propose managing that?"

"I'm not coming back."

By the look on his brother's face, Charles figured such a possibility had never occurred to him.

"Well, what will you do? Father will cut you off. What will you do for money?"

"I'll get a job."

Adolphus couldn't hold back a chuckle. "A job? You mean, like a common laborer?"

Charles didn't think it was funny. "The working people I have known are good people. Hard working and straight talking."

"They're *poor* is what they are. Be reasonable, Jehosaphat. You and I are the only heirs. The family fortune will one day be divided between the two of us. You're dangerously close to losing your half."

"I don't want my half. You can have it all."

Charles turned and walked away, leaving Adolphus standing on the brick sidewalk.

Charles was in a white shirt, dark pinstriped trousers and suspenders. He had left his coat and hat home, but refused to go back for them. He had no wallet, or money. Only the clothes he was wearing, but those clothes cost more than the average laborer made in a week. When he went to a local factory to ask for a job, he was laughed away. Not because of his height, but because of his clothes.

The foreman said, "Go home, rich boy."

Charles spent the night in an alley. He ate dinner by robbing a garbage barrel, taking scraps that had been thrown away from a restaurant. He spent a second night in an alley. After that, he didn't look so refined.

He saw a billboard tacked to a wall. A company was looking for drivers to take freight to Santa Fe, New Mexico Territory. He signed on. He had learned to drive a buggy from the family chauffer, and didn't think handling a freight wagon could be all that different.

By the time he arrived in Santa Fe, his hair was growing unkempt and he had a fine beard starting to cover his jaw. His once fine trousers had a hole in one knee and his shirt was stained from dust, sweat and campfire smoke.

He got the job as a drover, then with his money from driving the freight wagon, he bought clothes for the job. Tight-fitting riding boots. Trousers of that canvas-like material they were starting to call denim. He knew little about firing a gun, but it was said a cowhand needed one so he bought a pistol and a gunbelt. Turned out the main reason a cowhand or a drover needed a gun was so if you were thrown from the saddle and your foot stuck in the stirrup, you had a chance to shoot your horse before you were dragged to death. The dime novels would tell you about shootouts with outlaws and attacks by Indians, but the actual number-one cause of death among cowhands and drovers was being thrown from your horse and dragged.

His adventures eventually led him north, to Montana Territory. Three cowhands had gotten themselves into a tussle with Josh McCabe. Utter foolish to even try that, Charles thought. But they had tried it anyway. One of them wound up with a bullet in his shoulder. Another was a man named Reno, and he was taken down by Josh in an epic fight at Hunter's that was still being talked about. Because of this, there some openings and Josh hired Charles.

Josh never asked Charles about his background. He just asked him what he knew about cattle and horses. By the time Josh hired him, Charles had worked as a drover on two herds brought north to the railheads from Texas and then worked at a number of ranches. Josh asked Charles what name he used, and Charles told him Fat Cole. That's what most folks had taken to calling him.

Josh said, "Fat, you've got yourself a job."

Charles had never stayed in one job for long, but he found a home on the McCabe ranch. Partly because of Bree, and partly because of the McCabe family itself.

As much as Charles loved Bree, though, he had never told her a lot about his family. Only that his father was physically rough with him and that he had left home. He never talked about the family money. He had never told anyone about that. He didn't want people looking at him any different. Once they find out your father made more money in a week than most cowhands did in a year, they didn't look at you the same. Money made you somehow a prince, and Charles didn't want to be a prince. He wanted to make an honest living with his own two hands, and to eventually find the love of a good woman and raise children. Values he came by because of his friends, the boys who were sons of working men, back in New York.

Charles had seen something in their families that was absent in his own. He realized at fifteen what was truly valuable in the world were the intangibles. These working families were richer in what really mattered than his own could ever be. But to find what they had, he had to leave his family's money behind and go out into the world. He had been coming to this realization on his own, but his father had hastened things along.

On this cool morning early summer morning, while most of the men were off on a trail drive and Charles and Fred were minding the store here at the ranch, he was swinging an axe and splitting some firewood. He was going to fill the wood box in the kitchen and then the other one in the parlor. He was also going to fill the small wood box in the bunkhouse.

Even though he was built long and narrow, he was strong and he brought the axe down through the wood like a knife through butter. The two chunks of wood sprang away as if with a life of their own.

Most cowhands hated to work on their feet. Josh and Dusty would do it, but complained like an old woman about it. *A real cattleman works in the saddle,* they would say. But Charles didn't mind it. He didn't mind any kind of work that had him outdoors, working with his hands.

He didn't wear gloves. He had found he liked the calluses on his hands. Calluses gained from honest work.

Even though it was cool, he had tossed his hat and jacket to the grass. Splitting wood can work up a sweat.

As he worked, the kitchen door opened and Bree came bursting out. She seemed to never just walk, she bounded. She didn't just walk down the back steps, she skipped down. And she did it with a sort of moving poetry that captivated him. She was carrying two steaming cups of coffee, one in each hand, and managed to somehow not spill a drop as she sort of half-walked, half-skipped over to him. Her pony tail was long and dark, and it bounced and swayed as she moved.

She rose up on her toes and he bent down a little, and they gave each other a quick peck. The kind a loving couple does when they have been together a while and become familiar with each other.

"I brought some coffee out for you, sir," she said with a smile.

"Why, thank you, ma'am." He swung the axe with one hand and buried the edge in the chopping block, and then took the cup.

"It's cool this morning," she said, holding her cup with both hands so the heat of the coffee would keep her hands warm.

"The breeze is coming from the northwest. Just the way I like it. It's good weather to work hard in. Hard work warms you up."

Charles took a sip of the coffee. It was thick and black and bitter. Trail coffee. He had gotten used to it on that first trail drive, all those years ago. Regular coffee now struck him as thin and watery.

Bree gave Charles a smile. Not for any reason in particular, just the smile of a woman who was in love with her man. A smile he had dreamed of seeing her give him, but never thought she would. As he stood there, hot coffee in one hand, the cool morning Montana breeze washing over him and a beautiful girl like Bree flashing him a smile full of love, he thought that he was the luckiest man alive.

"Hey, Chuck!" Fred called from somewhere over toward the barn.

Bree rolled her eyes. "I hate that. I told them all to start calling you *Charles*."

"Well," Charles said, "you gotta admit, it's better than *Fat*."

She gave a sigh and a reluctant nod. "It's better than *Fat*."

Charles looked over toward the barn. Fred was walking away from it with a saddle slung over one shoulder. He was going to move some horses to a large corral he and Charles had been building down a little ways toward the center of the valley.

Charles called back, "Yeah, Fred?"

Fred said, "Rider comin'."

Then Charles heard the clatter of iron horse shoes on the wooden bridge out yonder.

He said to Bree, "I could look in your eyes all day, but I guess we better go see who our guest is."

She said, "You always know the right thing to say, you know that?"

He shrugged. "There are those who would say I never say anything right. I guess you just bring it out in me."

With his coffee in one hand, he took her hand with his other one and the two of them strolled toward the front of the house.

They stood just beyond the front porch. She let go of him and gripped her cup with both hands again, and took a sip. From where they stood, the barn blocked their view of the trail that led down to the wooden bridge, but within a few seconds the rider came around the barn and within sight.

Charles said, "It's Marshal Falcone."

"Dang," she said. "Where's my gun?"

31

When Vic Falcone had first taken the marshal's job in town, he had been a dapper dresser. Usually a black or gray jacket and a checkered vest and either a string tie or a bolo. But today he was in a blue range shirt and a leather vest, and jeans. His gun was hanging low and tied down, and his tin star was pinned to his shirt.

Bree and Charles watched him ride toward them, and she said, "I still don't trust that man."

Charles said, "Can't blame you. Many folks around here probably never will."

Falcone reined up in front of them.

"Mister Cole," he said, in his theatrical baritone. "Miss Bree."

He tipped his hat to her. She nodded curtly.

"Mornin,' Marshal," Charles said. "Nice day for a ride."

"Indeed it is. Mind if I step down and rest my horse?"

Fred had dropped his saddle and walked over, and reached for the reins. "I'll take care of him."

"Thank you kindly."

Bree said, "I suppose the neighborly thing would be to offer you some coffee."

"That would be greatly appreciated."

They went to the porch where there was a rocker, two straight back chairs, and a bench. From here, they had a good view of the wooden bridge down below, and the low, grassy hills that stretched off toward the center of the valley.

Bree went in to fetch the marshal a cup of coffee. She came back with a tray that held a coffee pot and a cup. Charles also noticed she had buckled on her gun.

Aunt Ginny followed her out.

"Marshal," she said, in her grand, high-society

way.

"Miss Ginny." He rose to his feet and fully removed his hat.

Everything this man did was with a theatrical flair. Charles imagined he couldn't scratch his nose without doing it like an audience was watching.

She lowered herself to her rocker. She didn't just drop into it. She lowered herself gracefully. In one hand was a small saucer and balancing on it flawlessly was a cup of tea.

"Please, sit," she said.

Falcone did so, and dropped his hat to the floor beside his chair.

He took a sip of coffee. Bree had brought him the raw trail coffee. Charles could tell by the smell of it.

"Ah, excellent," he said.

"So, Marshal," Aunt Ginny said, "I would like to congratulate you on the election."

He nodded his head in a short bow. "Why, thank you. I'll admit, I was a little surprised by the result."

"You didn't expect to win?"

He shook his head. "No, ma'am. Not really. Not considering the grudge I'm sure many people in the area hold against me."

Bree said, "Can you blame them?"

"Bree," Aunt Ginny said.

"No, it's quite all right," Falcone said to Aunt Ginny, then to Bree, "No, I cannot blame them."

"There are many who feel you owe a debt to society, regardless of how you managed to get those charges against you dropped."

Aunt Ginny gave a sigh of resignation, and shook her head.

But Charles admired Bree for her gumption. She didn't back down from anyone. She would stand toe-to-toe with a grizzly if that grizzly had gotten her dander up.

Charles wasn't here three summers ago when Falcone and his band of raiders attacked this ranch, but he had heard about it. Josh and Dusty had talked about it in detail one night over a campfire. And Bree still talked about it some. Charles couldn't blame these folks for the way they felt.

What the marshal said was, "I don't know what prison would do, Miss Bree. It wouldn't in any way make up for what I did. The kind of man I had let myself become. As for debts, I feel the debt I owe is to your father. And to the people of this valley. That's one of the reasons I took this job."

She wanted to say something. Charles could see the fire in her eyes. But at the moment, the marshal didn't sound like an actor in front of an audience. He just sounded like a man baring his soul.

Bree said nothing, and took a sip of her coffee.

"So, Marshal," Aunt Ginny said. "What brings you all the way from town this fair morning?"

"Well," he glanced at Charles. "I actually came out here to see Mister Cole."

Charles blinked with surprise. "Me?"

"Indeed. You see, we've had a small situation in town that I thought I should make you aware of."

Charles was listening.

"There's a man who rode in on the stage a couple weeks ago. He's been asking about you."

"Who is he?"

"He said his name is Harris Wellington. Does the name mean anything to you?"

The name meant nothing. Charles shook his head and said, "It's no name I've ever heard before."

"He's probably about my age. A little heavy-set. A grayish handlebar mustache."

Charles shook his head again.

"He has been asking for you at various places. The Second Chance. The hotel. Johansen's. Flossy told me about it first, then Hunter mentioned it yesterday morning when I went there for coffee."

Bree said, "Did you think of maybe asking him?"

Aunt Ginny shot her a look that said, *mind your manners*. Charles couldn't help but crack a grin.

If Falcone was perturbed, he didn't let on. He said, "A lawman has to be careful. To simply approach him with questions might imply that I suspected him of being some sort of a threat. He hasn't broken any laws."

"All right, marshal," Charles said, "I'll ride in with you. Have a look at this man."

Bree gave Charles a look that told him she didn't like that idea. She didn't trust Falcone. Bree was sweet and kind, unless you ticked her off. Once her dander was up, it didn't let down easily. And when it came to Falcone, Charles supposed she had reason to have her dander up.

Charles saddled up while the marshal finished his coffee, then they both swung into the saddle.

Bree said to him, "Please be careful. And don't trust this man."

Charles said, "I think it'll be all right."

"Come home to me safe."

He nodded and said, "It's a promise."

Bree stood and watched the man she loved riding down toward the wooden bridge with Victor Falcone.

If any harm comes to Charles, Bree thought, *Falcone won't live much longer.* She could guarantee that.

32

Charles and Falcone rode along Jubilee's main street.

Falcone said, "He's been spending much of each day at the Second Chance. A saloon's usually a good place when you're looking for someone. They're like clearing houses for information."

"I'll take a ride over."

"Before you do," Falcone said, "is there anything I should know? Any reason a man should be looking for you? I ask because if there is to be trouble, it would make my job a lot easier if I were aware of it beforehand."

Charles shook his head. "I don't have any enemies in the world. At least as far as I know. I can't imagine who would be looking for me, or why."

"One thing—I've also heard he might have a gunfighter with him. I don't know how accurate this is. I've seen Wellington but he's always been alone."

"With all due respect, I would think as marshal you would keep track of anyone in town who has the look of a gunfighter."

"I do. I've seen some. They come and go and so far none of them has caused any trouble. In a boom town like this attracts people from pretty much all walks of life. Mines want to hire guards, and gunfighters have the right resume for such a thing."

Falcone reined up in front of his office. "I recommend you ride on down to the Second Chance and see if Wellington is there. I won't be far away."

"Thank you, Marshal."

Charles rode with his gun belted high on his hip. He was no gunfighter and had no pretense about it. He was in jeans and wore an old, tattered vest over a range shirt. His hat was a dark gray and had been freshly blocked a year ago in town, with a rigid, flat brim and a flat crown. Over the past year, the crown had gotten rounded up and the brim was starting to become a little floppy.

He swung out of the saddle in front of the Second Chance and gave the rein a turn around the hitching rail, and went on in.

The old Chinese man he knew as Mister Chen was pushing a broom. Mister Chen was thin and no taller than Bree. His hair was white and he had a wispy goatee.

"Mornin', Mister Chen," Charles said.

"Morning, Fat. Excuse me," Chen said with a smile. "Charles."

Charles grinned. "The marshal told me there's a man here in town looking for me."

Chen nodded his head toward the corner of the room. A man was sitting alone at a table, his back to the room. He was the only one in the room, aside from Chen and Charles.

Charles walked over to the table and said, "Excuse me."

The man turned around in his chair. He was in a gray jacket and a checkered vest and string tie. He looked to be about the same age as Mister McCabe, but had the soft look of a man who doesn't do much hard work.

The man said, "Jehosaphat Cole?"

Charles nodded, repressing a grin at the name. The name had always struck him as a little outlandish. Not as bad as his brother's name, though.

Charles said, "I understand you've been asking for me."

He nodded. "You're a hard man to track down. Please, sit. Join me for a coffee."

Charles agreed. The man had a cup in front of him, and Chen fetched another one for Charles.

The man said, "My name is Harris Wellington,

Esquire. I'm an attorney for one Adolphus Cole."

"My brother."

He nodded. "The very same."

Chen set the cup in front of Cole. The man called Harris Wellington, Esquire ignored Chen, but Charles said, "Thank you, Mister Chen."

Charles then said to Wellington, "I have to ask, why would my brother send his attorney looking for me? I haven't seen the family in years."

Wellington nodded. "So, am I to presume you haven't heard the news?"

"What news? When I left New York, I left my old life behind me. I haven't looked back."

"Then, I'm afraid I have to inform you of some bad news. Your parents have passed from this Earth. Your father died in a riding accent. He was at the club and was thrown from his saddle. It was said he died instantly. Your mother died in her sleep a few weeks later. She apparently never recovered from the shock of losing your father."

Charles let the news settle in. His parents, dead. He realized he felt nothing. He supposed they had all been essentially dead to him the moment he walked away from them.

Wellington said, "Your brother Adolphus is the only family you have left."

Charles said, "Mister Wellington, I don't mean to sound callous, but they stopped being my family years ago. There was little love in that household, and I walked away from it. Like I said, I haven't looked back. I doubt Dolph considers me family, and I'm not sure I consider him to be."

"That's a harsh thing to say about one's family."

Charles shrugged. "I don't mean it to sound harsh. But you didn't grow up in that household."

"Well, whether you consider your brother to be family or not, you are officially half-owner of a huge estate. You are a very rich man, Mister Cole."

"You're right. I *am* rich. Rich in the ways that truly count. I'm now surrounded by good people in my life, and I have work that I love. I don't want the money. I'm willing to sign whatever I have to sign. Dolph can have it all."

Wellington shook his head. "Mister Cole, it's not that simple. You can't simply sign your inheritance away. Oh, there are documents you can sign, yes. But there is nothing to stop you from going to court at some point down the road and suing to reclaim it. When there is money of this magnitude involved, really anything is possible."

Charles got to his feet. "I don't mean to be rude, Mister Wellington. But I don't want the money. I'm not taking it. Please try to get that through my brother's head. My life is here, and that's all there is to it. Now, if you'll excuse me, I have a ranch to run."

Charles stepped out the front door. Hunter was there, a smoldering cigar in one hand.

He said, "What's that all about, in there?"

"Just a man, trying to draw me back into a life I left behind."

Hunter nodded. "A lot of folks I've met in the West are running from a life they left behind. Are you in any kind of trouble?"

Charles shook his head. "No. Nothing like that."

Charles swung into the saddle and cut around the side of the saloon, and to the back trail that would lead him to the ranch.

He had left behind the life he no longer wanted. Now he was having to do it again. He wondered how many times he was going to have to do this. He truly hoped his brother would understand and leave him alone.

33

Bree understood that when a man ran a cattle ranch, he sometimes had to be gone for a day or two. Those cow farms back east had pastures that were fenced off, and the white-faced cattle were short-legged and couldn't move all that fast. But out here in the west, they raised longhorns. Cows that had magnificent horns stretching away to either side of the head, and the cows were longer legged and could run like a horse. As such, a ranch in the west needed acres and acres for these critters to graze.

Bree was proud of Charles. Pa had left him in charge of the ranch while the rest of them were gone on the trail drive, and Charles was taking the responsibility seriously. But she also hated to see him go.

She stood on the front porch and said, "I'm going to miss you."

He put his hands on her shoulders and said, "I'll probably be back tomorrow. Midday, or so.

She nodded. She understood. Pa had left two line riders out there to patrol the outreaches of the ranch. They stayed in a small dugout cabin that served as a line shack. Pa had always said that this was a working ranch, and it was good for the ramrod to make an appearance out there every so often. Now that Josh was the ramrod, he operated on that belief, so Charles thought he should do the same while he was acting ramrod.

His horse was saddled and waiting for him, tethered to a hitching rail in front of the porch. His soogan was tied to the back of his saddle, and a Winchester was in the saddle boot. Two canteens were draped over the saddle horn.

He stood tall in front of her. His Boss of the Plains hat had a crown that was a little taller than the flat-crowned hats you saw worn by the men on a cattle outfit, and it made him seem even taller.

A pair of leather chaps were strapped over his jeans, and his gunbelt was buckled over his hips. He was no gunfighter, and the way he wore his gun showed it. Bree thought she liked that, though. Josh and Dusty wore their guns like they knew how to use them—Pa said Dusty was the best he ever saw with a gun, and coming from Pa, that meant something. Even though Jack was a scholar, he was at heart a gunhawk. But as much as she respected Pa and the boys, she was glad Charles was not a gunhawk. She was glad he was just a normal cowpoke. Good-hearted and hard-working, and she had no doubt he loved her. She could see it in his eyes every time he looked at her. But he didn't know how to kill, and there was no trail of bodies left in his wake. He wouldn't be jumpy the way Pa was, ready to draw and shoot every time the fire in the hearth snapped.

He gave her a kiss, which had started out like a *see you tomorrow* kiss, but then she wrapped her arms around the back of his neck and his arms were around her back pulling her toward him, and it turned into a *I love you so much I can't stand it* kiss.

Then he said, "I'm going to miss you too, you know."

She nodded her head.

He said, "But your Pa left me in charge of the place. He's trusting me, and I have to show I've earned that trust."

She nodded again. She said, "Go. But come back to me safe."

"That I will." He grinned. "Maybe a little dusty and saddle-sore, but I'll be back."

She returned the grin.

He said, "You sure you'll be all right while I'm gone?."

"We'll be all right. Mister Middleton has gone on

some sort of business trip, but Fred's here."

Sam Middleton had lit out two days earlier. He was vague about where he was going and so was Aunt Ginny. She had said he had a small business trip to make and would be back when he could be. A lot about Sam struck Bree as mysterious, but when she tried to talk about it with Aunt Ginny, her aunt tried to assure her that everything was fine. Charles had told Bree that she had a suspicious nature. She thought maybe it was something she learned from Pa.

She watched as Charles went down the steps in his long, bow-legged gate, and then stepped up and into the saddle. He had a willowy way about him, and she thought she had never seen anyone step into the saddle as easily as he did.

He sat and looked at her for a moment, then he turned his horse and was away.

She stood on the porch, watching him ride off. She watched as he crossed the wooden bridge a quarter mile away. And she watched as he rode on, growing smaller in the distance. Then he went up and over a low, grassy hill, and was gone.

She turned and stepped back into the house, and gently closed the door behind her.

Bree had no idea that at the edge of the pine forest that covered the nearest ridge to the west, a man had fixed a spyglass on the house and had been watching her every move.

He had a floppy-brimmed dark hat that was dusty from the trail. It would have to be re-blocked to make the brim firm, but that would wait. He stood with his back to a tall pine, and he turned the spyglass to fix on the rider who was moving away across the valley.

The man wore a Remington .44 low on his right leg, and had another tucked into the front of his belt. A bandolier of cartridges was draped across his chest.

He worked for Harris Wellington, and Wellington had contacted him and told him it was time to do what he had been hired for.

"You keep on riding, boy," he said, talking to himself the way a man will sometimes do when he's alone in the wilderness for too long. "I'll be waitin' for you when you get back."

A horse waited for him. A gray colored roan that stood fourteen and a half hands tall. Normal size for a wild one that had been caught and broken for the saddle. The man tucked the spyglass into a saddle bag, then swung up and into the saddle, and started across the grassy expanse between the edge of the pines and the McCabe house.

34

The man rode right up to the house. With Cole gone, and so was the mysterious man who went by the name of Sam Middleton, there were only women at the house. The man had been watching the house off and on for weeks, and had gained a fairly good idea of how many people lived here. A middle-aged woman and four younger ones. He wasn't exactly sure if the older one was the mother of the others, but he didn't really need to be. All he needed to know was there were five women in this house, but no men.

He knew what he had to do, what he was being paid to do, and he intended to do it. And what he was being paid to do was to make sure Jehosaphat Cole didn't get another day older. He didn't really want to hurt the women, but he would do what he had to do to earn his money.

He reined up at the corral that was a short distance from the main house. That was when he was caught by surprise—a man walked around from the back of the house.

That's right. The wrangler. The man had plumb forgotten about him. *Must be getting old,* he thought. Getting old, or too much whiskey over the years.

In town, the wrangler had been referred to as Fred. The man had actually stood at the bar one evening as Fred and Charles Cole and some of the men from the ranch came in for drinks.

"Howdy," Fred called to him and started walking over. "Somethin' I can do for you?"

The man drew his gun and fired. The bullet caught Fred square on, and he tumbled backward into the grass. He was confident Fred was dead, or would be soon. The man was a good shot and had placed the bullet at the center of the chest.

Dang, he thought as he stepped down from the

horse. He had wanted to get into the house without any noise. He didn't want the women to even know he was there until he was in front of them with his pistol aimed at them. These were women of the west, and many women of the west could shoot. The young dark-haired one he had seen on the front porch romancing Cole wore a pistol, and since she was a McCabe, he figured it wasn't for show. The idea was to get the drop on them without getting himself shot. He wouldn't be able to spend the money he was going to earn for killing Cole if one of the women killed him first. But he had forgotten about Fred.

Now he would have to change his plans a little.

35

Bree was in the kitchen when they heard the shot. She was at the table with Aunt Ginny and Jessica and they each had a cup of tea in front of them. Haley was upstairs with Jonathan. Temperance was in the parlor with a broom, and little Cora was with her, with a half-sized broom Pa had made for her. Cora loved to clean house with Temperance and Haley.

When they heard the gunshot, Bree looked at her aunt and Jessica and then got to her feet.

"No," Aunt Ginny said. "Fred's out there. He'll handle it."

But Bree couldn't just stand still and wait, if someone was in trouble. It was morning and Fred was outside working. There should be no reason for anyone to fire a pistol. And Bree knew by the sound of the gunshot that it was indeed a pistol. A .44 or a .45.

Her own was still buckled on, so she pulled it and checked the loads real quick.

"You all stay in here," she said, and headed for the door.

She was on the top step when she saw Fred lying on his back in the grass.

"Fred!" she called out and leaped over the two remaining back steps to the grass.

And a pistol cocked from beside her.

A voice, coarse and gravelly. "He's dead, missy. Drop that gun, or you will be too."

The man holding the gun looked like he had been on the trail a long time. But he had the look of a man who done lots of killing and was willing to do so again.

"I mean it," he said. "Last chance. Drop that gun. I don't like killin' a woman, but I've done it before and I'm willin' to do it again."

She let the gun fall to the grass.

She said, "What do you want?"

"You'll find out soon enough. Now, keep your hands where I can see 'em, and we're gonna go up into the kitchen."

With a gun aimed at Bree's head, Ginny and Jessica were willing to cooperate, which meant they were soon each tied to a kitchen chair. First the man had Jessica tie Ginny, then he had Bree tie Jessica.

"I don't want to hurt any of you ladies," he said. "But I will. I'll hurt you all sorts of ways if you give me any trouble."

Ginny said, "What on Earth do you possibly want?"

"At the moment, ma'am, I'll settle for you bein' quiet."

He said to Bree, "There should be one more here. Call her into this room. And the children, too."

Bree was so mad she could put a bullet in this man's head and not think twice about it. She said, "You leave those children alone."

"I won't hurt anyone, if you call to the girl and have her bring those children in here. And do it right now."

Bree looked to Aunt Ginny, who gave a subtle nod of her head. Bree called out, "Haley! Can you come here a minute? And bring the kids!"

Haley did.

The man had Haley tie Bree to a chair. He ordered Haley to put both children in the playpen.

"I'll leave you loose to tend to 'em," he said. "But keep 'em quiet, or I'll hogtie all three of you and gag you."

"What do you possibly want?" Bree said.

"What I want, missy, is to wait. And that's what we're gonna do."

"Wait for what?"

He pulled a chair away from the table and turned

it so he could have a view of all of them. He lowered himself into the chair and said, "We're gonna wait for that boy you were kissin' on the porch to get back. Then I'm gonna put a bullet in his head."

36

Harlan Carter stepped out the kitchen door with a bucket in his hand, and headed for the well. He had dug the well when he and Emily and Nina had first arrived in this valley a couple summers earlier. Hand-dug wells often didn't have water that was good for drinking, but this water was cold and clear. Emily needed the water to make coffee, and he was a man who woke in the morning with a powerful hankering for coffee.

He saw a rider a ways off, and knew by the rider's height and the set of his shoulders that it was Fat Cole. Everyone was starting to call him Charles. Harlan threw a wave at him and Charles waved back.

Harlan knew the McCabe men were off on a cattle drive. Charles and Fred were the only two men at the house, and the two line riders out in one of the line shacks were the only other men on the entire ranch.

Harlan fetched the water, then once three cups had taken care of his coffee-hankering, he lifted the double-barrel scattergun from its perch above the door and fit two cartridges of buckshot into it.

"Fixin' to do some huntin'," he said. "Kind of in the mood for some deer."

"That'd be good," Emily said. She had taken some of the water she had heated in the coffee kettle and was about to start cleaning the breakfast dishes.

"I won't be gone long."

He headed out. He was tall, even more so than Charles Cole. With a black, floppy hat perched atop his head, a white shirt with suspenders, dark gray linsey-woolsey pants tucked into laced-up boots, he looked very much a farmer, which he was. Wasn't always, though. The McCabes knew his story. He figured Vic Falcone in town had figured it out, too. You couldn't put much past that man. But as far as everyone else around here knew, he was Carter Harding. Farmer from New

England.

There was a half mile of long, low grassy hills between the house and the nearest ridge. With his scattergun in his hand, he took long strides through the grass, heading toward the ridge. He loved the peace and solitude of the life he now led. Working the corn field, hunting in the wooded ridges. Sometimes just taking long walks on the grassy floor of the valley. He now had something he had never known before coming here— friends. And he liked seeing them occasionally, but mostly he just liked to be with his wife, or to be alone. He had a lot of weight he carried with him, the weight of his past life. A life he had left behind years ago, but that still continued to ride with him. He doubted he would ever fully find peace from it. Considering the things he had done, he figured maybe that was the way it should be.

He was maybe a quarter mile from the house when he came across it. Something that shouldn't be here. The trail of a rider.

He knelt by the tracks and noted they were maybe a few hours old. The sun had been in the sky not much more than an hour, which meant a rider had come out here while it was still dark.

He rubbed the dark whiskers that covered his chin like a bush growing wild. Ain't much reason for a rider to be out here before first light, especially one who is keeping away from the main trail.

Harlan Carter knew trouble. At one time, he had been the living personification of the word. He knew just about everything there was to know about living on the run, and about how to travel about and avoid being seen.

He glanced at the direction of the tracks. They went to the ridge, at a point between here and the McCabe ranch.

He rose to his feet and began walking back to the

house.

Emily didn't realize he was back until he stepped into the kitchen.

"Harlan," she said. "I didn't expect you back so soon."

He set the scattergun on the table, then went to a small chest of drawers against one wall, pulled open the top drawer, and reached in and came out with a gunbelt. The one he had taken from an outlaw when they had been on their way to this valley, and then he had worn it while he helped their son-in-law Jack defend the town.

Emily knew his background. He seldom talked about it because he couldn't without tears streaming down his face, and a man as tough and strong as Harlan Carter was embarrassed by his own tears. She had never seen him wear a gun until two summers ago, and she had hoped he would get rid of it. But he never had.

She now watched as he buckled it on and pulled the pistol and turned the cylinder one click at a time, looking at it from the backside of it. What she had learned was called *checking the loads.*

"Harlan, what are you doing?"

He told her about the tracks he had found.

She said, "It might be nothing."

He nodded, and slid the gun back into the holster. "Might be. But I got good trail sense. My hackles got up when I saw it. Somethin' ain't right. I'm gonna ride out to the McCabe place and check on things."

"Harlan..," she didn't want him doing this. Not him. She didn't like anything that caused him to in any way revert to the man he once was.

"If I had to be away, they'd be checkin' on you. And besides, they're family now, through marriage."

"Harlan, please be careful."

"I got my horse saddled outside, and I hitched up the wagon. I want you to go into town. Tell Marshall Falcone to get hisself out to the McCabe place."

"Will he come? His jurisdiction ends at the town line."

"Tell him Harlan Carter says to do it, and I'm bettin' he'll do it."

She left her chores behind, and went outside and climbed into the wagon.

"But will I be safe?" she said. "With that rider around..."

"You'll be goin' in the opposite direction of the one he was ridin' in."

"Harlan, please be careful."

"Best get goin'."

He was tall enough that he could kiss her even while she was in the wagon seat and he was standing on the ground.

Then she clucked the horses into motion.

Harlan watched her ride away from the farm and then out to the trail and turn right.

He then saddled up, and with his scattergun held over the saddle in front of him, he started for the McCabe place.

37

In Harlan Carter's earlier years, he had gained more skill than he was comfortable with at learning how to attack a facility. Whether that facility was a ranch or a farm, a stage depot, or a town itself. Every facility, no matter how well fortified, had points of weakness. Even now, without even really trying, he found his mind working this way with every building he saw. The Second Chance Saloon, in town. The Brewster farm, which wasn't far from his own. Even the church. It was just something that happened in the back of his mind without him really trying to make it happen. Points of entry. Which windows gave the best visibility, which the worst. How much hurt could a sniper on a roof cause you as you approached the place?

And once he knew the people who lived there, then without even trying he evaluated the ability of each of them. Not only how well he thought they might be able to shoot, but how good they were at strategic thinking, and even how aware they were of what was going on around them.

The McCabe house would be a hard one to attack. Johnny McCabe had situated it and designed it with defense in mind. But no place was entirely attack-proof.

As Harlan understood it, Victor Falcone and his former gang of raiders had attacked from the ridge to the west, covering the quarter or so mile between there and the ranch after dark. They came in two groups and tried to use the element of surprise. They carried torches so they could see, and there was also something about a mob attacking you with torches in their hands that created a sort of primeval fear reaction. Surprise and fear were what Falcone was banking on. He had banked wrong.

From what Harlan could figure, Falcone made two mistakes. One was trying to use the element of surprise on a man like Johnny McCabe. When you have a man as battle-weary and jumpy as McCabe, you really couldn't surprise him. He was always ready, always alert. The second mistake was trying to instill fear in him. Harlan figured McCabe was afraid of very little, and from the life he had lived and the things he had done, a group of raiders riding down on the ranch would not be one of them.

Harlan hadn't given this a lot of thought, intentionally. Just one day when he and Emily were at the ranch, at a little reception given after Nina and Jack's wedding, Harlan stood with a cup of coffee in hand and glanced about the ranch grounds, and these thoughts just sort of flooded into him. The way they did no matter where he was.

So as he rode toward the ranch after finding the lone set of tracks where there should be none, he didn't even have to think about how he was going to approach the place. That strategy was formed the day Nina and Jack were married. He just never thought he would actually have to carry through with it.

McCabe had built the house near a tangle of bushes, brambles and small trees. This way he didn't have to worry about being attacked on that side of the house. Anyone trying to get through there on foot, let alone with a horse, would be scratched up and make his fair share of noise. Anyone wanting to approach the house would have to do it from behind, where there was a large open section of valley floor where the McCabe remuda usually grazed. Or west of the house, the direction Falcone had used. Or north, where the center of the valley lay. Where Harlan and Emily had their small farm. It was south, west and north that anyone defending this house would be devoting most of their attention. They wouldn't give much thought to the tangle of brambles east of the house. So Harlan approached the house by skirting the edge of these brambles.

He kept his horse to a quiet walk. When he was within a hundred yards, he swung out of the saddle. He turned the horse back toward the farm and gave it a slap on the rump, and the horse took off at a slow trot. It would graze and frolic its way back to its home.

With the scattergun in one hand and his pistol on his belt, he got down on all fours and crawled his way through the tall grass between here and the barn, which was in front of the house and to the left a little, if you were standing on the porch looking out.

He moved slow. He was in no hurry. The faster you move, the easier it is for the human eye to pick up the motion. If there was some sort of trouble going on at the house, the last thing he needed was a gunman glancing out a window and seeing the motion and realizing there was a man out there, and firing a shot at him.

He stopped and held motionless. He was now directly in front of the house, about a hundred yards out. The house looked quiet. No sign of activity at all.

Maybe he was being foolish. Maybe he was just an old outlaw who was jumpy and overly cautious, like McCabe himself. Maybe he would knock on the door and find everything was all right, and find himself feeling foolish for being out here crawling through the grass. And he would have to borrow a horse to get back home. But he would rather feel foolish than not check on the women and have it be that they were in real trouble.

He looked at the roof. During the Falcone attack three years earlier, McCabe had positioned his son Josh up there with a rifle. A man on the roof right now would have a clear shot at Harlan—one of the risks Harlan had to take with this approach to the house. He was easily within a Winchester's range. A man sitting on the roof with a Winchester or any good rifle would be able to just draw a bead and pick him off. But the house was too far away for Harlan's revolver or his scattergun.

Gotta get me a rifle one of these days, he thought.

The strategy he had mapped out the day of Nina and Jack's reception was really designed for night-time approach. Wouldn't even matter if McCabe and his sons were all armed and waiting. Give him five good men crawling toward the house this way, he thought. Torches, but not lit up. Harlan would have two men at the parlor windows on the east side of the house and one at the kitchen windows. Light the torches and throw them in the windows. All sorts of chaos breaks out when a house is bursting into flames. While the people inside are trying to put the fires out, his men would pick them off. While other men McCabe might have positioned outside came running, Harlan's two remaining men would pick them off as they approached the house. Five men and five minutes, Harlan thought, was all he would have needed to do what Victor Falcone hadn't been able to do with more than twice that number of men.

He continued on, working his way through the grass. Eventually he reached a point where the barn obscured his view of the house, which meant anyone inside would find their view of him obscured, also. He stood and ran toward the back side of the barn.

Harlan flattened against the back wall of the barn and peered around the corner toward the house. He now had a clear view of the kitchen door and the stretch of ground between the kitchen door and the corral.

That was when he saw the man lying on his back in the grass. Fred Mitchum, he realized. The wrangler. This confirmed to Harlan that he wasn't being foolish. There was real danger, here.

A horse was standing idly by the outside of the corral. Looked to be ground-hitched. Cowboy talk for when a rider leaves a horse with a rein trailing on the ground. A horse will act like he's been tied to something, and will tend not to roam. This horse seemed contented to stand with his head down and chew at the grass.

The saddle had saddlebags and a soogan. Harlan didn't recognize the horse but he recognized the look of a man traveling. This could very well be the horse that made the tracks he had seen.

He decided to abandon his plan of stealth. Fred was dead and the women were probably in real danger. He decided speed was now what was needed.

Holding his scattergun in both hands, ready to snap off a shot if necessary, he began a hard run from the barn toward the house. When he walked his gate was long, and when he ran it was even moreso. Long striding steps. He expected a shot to be fired at him at any moment, but there was none and he made it to the wall of the house. He was now at the west side, and the kitchen door was ahead of him.

He went to a kitchen window and allowed himself a quick look.

Miss Brackston, Bree McCabe, Johnny's wife Jessica and Josh's new bride Temperance were all tied to kitchen chairs. A man sat in a chair with a gun in his hand. The girl Haley was kneeling on the floor and the two young'uns were in the playpen McCabe had made over the winter.

Harlan had never seen the man before, but he knew the look. He actually had the look, himself. Trail weary, and with some of the light gone from his soul because of all the killing he had done. And this man had the look of a man who was willing to kill again.

Harlan had no idea why the man was here, and had little interest. A man like McCabe makes enemies. Dusty, too. Even Josh and Jack. Harlan's main concern was ending the threat without any of the women or the two young'uns getting hurt.

He had promised the Lord he would never kill again. He had broken that promise a couple summers earlier, when he helped Jack defend the town against outlaws. He had again promised the Lord no more killing.

"Lord forgive me," he said quietly.

He reached over and knocked on the kitchen door, and then turned and ran toward the barn.

38

Sitting and waiting has a way of lulling your mind into a sort of awake-but-not-really state, and that was what the man was falling into as he sat with his gun in his hand. The women tied to the chairs looked scared and a little restless. The one kneeling on the floor was focusing on the children.

But then the knock at the kitchen door jarred him back to full awareness.

"Huh?" he said.

The girl on the floor looked toward the door.

"Don't you even think about it, missy," the man said and got to his feet.

The ones who were tied to the chairs were looking at the door, and then at each other.

The man said, "Don't none of you make a sound. Not one of you. I don't like to kill a woman, but I'll put a bullet in you if'n I have to, and won't lose a minute of sleep over it."

The door had a window with curtains, and he pushed one curtain back for a look at the side yard. No one was there.

"What in tarnation," he muttered.

He opened the door, gun ready. The steps leading up to the door were empty.

He stepped out, looking toward the corral where his horse stood, idly grazing. Then he looked toward the barn and saw a man running from the house.

The man raised his gun, cocking it as he did so, and fired off a shot toward the man who was running, but his target pushed in through the barn doors at the last second and the shot missed him.

Who could that feller be, the man asked himself. He thought he had accounted for everyone. But he had forgotten about the wrangler, so he might have missed someone else. When you're observing a house from a distance through a spyglass, you don't always get a totally complete picture.

Then it occurred to him who this man he was. He hadn't seen him in a number of years—he had lost count.

He ran for the barn, keeping his gun ready. If the man tried to step out and snap off a shot at him, this man would be ready.

But there were no shots fired.

He stepped into the barn. It was dark in there, but not so dark he couldn't see. Not like a nighttime dark. More like a room that's been closed up and the curtains drawn.

There were stalls at the far wall, and a couple sawhorses with saddles draped across them. The place smelled like horses and hay, the way barns usually did.

The stalls were empty, but the man he saw had to be here.

He called out. "Harlan? Harlan Carter? That you?"

There was no response. As if there was no one else in the barn.

He started forward, and checked the first stall. No one was there.

Had he been seeing things? The way the man had run. The way he moved. Not to mention how tall he was. It had to be Carter.

"Harlan," he called out. "I thought you was dead all these years. Come on out so we can talk."

He tried the next stall. It was empty.

It couldn't be Harlan Carter, he decided. It had to be have been fifteen years. Maybe twenty. No one had heard from him in all that time. Many assumed he had to be dead. But the resemblance was startling.

And what would Harlan Carter be doing here? Was he working for Johnny McCabe? Maybe McCabe had hired him to protect the women while all the men were gone on their cattle drive?

There were very few in the world as dangerous as Harlan Carter. He would be the ideal man to hire for such a job. And yet, the man with the gun couldn't imagine the Harlan Carter he remembered taking a job like that. Carter had been the leader of their gang of raiders and outlaws. He didn't take orders from any man. He gave them.

He checked the third stall. It was empty.

He checked the other stalls one by one, and found they were the same. The man he thought might be Harlan Carter wasn't there.

Then he found the second door. It wasn't like the double doors at the other side of the barn. The double doors most barns had. This was a single door, like what you would find in a house. And it was hanging open.

The man let out a curse, then charged through the door and ran back to the house. He had left the women unattended in there, and he had been in the barn long enough to allow the man he was hunting to have made his way back to the house. A good piece of strategy, keeping him preoccupied with the barn. Something the Harlan Carter he remembered might have thought up.

The kitchen door was hanging open, also. He had left it that way. He took the three steps in one leaping stride and charged into the kitchen, and found Harlan Carter standing alone in the middle of the kitchen, facing the door. A gun was in his hand.

"Howdy," Harlan said, and pulled the trigger.

The gun went off like a cannon, belching flame and smoke. The man felt an impact like a strong punch in his chest, and was driven back through the doorway. He landed hard on the ground beyond the back steps.

Harlan followed the man outside, his gun ready in case his shot hadn't been as good as he thought it was. In case the man was outside waiting with his own gun ready. But Harlan found his shot had been true. The man was lying on his back in the dirt, and a dark blood stain was growing on the front of his shirt.

Harlan kicked the gun out of the man's grip, then knelt down by him. That was when he realized he had seen this man before.

"Summers?" Harlan said.

The man was dying. His eyes were fixed toward the sky and had the haunted look of a man whose spirit was about to leave his body. But he was still breathing, and he heard what Harlan said, and he nodded his head.

"What're you doing here?" Harlan said. "What did you want with these women?"

Harlan heard the scuff of a boot sole on the dirt and saw motion with his side vision. He glanced over and up to see Bree was there. And Jessica. Harlan had come into the kitchen to find Haley already cutting the others loose from where Summers had tied them to chairs, and he had them all take the young'uns and get into the parlor. Less likely to be hit by stray bullets, in case there was a gunfight. But now Bree and Jessica had followed him outside.

"Who is he?" Jessica said.

"A man who used to ride with me. A long time ago."

Bree was a little incredulous at this. She said, "A friend of yours?"

Harlan shook his head. "No, ma'am. The life I led back then—I didn't have no friends."

Summers was still breathing, but barely. Raspy, shallow breaths. Harlan wished he had shot a little lower. Gut shot him, maybe. He would have lasted longer. As it was, with the bullet dead center in his chest, Summers didn't have more than another minute or two left on this Earth.

"Moody," Harlan said. "What do you want here?

What do you want with these women?"

Bree said, "Why do you want to kill Charles Cole?"

Moody said, "Carter. You ever thought it would end like this?"

Harlan nodded. "I'm surprised you and I both lived this long."

Then Moody took one rasping breath, and he breathed no more.

Harlan rose to his feet. He said, "Now we'll never know who sent him."

Jessica stood with one arm folded over her stomach, and the other arm across her chest and her hand on her shoulder. Covering herself in a sort of defensive way Harlan had seen women do over the years when they were afraid.

She said, "What makes you think someone sent him?"

"Man like Moody, he didn't kill just for the sake of killin'. In a way, he was one of the least violent men I ever met. Never saw him raise a hand or fire a shot in anger. But if he was paid to kill, then it was a whole different thing. He wasn't the best I ever seen, but he was good. He wouldn't have done this, holdin' you ladies at gunpoint, unless he was paid to. And now we'll never know who hired him."

Jessica said, "He was waiting for Charles, and said he intended to put a bullet in him. I don't think we're going to get any answers until Charles gets home. Maybe he'll have some idea as to who would hire a man to kill him."

Harlan's gaze drifted over to the body of Fred Mitchum, lying on the dirt. And he noticed something. Fred's foot was twitching. *Could just be death spasms*, he thought. Depending on how long he had been laying there.

He said, "How long ago was your wrangler shot?"

Bree said, "An hour, maybe. Poor Fred."

"He ain't dead."

39

Fred had taken a bullet to the chest. The bullet Summers had fired was a .44 caliber, and it had torn a large and ragged hole into Fred's ribcage. The front of his shirt was bloodied, and it looked like there was more bleeding inside.

Bree was the best rider there, so Aunt Ginny sent her galloping to get Granny Tate. The fastest horse on the ranch was Rabbit, one of Josh's horses, but Josh had taken him on the trail drive. Rabbit was a mountain-bred mustang, but also had turned into a great cutting horse. So Bree grabbed a horse she called Flame. With Fred down, Bree saddled the horse herself, and then was off at a break-neck speed to get Granny Tate.

Aunt Ginny said, "Maybe we should move him into the house."

She and Jessica were standing over Fred. Harlan was kneeling beside him, and they were using a fresh bedsheet torn into strips to cover the wound and maybe hold back the bleeding.

Harlan said, "He's bleedin' from the inside, too. That's why he ain't woken up. But at least the wound ain't bubbling. Means a lung ain't hit."

Haley was there, standing a little behind Aunt Ginny and Jessica.

She said, "Have you seen this kind of wound before, Mister Harding?"

"All too many times."

Aunt Ginny said, "Should we move him inside?"

Harlan shook his head. "Let's wait for Granny Tate to get here. See what she thinks. She might want him upstairs, or she might want him in the bunkhouse. But too much movin' him around won't be good for him. Could make the bleedin' worse."

Charles returned that night, riding up to the ranch house when it was almost fully dark. The lighted windows of the first floor were like a beacon to him.

His work had been finished by late afternoon. He could have easily spent one more night at the line shack, but he missed Bree.

As he was riding up toward the house, he got a sense of strange quietness from the house. It should be near dinner time, but there seemed to be no activity. He knew they must have heard his horse clattering across the bridge. He almost expected Bree to be out on the front porch to see if it was him. And yet there was nothing. It was like they had left the lamps burning on the first floor, but had all gone away somewhere.

How strange, he thought.

He swung out of the saddle by the corral and gave the rein a couple of turns around the hitching rail. He would go in and see the family. Maybe get a kiss from Bree. Then he would come out and tend the horse himself. No need to bother Fred.

There were three steps leading up to the kitchen door, and he put a foot on the first step and was reaching for the door handle when the door was pulled wide open, and Charles found himself facing the working end of a revolver.

Harlan Carter was holding it. Harlan said, in his tight-mouthed way, "Charles. Good to have you home."

Carter raised the pistol up and away from Charles, and released the hammer.

Charles stepped up and into the kitchen. "What in the world is going on here?"

"I'm hopin' you can tell us."

Bree came running from the parlor out into the kitchen and threw her arms around Charles. "I'm so glad you're home!"

She was almost crying.

"What's happened?" he said.

"It's Fred. He's been shot."

"Shot? How?"

"Some man. Claimed he was here to kill you. And he shot Fred."

Charles wasn't sure he was hearing this right. He glanced to Carter, then back down to Bree, who was still hanging onto him tight.

Charles said, "Shot? How bad off is he? Is he going to make it?"

He looked at Carter, and Carter silently shook his head.

PART FOUR

The Scout

40

It was early evening when they bedded the herd down for the night. Johnny stood by the chuck wagon, a tin cup filled with coffee in one hand. Ches was working on a pot of chili, and he had two large kettles of coffee going.

Zack came walking over, covered with dust. He said, "Hot out there."

"Did you find anything we should know about?"

Zack had been scouting along their back trail.

Zack said, "If anyone's following us, they're better at this than I am."

Johnny grinned. "There's no one better than you."

Zack returned the grin. "Then I guess there's no one back there."

Johnny said, "Get a good night's sleep. In the morning, I want you to ride ahead of us. We're a few miles from a stream Josh and I saw when we were scouting the area a month ago. Spring runoff was strong then, and at one point the stream widens out into a small pool. I'd like to know if that pool still has enough water for this herd to drink. They'll drink it dry. But if it's still full, or even part full, I don't want to pass it by. Then we'll have to take a sharp swing southeast. There's a farm maybe a mile from that stream and I don't want to take a chance on trampling any crops."

"A farm? Out here? How can you grow anything out here?"

There was grass where they had camped for the night, but in the distance, maybe five miles to the west, was a rocky looking arroyo and much of the land between here and there looked like gravel and sage.

Johnny said, "Irrigation. Jack's talked about it. The farm has a windmill to pull water from a well they dug, and then the water runs down into their fields.

Corn, potatoes. They're even thinking on trying wheat. Josh and I met them. A Mrs. Watkins. Her husband was away at the time. I promised her we'd keep our herd away from their fields."

"All right. I'll take a ride out in the morning."

At first light, Zack had Ramon fetch him a horse, and he rode south to find the stream Johnny had mentioned.

Zack didn't like the looks of the clouds off to the south. Dark and low-hanging. The wind had shifted in the night and was now coming directly from the south. If this continued, it would bring that bank of clouds right at them. Sudden rain could pound the ground hard out here in the grasslands and prairies, and sometimes bring hail stones with it. Not pleasant to ride through. Johnny would have to stop the herd and wait it out.

Zack had a rifle with him, tucked into his saddle boot. A canteen was tied to the front of his saddle. He rode light and easy, his eyes scanning the ground in front of him for tracks, then he would shift his gaze to distances further out, looking for any signs of motion. A couple of times he looked back and saw a large dust cloud that would be the herd in motion, but nothing else that might indicate anyone was on their back trail.

When he had ridden maybe three miles from the herd, the clouds has spread out and were now fully covering the sky. Zack could smell rain in the air. The wind was getting stronger and shaking the brim of his hat.

He got down from the saddle and loosened the cinch so the horse could breathe a bit.

He said, "We have a storm coming, boy."

The horse didn't graze. Often when a storm is coming, a horse won't stand idly and pull grass loose with its teeth. This horse was a tan mustang with three white stockings, and it looked like it wanted to be anywhere else. Zack understood the feeling.

Storms were different out on the open grasslands, east of the mountains. They could come fast and the rain could be hard. Not that storms in the mountains or the valley he called home were easy, but there was sometimes an explosive quality to them out here. He had seen more than one herd stampeded by a sudden storm blasting down at them.

He decided the horse wasn't going to graze or get any rest, so he tightened the cinch and swung back into the saddle.

Zack rode further south, up one low grassy hill and down another. He came across a barren stretch where the ground was mostly hard gravel, with occasional strands of grass trying to stand tall. Then he was back riding over sod again.

The grass was starting to show brown, but some of the springtime green was still there. The wind was strong, and rich with the smell of earth and rain, though no drops had yet started to fall. He hoped he could be back at the chuck wagon before it did. Maybe hunker down under the awning. He had been shortsighted when he left camp this morning, and left his slicker in the wagon.

After about half a mile, he came to the stream Johnny and Josh had spoken of. He followed it along as it bent southwest, and came to the pond Johnny had mentioned. It was maybe fifty feet across and stretched along for a couple hundred feet more. A sizeable amount of water. It would make a grand swimming hole in the hot, summer months, except by then it would probably be little more than a large puddle. At the moment, there should be enough water here to handle the herd and for Ches to fill his water barrel.

Zack swung out of the saddle again and let his horse drink a little. He cupped his hands and drank a few mouthfuls, the water spilling out between his fingers, and then he pulled his canteen from the saddle and filled it.

Johnny had said there was a farmhouse not far beyond this pond. Zack wanted to reach the farmhouse and then get back to the chuck wagon before the rain hit. He swung back into the saddle.

He rode what he estimated to be a little more than half a mile when he saw a windmill standing tall, and spinning hard in the wind. Not far from it was a barn with a peaked roof. The barn was painted red, but in this light it looked more like a muted purple. Out behind it was a buckboard.

Zack saw someone coming out of a long, narrow building. Zack had never been a farmer, but he knew enough about it to know this was the henhouse. The person coming out of it was a woman, her hair tied back in what was probably a bun—he couldn't see from this distance—and she had a wicker basket in one hand.

He thought he would ride in and talk to her husband a bit about the herd, and then start back.

She heard him coming and stopped to wait for him. He reined up beside her and touched the brim of his hat.

"'Morning, Ma'am."

She said, "Good morning."

He would have placed her somewhere in her early thirties, and was struck by how pretty she was. Her eyes were a gray-blue, and her nose and the curve of her cheek were what struck him as perfection. He almost forgot what he was going to say.

He felt a little ashamed of himself, acting like a schoolboy over a married woman.

He said, "I was just wondering if I could talk with your husband for a bit."

"You could," she said. "But he's not home right at the moment."

The wind whipped at Zack, and the hat almost came off his head. "Well, I hope he's not on the trail right now. We have some bad weather coming in."

As he said that, a large rain drop splattered on the brim of his hat. This drop was followed by a few more, falling in quick succession.

She grinned. "It would seem so. He went into town for supplies. I'm sure he'll wait it out before he comes back."

"Well, ma'am," he said. The rain was coming down harder. "I'm with a bunch of drovers and we have a herd back there..."

Then the sky opened and a sheet of rain washed over the land. She turned her back to it and Zack held onto his hat, and his horse turned and wanted to run. No need to keep talking, he figured. She wouldn't hear him anyway.

She started to head back to the house, and turned to him. She shouted over the roar of the rain, "You can wait in the barn if you like!"

He was about to shout back, *Thank you kindly*, when he saw it. A long black tendril dropping out a cloud. It snaked its way down, touching the land not a quarter mile from the house.

She saw it too. She called out, "Twister!"

His horse reared. He tried to keep control of it. He was going to ask her if they had a storm shelter, but his horse bucked and then reared again, and Zack fell backwards and slammed hard on the wet sod.

It was a moment before he could catch his breath, and he rolled over onto his hands and knees. He looked up and saw the funnel was looming large just beyond the corn fields. It was coming toward the farm, and it was coming fast.

41

Zack's hat had tumbled away somewhere into the rain. He held his hand up over his eyes as he pushed himself to his feet. The rain was cold and his clothes were already soaking with it. His horse was gone.

The woman was beside him but looking off toward the barn and calling something out. Zack couldn't hear her because of the roar of the rain, and the oncoming twister sounded like a locomotive.

Zack grabbed her and spun her around. Her bun had come loose in the wind and rain and her hair was falling down her back, as wet as if she'd just come in from a swimming hole.

"Do you have a storm cellar?" Zack shouted the words and still wasn't sure she heard him, but she nodded.

She pointed to an area behind him. Maybe thirty feet away was a wooden door on the ground, with a handle something like what you would see on a barn door.

"Get down in there!" he called out to her.

A boy ran from the barn. He was maybe twelve, and he was calling out, "Ma!"

"Both of you!" Zack called out to them. "Get down into the cellar!"

She shouted to Zack, "My daughter! She's in the house!"

Zack looked to the twister. It had been a quarter mile away but had already cut that distance in half. The wind was whipping the rain at him so fiercely that it stung his face. He had to raise a hand to protect his eyes. The twister was writhing in the air as it moved along, and it looked like it was coming right at them.

"Get into the cellar!" he shouted to the woman and boy, and he started for the house at a dead run.

The farmyard was muddy and in places flooding

because of the rain. He splashed through it and then went sliding in his smooth boot soles and went face-down in the mud. He didn't have time to think about it. He pushed himself to his feet and continued running. When he got to the kitchen door, the pounding rain had already washed all of the mud from him.

"Hello!" he called out. "Where are you?"

He heard a girl's voice. Small and meek. "In here."

He found her in the parlor. Maybe five years old, in a dress and with a little apron tied about her waist. Her hair was in braids.

He didn't have time to talk to her, to tell her he was here to help and don't be afraid. The wind from the twister was getting violent. The window panes were rattling and the front door was torn open.

He grabbed her around the waist without a word and began running through the house to the kitchen door. A window pane came free and crashed to the kitchen floor and the girl screamed.

Zack didn't have time to ask if she was hurt. He kept running.

He splashed through the puddles and the small areas of flooding in the back yard. One maple that stood solitary behind the house was bending nearly to the ground. A loose board went flying by. The sky was nearly black. The twister was now close and so loud Zack couldn't hear if the girl was crying or screaming.

He got to the cellar door and pulled it open and dropped the girl in and then climbed down in and pulled the door shut. There was a timber to slide in place and hold the door shut.

It was dark inside.

"Are you all right?" he called out.

"Yes!" the woman called back.

"Momma!" the girl was crying.

"Get to the back wall!" Zack called out, and made his way through the darkness toward the back.

The cellar wasn't very large. The walls and floor were earthen. It had been dug from the ground and was functional but nothing more.

The woman was beside him. She was holding onto the girl tightly, and Zack pulled them both in and wrapped his arms around them.

The roar outside was making his ears ring. It was what it must have sounded like to be caught underneath a train. He felt the ground shaking. Then it was hard to breathe, as though the air was being sucked out of the cellar. Dirt was being whipped up and was catching him in the face.

Then it began to grow quieter and there was air again. The rumbling in the ground began to fade.

"Is everyone all right?" he said. He didn't have to shout this time.

The woman nodded. He couldn't see her in the darkness but he could feel the motion.

She said, "Luke?"

Zack heard the boy's voice. "I'm here, Ma. Is it over?"

"Sounds like it," Zack said. "You all wait here. I'm gonna check."

Zack slid the timber aside to free the door, the pushed the door open and looked out.

The clouds were still dark and heavy, the rain was easing off. There was wind, but nothing more than you would normally expect in the open country, where there was almost always wind.

He climbed out. The twister was gone. They often dissipated as quickly as they appeared.

He looked to where the farmhouse had been. In its place were scattered and broken boards, and more boards were scattered all about the yard. The barn was in the same condition as the house. Just like if you built a house of cards on a table, then swept your hand through it and watched the cards scatter about the table top.

It was gone. The home these people had worked so hard to build. Gone almost like it had never been there at all.

42

The rain was falling lightly. Zack was soaked as though he had fallen into a lake, and chilled to the bone. The pistol at his side was drenched, and he was sure the powder in the cartridges in the gun and the loops on his belt was wet and useless.

The clouds overhead covered the sky from one horizon to the other, so Zack couldn't get a fix on what time it was. He never carried a watch, and usually relied on the position of the sun for such a thing, or the stars or moon at night.

He had walked out for a look at the crops, and was now returning to the farmhouse. Or, where the house had been.

The boy called Luke was trying to sift through the wreckage. The woman was standing by, holding the young girl close to her.

Luke said, "We're left with nothin'. Nothin' at all, 'cept the clothes on our backs."

The woman said, "That's not true, Luke. We are all alive, and we have each other."

She heard Zack approaching and looked over her shoulder at him. He was again struck by her beauty. Like something out of a painting.

He shook his head and said, "The crops are gone. The twister tore right through the corn field. It dug a path of dirt maybe fifty feet wide. What it didn't tear up directly was torn up by the wind it threw off. There's nothing left at all."

She nodded.

Zack's hat was long gone. His horse had run off, and he hoped the animal had somehow been able to evade the funnel.

He said, "My name's Zack Johnson, by the way."

She sighed and allowed herself almost a grin. "We didn't have time for proper introductions. Crystal

Watkins. This is my daughter Mary and my son Luke."

For the first time, Zack noticed a little lilt to her voice. Like a trace of a British inflection.

Luke was standing where the kitchen had been. He said, "The stove's gone. You'd think it would be here in pieces. But it's just plain gone. What'd the storm do? Suck it right up?"

Zack nodded. He said, "I've seen such a thing."

The boy looked over at where the maple had stood. "And the tree's gone. Pulled right up and out of the ground, the way you'd pull a weed."

Zack nodded again.

He said to the woman, "I'm sure your husband will be all right. If he stays in town and waits out the weather. I'll stay with you until he comes back. We'll make a fire. It may not be easy, but some of the boards might be dry. We can even stay the night in the storm cellar if we need to."

She looked at her son and said, "Luke, why don't you take Mary and look for Bessie?"

She said to Zack, "Bessie's our milk cow."

Luke said, "Do you think she lived through this?"

She said, "We won't know until we look for her, will we?"

Luke gave his mother a look like he wasn't sure she was being reasonable, but gave in to parental authority. He waded out of the mess of broken boards and took Mary's hand.

"Come on," he said. "Let's go look for Bessie."

When the children were out of earshot, she said to Zack, "I don't know you all that well, but somehow, I feel I can trust you."

He nodded.

She said, "My husband won't be coming back."

He waited for her to say what she had to say. She took a few paces, her arms folded about her. She was as soaked as Zack, and he was sure she was cold. He wished he had a jacket or blanket he could put about her shoulders.

She said, "The children don't know this, but Conner died almost two years ago."

Zack wanted to ask how it was possible to keep something like this from her children for so long, but before he could, she continued on.

"He wasn't a good man, Mister Johnson. He drank. He was abusive. He never laid a hand on the children, but there were times at night, after he had been working the whiskey bottle, when he might backhand me."

"I'm sorry," he said.

"He always was, too, afterward. He would beg forgiveness. And he had spells of ambitiousness. Building this windmill," she waved a hand to where the windmill had been, though there was not a trace of it now. "But there were times when he just sat and drank and stared off at the wall, as though he was reliving some unimaginable horror from his past. I can't imagine what it might have been. He talked little of his past. He was Maryland and fought in the War, your War Between the States. But I know little of his experiences in it."

"You sound like you're not from around here."

She shook her head. "Scotland, originally. We came to this country when I was but a child. I met Conner fourteen years ago."

She was silent a moment, looking off at the children. They were now beyond where the barn had been. The land dropped off and away, and Luke was looking down the decline and calling out, "Bes-sie!"

The woman said, "Conner went to town for supplies, that he did, but eighteen months ago. You must understand, the nearest town is thirty miles away. To go is an overnight venture. The children attend a small schoolhouse two miles away, but any actual town involves a thirty-mile trek by wagon. Well, needless to say, he didn't come back. I heard second-hand he had gotten into a card game after a few too many glasses of whiskey. He accused a man of cheating and the man didn't take kindly to it. Conner carried a pistol and so did the other man, and you can imagine what happened. Conner was shot and killed."

Zack was shaking his head. "I don't know what to say."

"There's not much to say." She was still looking off toward the children and her back was to him.

"You never told the children."

"I didn't know how to. Luke is fast on his way to becoming a man, but he's not a man yet. In many ways, he's still but a boy. How can you tell a boy about his father, when his father was a man like Conner? Someday I will. But not yet. He needs to have the image of his father as a good man, something to aspire to."

"The crop you were growing..."

She turned to look at him. "I put it in myself. Luke and I. He has taken on much of the work of a man."

"A boy grows up fast out here."

"And now it's all gone." Tears began running down her face. There were no sobs, but the water flowed.

"Mrs. Watkins," he said, "you can't stay here. There's nothing left."

She wiped away the tears and Zack thought she looked a little embarrassed. "Crystal, please."

"Well, only if you call me Zack."

She smiled and nodded. He returned the smile.

He said, "We have a herd maybe five miles back. It's a walk we'll have to make on foot because my horse is long gone. I'm not sure what time it is, but if we get started now we ought to be able to make it before nightfall."

She said, "I can't impose."

He couldn't help but smile. "It's no imposition at

all. It's called bein' neighborly. I can't just leave you and the children. You have nothing left here. We have food back at the chuck wagon, and you can dry off by the fire. We have extra blankets."

"You're too kind."

He wanted to take her in his arms and not let go. But what he said was, "Nothin' of the sort."

She called out to the children and they came back.

Luke said, "I'm afraid Bessie's long gone, Ma."

"It's all right. Now, I have to ask you a question? We have a five mile walk ahead of us. Do you think you're up to it?"

43

Johnny didn't have to bring the herd to a stop, because it was doing so on its own. No critter is going to want to run face-first into cold, hard rain. Johnny sure didn't want to and he couldn't blame the cows for not wanting to, either.

He was riding over to Josh to tell him they would wait out the storm there, but then overheard came a sort of whistling and a roaring.

Johnny looked up to see a funnel cloud descending. He had seen them before, but this one was coming right at him.

His horse spun in a complete circle then reared up violently. With the funnel descending right down on him, Johnny didn't have the presence of mind to hang on, and he slid off and away and landed in a backward somersault on the ground. Josh's horse was rearing and bucking, and he was managing to hold on, but just barely.

Johnny looked up at the funnel and saw it bending back upward, forming almost a loop. Then it began to dissipate.

Even though it wasn't touching down, it was throwing off enough wind that his hat went flying away and the rain was catching him in the side of the head like pebbles. He saw the canvas of the chuck wagon ripping partly away, and whipping in the wind like a bedsheet clipped to a clothes line.

The herd wasn't standing still for any of this. They let out a chorus of bellows, then began to run.

Josh and his horse went down and the cows seemed to be running over him. Johnny screamed out his name, though his own voice sounded distant in the din all around him. The ground was shaking and the rain was driving into his face.

Then Josh was up and running toward him. Josh

was at the edge of the stampeding herd, and he managed to run past a few charging beasts and was then at his father's side.

Visibility was limited with the rain so strong, but Johnny could see Matt out there, still on his horse and riding hard, trying to stay with the herd. Coyote Gomez was there, too, and Kennedy.

The chuck wagon's team was turning and bucking, and Johnny saw old Ches fall away from the wagon seat, and then the team bolted into a full gallop. A loud boom of thunder echoed around them, and the team turned to their left and the wagon pitched over. The team dragged the wagon along for another fifty feet before stopping.

Johnny and Josh ran over to Ches.

"I'm all right," he said, pushing himself up onto one elbow. "I been through worse."

Johnny saw another twister drop, off in the distance. It looked like a strand of black yarn from where he stood. It twisted and danced for a few seconds, and then was gone.

They got Ches to his feet and then Johnny ran to the chuck wagon. The team was panicking, partly because of the storm and partly because they probably felt trapped. They tried to bolt again, and dragged the wagon along for a few more yards.

Johnny worked fast and unhitched the team and let them run. It would be safer this way. Hitched, they would only hurt themselves and do more damage to the wagon.

Johnny found the herd was long gone. The ground was still shaking the way it will when a herd this size runs, but the shaking was dying down as they pulled away.

The rain was now starting to let up a little. A streak of lightning snaked its way to the ground in the distance and there was another clap of thunder. Then the wind began to ease a bit, and the pounding rain slowed to a light drizzle.

Ches said, "I'm gonna see what I can salvage from the chuck wagon."

Dusty and Ramon came riding over. Ramon was riding slumped over in the saddle, holding onto the side of his ribs.

"Lost the remuda," Dusty said, "and Ramon's hurt. Got run over by a horse."

Kennedy returned to camp.

Kennedy said, "They're gone. Scattered all over the countryside. I never seen a worse stampede. Even worse than the last one."

Coyote came riding in. He shook his head and said, "They're scattered for miles."

They all managed to get the chuck wagon uprighted again. The axels and wheels didn't seem to be damaged.

Johnny said to Ches, "See what kind of shape things are in. And see if you can get a fire going, and a pot of coffee. These men are gonna be wet and cold."

Josh said, "We've got four horses. That's it. And five men missing."

"All right. Grab a cup of coffee and get warmed up, as soon as it's ready. Once the rain fully stops, we'll start a search."

Taggart came riding in. And Matt walked in on foot.

"Got throwed," he said. "My horse was killed in the stampede."

Taggart said, "No sign of Palmer and Patterson, or your brother Joe."

Johnny nodded. "Grab some coffee."

Dusty got the saddles off the horses. "One horse has thrown a shoe," he said, "but otherwise they seem all right."

The drizzle eased off to a fine mist, and then was gone entirely. And then the drizzle came back, and then disappeared again. Johnny finally saw a break in the clouds to the west, and some blue sky.

He said, "I think we're through the worst of it."

Dusty said, "I'm going to saddle up and begin trying to round up the remuda."

Ramon was sitting against a wagon wheel, a cup of coffee in one hand. Ches thought he might have broken a rib. Ramon tried lying down, but found it was more comfortable to sit up.

Ches said, "We gotta find somethin' to wrap around those ribs."

Johnny took a cup of coffee. He checked the rifles and found they were dry, which was more than he could say for the cartridges in his revolver and his belt loops. He unloaded his gun and loaded in five dry .44-40 cartridges, and then filled his belt with them.

"Let's saddle up," Johnny said. "And go find our missing men."

Johnny and Josh found the body of Patterson. Looked like he was just lying in the wet grass sleeping, but Josh dismounted and rolled him over. He could see Patterson's neck was broken.

Johnny said, "Might have happened when he got thrown, or maybe a steer ran over him."

Kennedy and Taggart came riding up. Kennedy said, "We didn't find Palmer, but we found this."

He held up a tattered and torn piece of rawhide. "This was his vest. All that's left of it."

The clouds broke up and the sun was once again out, just long enough to drift down toward the horizon. The day warmed a little, but not enough to help. Johnny's clothes were still damp and he felt a chill.

It was nearly dark and a fire was blazing away

beside the chuck wagon when Johnny and Josh rode in. The wood in the possum belly was still dry. A fresh pot of coffee was boiling away and Ches had dumped some cans of beans into a pot and was heating them.

Johnny said, "Is that coffee ready?"

"Will be in a few minutes," Ches said.

Ramon was on his feet. Ches had taken an extra blanket and cut it into strips and wrapped them around Ramon's ribs.

Ches said, "He needs a doctor. He's got one rib that's broken right good. I seen one like that puncture a lung, once."

Johnny stripped the saddles from the horses and when he was done, the coffee was ready. He filled a cup.

He said, "No sign of Palmer at all. I've seen it before. A man gets so run over by a herd there's just nothing left of him. And Joe's still missing."

Josh said to Dusty, "Any luck with the remuda?"

Dusty said. "I found four of 'em. One with Pa's saddle."

Johnny said, "In the morning, we'll get to work. Round up the remuda first. We'll need them before we can start rounding up the herd."

Kennedy was standing off a ways, with a cup of coffee. He said, "Hey, someone's coming."

Johnny walked around the wagon so he could get a better look. It was a man on foot.

"Hello, the camp," the man called out.

It was Joe.

He was soaking wet and his hat was gone, and he was favoring his left leg a little.

Johnny shook his hand and said, "We were worrying about you."

"That coffee sure smells good."

Ches filled him a cup and Joe stood by the fire to try and warm up.

He said, "I tried to stay with the herd but I got

throwed. Landed hard and hurt my leg. Walked all the way in. Probably five miles. I couldn't make very good time with my leg the way it is."

"Did you see any of the herd?"

Joe shook his head. "They were still so skittish from the last stampede, and the grass fire. They're long gone."

Kennedy called out again, "Someone else out there."

Johnny went to the edge of the firelight and saw three people on foot. One was a man and he was carrying a child. One of those afoot was a woman, and another a boy.

He realized who the man was.

"Zack," he said.

Zack said, "You got four cold, wet, hungry people here."

44

Crystal Watkins sat with Luke at one side of her and Mary at the other. Her arm was around Mary, pulling her close, and Mary was dozing. Zack found his soogan was still dry in the back of the wagon, and he unrolled it and wrapped the blankets around Crystal and the children.

"But what about you?" she said. "You must be cold."

Zack waved off the suggestion, trying really hard not to shiver as he did so. "I've been cold before. A lot colder than this. Why, Johnny and me, we've ridden through blizzards and hail storms that make this kind of cold cold look mild."

But when Ches announced another pot of coffee was ready, Zack didn't hesitate. And he made sure he was standing as close to the fire as possible while he drank it.

Johnny came on over. "I was worried about you. I should have figured you were too tough for a storm like this to stop you."

"Like I was just sayin', you and me've been through worse."

Johnny glanced down at Zack's gun. "Your powder's probably wet."

Zack still carried a cap and ball revolver. Each chamber had to be loaded manually with powder and a ball. You could buy pre-rolled paper cartridges, but Zack knew he might have to depend on his gun to stay alive and didn't want to rely on cartridges rolled by a stranger.

He said, "We still got that can of powder in the wagon?"

Johnny nodded.

Zack said, "What's left of the herd?"

"Don't know yet. But it don't look good. We could

be ruined."

Crystal Watkins said, "We're in roughly the same situation. The children and I now have only the clothes on our back."

Josh was there, with a plate of hot beans. He said, "That stream we found, and the pool of water. Shouldn't be far ahead. Some of the beeves might make their way there. They can smell water sometimes from far off."

Zack shook his head. "Crystal and the children and I walked past there on the way here. A twister touched down and tore up the ground all around, and sucked the pond dry. There's nothing left."

Later on, Johnny took a walk out beyond the edge of the firelight, a cup of coffee in one hand. The sky was clear and the stars were shining big and bright. The camp was quiet and most everyone was asleep. The four horses remaining of the remuda were picketed nearby.

Though the sky was clear, the wind was a little cold. Nothing that would bother you normally. A cowhand would just wrap up in his soogan and sleep warm as could be. But the men were in clothes that were still damp from the rain, and the cold wind was just making matters worse.

Johnny looked at the stars. Not a cloud in the night sky. You wouldn't have thought that less than ten hours ago, there had been rain and lightning and twisters descending on them.

The herd was gone. They had recovered almost two thousand head after the last stampede, which wasn't quite half. Now he wondered if they would be able to recover enough to make the trail drive to Cheyenne worth their while at all.

He had seen other cattlemen lose their entire herd on the trail before, but it had never happened to him.

He threw his cup upward at the sky. Throwing it at God. The cup bounced off a ways, and the coffee splattered down nearby like brown rain. He kicked a clump of grass and sent some dirt flying.

"Don't do no good to be mad at God," his father had said once, years ago.

Johnny had been twelve, and a young colt he had helped deliver had died in the night. Didn't know why it had died, they had just found it dead.

Johnny hadn't wanted to cry, because when you're twelve you want nothing more than to be taken seriously as a man, and at twelve it had seemed to him like men never cried. Only boys did. But Johnny had loved that colt, and tears streamed down his face and he kicked the wall of the stall hard, and then grabbed a wooden stool and heaved it across the barn.

"Why'd he do it, Pa?" Johnny had screamed out. "Why'd God let the colt die?"

"Don't do no good to be mad at God, son. It's like the whole world, all that there is, is one big tapestry. Like when your mother is workin' a quilt. Every piece in place."

Pa had put his hand on Johnny's shoulder and said, "Everyone passes on when it's their time. That time is determined by God, based on His knowledge. And believe me, He knows more about everything around us than any of us know."

Johnny wiped away a tear, hoping Pa hadn't seen it. He said, "Does God ever make mistakes?"

Pa shook his head. "He's got more information than we do. Lots more. We have to trust that He's doing what's best for everyone involved. You never know— maybe that colt had a terrible fate waiting for it down the road. We'll never know the answers, son. But being mad at God is a waste of energy. The tapestry is as it is, and we're all a part of it."

Johnny thought of this now as he stood out beyond camp. He said out loud, "But, Pa, I've worked so hard to build this ranch. To build a life for my children.

For your grandchildren. And now we won't have enough to pay the bills."

He could almost see his father standing there in the darkness, listening to him. Pa stood a little taller than Johnny, with his shoulders a little stooped from all of the hard work he had done over the years.

Johnny shook his head and said, "I made a bad mistake, Pa. I got myself shot up three summers ago. Shot up bad. We needed to make a cattle drive a year ago and the herd was ready, but I wasn't. I ain't been the same since I was shot up. And I had to go to California to see Lura's grave one more time."

Johnny looked at his father. "And I met Jessica and Cora. That part wasn't a mistake. You'd like them, Pa."

"I know I would."

"But now it's all gone. I waited too long, let the ranch's debt pile up too high. We had made a few sales to the Army and to a couple mining camps, but it wasn't enough. We needed this trail drive. We had almost four thousand head, Pa, between me and Zack. And with Matt's and Jessica's beeves thrown in."

Pa walked over and placed his hand on Johnny's shoulder. "You take too much onto yourself, son. You always did."

Johnny wiped away a tear. He hoped Pa hadn't seen.

"Son, are you mad at God?"

Johnny shook his head. "Not really. Mad at myself, is what I am."

"Do you trust in God?"

Johnny nodded. "I guess I do."

"God has given you a lot of know-how. A lot of knowledge you've picked up over the years. You got a good group of men who would follow you into hell if you asked them to. You have three great sons and a wonderful daughter, and now you have Jessica and

Cora, too."

Johnny nodded.

Pa said, "Everything will work out. Trust in God. Ask Him for guidance."

Johnny drew a breath and let it out. The feeling of crushing despair was starting to dissipate, just like the rain had earlier in the day.

Johnny said, "Thanks, Pa."

"Think nothing of it."

Johnny looked up and saw he was standing alone out in the night. But he realized he was never really alone.

45

The morning sun brought a much-needed warmth. Ches had the fire going and coffee was brewing. Dusty had woken up to the sight of an elk standing tall at the top of a low ridge in the distance. He had gone to the wagon and grabbed Pa's Sharps, and made a shot that woke the entire camp up, but now Ches was roasting freshly cut elk meat. The smell made Johnny's mouth water.

Joe came over. He said, "I heard you out there talkin' in the night."

Johnny nodded. "Talking to Pa."

Joe nodded, too. "I do that sometimes, too."

Johnny knew they needed to start trying to round up as many beeves as they could, and as much of the remuda as possible. But at the moment, they were alive and the sun was warm and the smell of coffee and roasting elk was what these people needed.

When the first of the meat was ready and cut into plates, Zack brought it over to Crystal and the children. Luke and Mary chewed into it like they hadn't eaten in days. Zack was sure their stomachs were telling them that.

He said to Crystal, "You eat, too."

"No," she said. "You're hungry. And so are the men."

Johnny walked over. He said, "We insist. Please, eat. There's more than enough for all of us."

As she ate, Zack went over to the fire and refilled his coffee cup. Johnny walked with him.

Johnny said, "She's a pretty woman."

Zack shrugged. "Hadn't noticed."

Johnny gave him a look that said, *like heck you haven't noticed.*

He said, "Where's her husband?"

"Gone. The children don't know it, but he's dead."

Johnny gave him a curious look, and Zack said, "It's a long story."

Johnny said, "So, she might be welcome addition at your ranch house."

"Haven't given it any thought at all."

Johnny grinned and have him that look again.

Zack said, "So, boss, what's next?"

"Well," Johnny scooped up his tin cup from where he had set it in the grass and poured himself some coffee. "We get to work rounding up the horses and the herd. Again."

Four horses meant the search for strays would be limited. Horses had to be rested, and the option of switching off to a fresh mount wasn't there.

Zack rode most of the morning and found two horses. One was a bay he had ridden a few times during this trail drive, and the horse knew him and came over. The second one wasn't quite so sure. Once he had them roped, he thought about switching his saddle onto one of the fresh horses, but then decided against it. These horses had been scared by a storm and then spent the night in the wild. They might be a little skittish. He wanted to get them back to camp and let them get settled in before anyone rode them.

On the way back to camp, he saw a third horse. But that horse cut and run. He knew he could never catch it on the tired mount he was on.

He rode into camp with the two horses. Crystal was at the fire working with a pot. Zack stripped off the saddle then walked over.

She said, "I found some wild onions, and I'm using some of the elk Dusty shot this morning to make a stew. I'm kind of improvising as I go."

"Sure smells good."

She grinned. "I think you're just hungry."

He shrugged. "I am a little hungry. But that

doesn't mean it don't smell good."

His eyes held hers for a moment. She smiled then looked away.

"Crystal," he said.

She looked at him. He saw a look in her eyes that every man wants a woman like her to have when she looks at him. He wanted to say so much, and yet it was so soon and he didn't want to frighten her away.

Then, Ches came walking around from the back of the wagon. He said, "That stew yer workin' on sure does smell good."

Zack said, "That's what I said."

Johnny and Dusty came riding in. They swung out of the saddle, and Johnny said, "You found two horses. Good."

Zack said, "Found me a third one, but there was no way I could catch him. They're still a little skittish, and the one I was riding was too winded."

"We've found five head of cattle. One with your brand and four with ours. Josh is staying with them so they won't wander too far."

Johnny got a cup of coffee and said to Josh, "I'm gonna take a fresh horse and ride out and check that pond. See if it's filled up at all. I'd like you to come with me."

Johnny and Josh saddled up and headed out. There was really no need for both of them to check out the water. In fact, since Zack was the scout, it probably would have fallen into his line of duties. But Johnny wanted to talk to Josh about the hard realities that might be facing the ranch.

They found the land around the pool mostly torn up, like Zack had said. A twister had touched down and ripped up sod and a couple small trees, and they could even see a hollowed out section that had probably been the resting place for a large rock.

The twister had gone along a hundred yards and then straight through the pond, sucking up the water. The stream was still running and the pool was about a foot high with water again.

"It's not enough," Johnny said, as he and Josh stood on the bank looking at the water. They were letting their horses drink a bit. "The steam's still flowing, but since it's spring runoff and it's now June, there's not enough water in the stream to fill this pond all the way up. There won't be enough to water two thousand head here again until next spring."

"At this rate, I'm wondering if we're going to be able to put together a herd of two thousand head."

"That's something else I'd like to talk with you about. That's why I brought you out here. Since you're the ramrod of our ranch and our brand is on most of the cattle. We're running late as it is. We were originally planning to be in Cheyenne by next week, and we're hoping the buyers got our letter and are willing to wait. But we're going to be easily two weeks right here, trying to round up the herd. And that's if the weather's cooperating and luck is on our side."

"So, what are you proposing?"

"We take a couple of days, three at the most, and round up what we can. Then we head to Cheyenne with what we've got."

"It won't be enough to cover the ranch's debt."

Johnny nodded. "I've been thinking about that. We're going to have to sell off some land."

"Not to Bertram Reed."

"No. Not to him. Not unless he can convince me he had nothing to do with that grass fire and the murder of Bingum and his men, and those cattle thieves we had to shoot. But there are others. There's some good bottom land in the valley that's not really enough acreage for a herd our size, but it might make for some good farming with today's methods. Things like irrigation."

Josh was quiet. He paced forward a couple of steps. He pulled off his hat and ran his hand through his hair. The day was hot and his hair was wet with sweat.

He said, "To sell off land. We never had to do that before."

"It's not an easy decision, and I can't make it alone. We all need to be involved in the decision. We can talk to Dusty about it, and we'll talk to the women when we get back home. Maybe I'll wire Jack from Cheyenne. But I wanted to talk to you about it first because you now have a position of leadership."

Josh rubbed his hands through his hair again, and let his eyes roam about the land around them. The sod that had been ripped up by the twister, and the low grassy hill out beyond. Overhead the sky was mostly a clear, bright blue. A heavy white cloud looking like a big scoop of mashed potatoes hung low in the sky to the west.

He said, "The land, the ranch, isn't just our home. It's always seemed like it's almost an extension of you. Bree and Jack have said the same kind of thing over the years when we were growing up. I said this to Dusty a while back and he said he could easily see it. And since we all come from you, to sell any acreage would be like selling a part of you and a part of us. But a McCabe pays his bills, one way or another."

Johnny nodded. "That we do. I see this as a setback, but we have good brood stock back home. We'll rebuild."

Josh put his hat back on. "All right. Let's go back and talk to Dusty. Tell him the plan. And tell the others we'll round up what we can, and we're off to Cheyenne in three days."

46

Cheyenne was a cow town, and there were cattle pens set up near the railroad. Johnny and the others herded their cattle into the pens. All four hundred and seventy-two head.

The buyer was a man named Reaves from Chicago. A round stomach pulled tight against his vest and jacket, almost like a badge of his success. Johnny had noticed how many successful businessmen seemed to be fat. The chain of a pocket watch spread across the man's belly from one pocket to another, and it had to be a long chain. He had bushy white sideburns and a thick white mustache that covered his entire upper lip. Johnny didn't see how the man could drink coffee without getting brown stains on it.

Reaves said to Josh, "Young man, we were originally planning on a much larger herd."

Johnny let Josh do the speaking. As ramrod of the ranch, it had been Josh who had met with Reaves originally and negotiated the price.

Josh said, "Yes, sir. I'm not making excuses but it was a hard drive."

Zack was standing there too, as some of the cattle were his. And some of the stock belonged to the McCabe-Swan Cattle Company that Jessica had started with Matt and bore the Swan brand, so Matt was also there. Dusty was sitting on a fence, chewing a piece of grass.

Reaves said, "I'm a cattleman and I understand the hazards of the trail. I've seen some herds more decimated than yours. In your favor, the cattle you do have are in good shape."

Should be, Johnny thought. They spent enough time standing around grazing while they waited to be rounded up.

Reaves said, "Well, cattle prices have dropped a

bit since we last spoke, but we agreed to a certain price per head, and I'll stand by it."

He extended his hand and Josh shook it.

Luke had been concerned that when his father came home, he wouldn't know where to find them, so Crystal had decided it was time to tell him the truth. He hadn't taken it easy. She never expected him to.

He had said, "You could have told me right off. I'm not a little child, anymore."

"No," she said. "I suppose you're not. It's hard for me to realize sometimes how fast you're growing up. It seems to me like just yesterday you were in diapers and now, here you are almost a man. You'll understand when you're a parent."

He was silent for a moment. To her surprise, there were no tears.

Then he said, "I suppose in some way, I knew. You kind of know when you're father isn't coming back. I kind of knew it was you and Mary and me. The three of us. And I remember how Pa was. He was a rough man a lot of the time. I saw the way he treated you."

This had made Crystal's eyes well up. She thought she had kept Conner's abuse hidden from the children.

Luke said, "He wasn't a good man. Not like Zack. I wish he had been more like Zack."

She pulled Luke in for a hug. "Me too."

Josh paid the men, and there was a little money left over. Enough to cover a hotel room for Crystal and the children.

Zack was able to afford a bath, and there was a laundry in town, so when he knocked on Crystal's door, he did it freshly bathed and in clean clothes.

He invited her and the children to dinner, and later in the evening, once Luke and Mary were asleep,

Zack and Crystal sat at a small table in the hotel room. He had bought a bottle of wine and filled two glasses. He couldn't afford the fancy goblets Aunt Ginny used for wine, so they were using two tumblers that the hotel had supplied.

He said, "Do you have any plans?"

She shrugged. "The only family I have is back in Perth."

She saw by the look on his face he didn't know quite where that is. She said, "It's a small town in Scotland. I can't afford passage, so we'll have to remain here. I'm a fair seamstress. Maybe I can get some financing to open a shop here in town."

He nodded. He wasn't surprised she was a seamstress. Women on the frontier seemed to be able to do everything.

He said, "You know, there's a place for you back in Montana."

"Does that little town you talk about have room for a seamstress?"

He nodded. "They already have one, but the way the town's growing, I'm sure there's room for a second. But..."

He hesitated. He took a sip of wine to see if it would settle his nerves any at what he was about to say. He found it didn't.

He said, "I know a rancher who could sure use a good woman to be his wife."

Zack winced at the way it came out. He had never been good with words.

But she smiled. "Why, Zachary Johnson. Are you asking me to marry you?"

He found his face heating up. He hoped he wasn't blushing.

He said, "I suppose I am."

She looked over at the bed at the other side of the room. Luke and Mary were lying still. Too still, she thought. She knew they weren't sleeping.

She said, "Luke. Mary. I have something to ask you."

They both sat up in bed.

She said, "Zack has asked me to marry him. Do you like that idea?"

Mary nodded.

Luke broke into a big smile. He said, "Does this mean I'd be your son?"

Zack said, "Well, I guess it does. If you don't mind."

"Not at all."

Crystal said to Zack, "Well, then, Mister Johnson, I would very happily and joyfully consent to be your wife."

Mary jumped out of bed screaming out, "Yay!" and ran over to them. Zack scooped her up and sat her on one shoulder.

Luke walked over. After all, he was almost a man and very aware that a man didn't behave like a child.

They had lost everything but the clothes on their back in the tornado, but Zack had spent a little of the money from the sale of the herd and bought Luke and Mary each a night shirt.

Luke said, "Can my name be Luke Johnson?"

Crystal said, "It sure can."

Luke held out his hand like a man and Zack shook it. Then Zack pulled him in for a hug.

PART FIVE

The Gunhawk

47

Harlan Carter went and fetched Emily, and they stayed the night at the McCabe ranch. Harlan figured if Moody had a partner out there, then the folks at the ranch shouldn't be left alone. Charles was a good young man and a capable cowhand, but he wasn't a gunfighter. Harlan also didn't want Emily alone at the house.

While Granny and Aunt Ginny were tending to Fred, Harlan went out to the tool shed with Charles.

Harlan said, "I dragged the body out here. I wanted you to have a look at it. See if you knew him."

Charles carried a lantern in one hand. He had his pistol on his belt, but he was glad Harlan Carter was here. If trouble arose, he had to admit he wouldn't know what to do about it.

Once they were in the barn, Charles held the lantern out and over the body. It was covered with a blanket, and Carter pulled the blanket back. Charles took a long look at the face.

"Don't think I've ever seen him before."

Carter said, "His name is Moody. An outlaw I knew years ago. A former raider during the war, and a paid killer."

Charles shook his head. "Did he say specifically what he wanted?"

"Just to put a bullet in you, and this man wouldn't be coming after you unless he was paid. You got some enemies?"

Charles shrugged. "None that I know of. I'm just a cowhand."

"In my experience, no one ain't just anything."

Charles didn't quite know how to take that. Was it a compliment, or was Carter calling him a liar?

Carter said, "One man don't pay another to kill a man for no reason."

Charles stood in silence for a few moments, trying to let all of this digest. Trying to figure who could be paying a man to kill him.

He said, "One thing I know. I'm so grateful you were here to stop him. If he had been here waiting for me, he would have shot me before I got into the house."

"'Spect so."

"And there's no telling what he would have done with the women."

"Out here, even the most black-hearted types usually won't harm a woman. But you never can tell."

"How'd you know something was wrong?"

Carter shrugged. "Man like me, the life I've lived, you get so you can smell trouble on the wind."

Charles went back into the house. Emily was upstairs with Granny Tate and Aunt Ginny. Jessica and Haley were getting the children to bed, and Temperance was helping where she was needed.

Harlan Carter, or Carter Harding—Charles never really knew what to call him—was outside. Standing guard, he said, but he wasn't standing. He was pacing about. Sometimes on the porch, sometimes as far away as the barn.

Charles and Bree went to the kitchen, and Bree poured them each a coffee.

Charles said, "Carter is ever a restless one, isn't he?"

Bree said, "I've been around gunfighters all my life. I think maybe what he did today sort of awakened something in him, and he's trying to put it back to sleep."

"I'm sure glad he was here today, though."

Bree nodded, and took a sip of coffee.

Charles sat and stared at his cup. Bree had grown up around gunfighters. Her father and all three brothers were gunfighters. Even Bree was, to some extent. Even

Carter Harding, the farmer from down the trail, was a gunfighter. For the first time since Josh had hired him, Charles found himself feeling out of place.

He knew Bree loved him, even though he was a cowhand and nothing more, especially since he refused to claim his half of his family fortune. He knew Bree was satisfied with him being nothing more than a cowhand. But for the first time, he wondered if he was satisfied with it.

He realized as tall as he was, he felt small around these people. Maybe it had always been that way a little bit. Maybe that was why he had gotten so tongue-tied around Bree early on.

There was only one way not to feel small around these people. He knew what he had to do, and he knew whose help he needed.

48

Carter rode out in the morning and spent the better part of the day riding through the ridges cutting for sign.

He returned in the early afternoon. Emily was still at the ranch house, and had a hot dinner of steak and potatoes waiting for him.

"Found his trail," he said. "He rode alone. It should be safe for us to go home tonight."

He took a bite of potato, then said, "I followed his trail all the way back to town. I rode in to Falcone's office and told him. He's coming out in the morning to fetch the body, and see if anyone in town saw him. Maybe try to figure out who he was workin' for."

The following morning, Charles rode out to the Carter farmhouse. Carter had work to do, but when he saw Charles ride up, he came over. A couple of chickens scurried across the yard, and Smoke was drifting from the chimney.

"I want to talk," Charles said. "I gotta ask you something."

"Then get down off'n that horse and let's take a walk."

Once they were out behind the house, Charles told him, "I want to learn how to fight. I want to learn how to stand alongside the McCabe men and be their peer. Or at least somewhat close to it."

"That ain't enough," he said.

When this man talked, he barely opened his mouth, and he had a deep, coarse voice.

Carter stood in a white shirt that was dirty with sweat and smeared with garden earth. Suspenders were looped up and over his shoulders. His hair was cut short and his jaw and mouth were covered with a beard that looked as coarse as wire. If someone had said that he wore the beard because he was so tough there wasn't a razor made that could cut it, Charles might have been inclined to believe it.

Carter had put his gun away. He normally didn't carry one, anyway. Charles figured he probably didn't need to. No man in his right mind would have challenged Harlan Carter. The way he stood, the way he moved. The sound of his voice. It all had a way that said *I'm walking death and don't rile me up.*

But what Carter had just said got Charles a little riled up, and he wasn't afraid. He said, "What do you mean it's not good enough?"

Carter looked at Charles, but he never seemed to really make eye contact. He had a way of looking past you, or somehow through you.

He said, "Just to hold your own with the McCabes, it ain't reason enough for me to teach you what you want to know. Besides, there ain't all that many who can hold their own with them."

Charles took a couple of steps. He kicked at a clump of grass.

He said, "I have a girl in my life I want to marry. But she can out-shoot me. She can out-fight me. Last summer, when Aloysius Randall was trying to force his way on her, I tried to step in and save her. You know what happened? He whupped the tar out of me. She ended up having to beat him up to save the both of us. Jesus, do you know how that makes me feel?"

"Don't use the Lord's name in vain. Ain't right."

Charles looked at him. This man who had probably murdered more men than he could count in raids on farms and towns during the late War Between the States. This man who had robbed banks and stagecoaches. You wouldn't think he would quibble about using the Lord's name in vain. And yet, maybe it was because of all he had done that Charles found what he said meant more than it ever would have from a preacher.

Charles said, "And that man at the house, who was holding the women prisoner. That man who was waiting for me. He would have killed me, and there was nothing I could have done about it. But you handled him."

Carter looked down at the grass for a second, then off to the trees at the edge of the valley. "That's what I done."

"That's it right there. I want to be good enough to do what you did. You rode in and stopped him. Saved all of them. Saved me, too."

Carter said, "You don't know what you're asking."

Charles said, "I want to be good enough to stand alongside her. I want to feel like I deserve to be."

"She must think you are. She's a level-headed gal."

"I want to be able to protect her. Imagining what might have happened if you hadn't been there at the ranch kept me up half the night."

Charles almost said *Jesus* again, but thought better of it.

Harlan stood tall and looked off at his corn field. Tall, he was, too. Charles was dang tall, and had met few men he had to look up to in order to meet their gaze, but Carter was one of them.

Carter was silent. He pulled a long stem of grass and began chewing on it. The wind blew lightly and a chicken hawk circled high in the sky, off a ways.

Charles didn't know how he knew this, but he knew to just be quiet and let this man take the time he needed.

Finally, Carter said, "Be here tomorrow. Sunrise. Not a minute later, or the deal's off."

"What deal is that?"

"I'll tell you when you get here."

49

It was morning, and the sun was barely in the sky. Harlan Carter and Charles Cole stood out behind the house. A rail fence stood there, and Carter had some cans placed on it. Charles figured they were going to do some shooting. He had seen Josh and Dusty firing away at some cans back at the ranch. He had seen Bree do it, too. She wasn't nearly as good as her brothers, but she was a dang sight better'n he was.

Carter said, "You ever kill a man?"

Charles nodded. "Once. Back in Texas, before I come north. I was just a new hand. Eight Comanches come riding at us. They were painted for war and were whooping and screaming. It was on a trail drive. I was riding flank. All the rifles were in the chuck wagon but I had my pistol on me, and I pulled it out and fired a shot and took one of them clean out of the saddle. Damned luckiest shot I ever made in my life. A couple of the other men stated shooting and took three more, and the other four just turned and lit out."

"How'd it make you feel?"

Charles shrugged as he thought about the memory. "I don't know. I just sat in the saddle and looked down at the body. I was carrying a forty-four, and the ball caught him in the face and turned him into a gory mess. He was just layin' there dead. I guess I felt kind of empty and cold inside."

"Good. That's how you should feel. Takin' a man's life ain't no small thing. There ain't much worse you can do."

Charles was facing the fence, his gun buckled onto his hip. Carter stood beside him, still and stoic and yet with a sort of energy about him that gave the impression he could kill a bull with his bare hands. He was dressed like he had been the day before, like a farmer, but buckled around his hips was an old-style cap and ball Colt revolver. The one he had been wearing at the ranch house.

He didn't wear it hanging low and tied down like Johnny McCabe and his sons did. It was riding high on his hip.

Carter said, "You gotta watch your language. No more using the Lord's name in vain. And no more *damn* or *son-of-a-bitch*. Nothing like that. What I'm going to teach you, it's going to make you in some ways less than you are. The ability to kill a man ain't nothing to be proud of. You've gotta find balance. You've gotta make sure every other part of your life is lived above board. No foul language. No heavy drinkin'. You fall out of balance and you'll lose yourself. I'm speaking from experience, son."

"Yes, sir," Charles said.

"You'll notice old man McCabe don't hardly use a foul word. Neither do his sons. None of 'em."

"Yes, sir."

"All right. Let's begin. First thing you need to learn is how to shoot."

Charles felt a little indignant at that. After all, he had taken a Comanche out of the saddle back in Texas.

He said, "I know how to shoot."

Carter shook his head. "You know how to fire a gun. Ain't the same thing. I'm gonna show you how to shoot."

In one smooth, clean motion, Carter's gun was in his hand and his arm was brought out to full extension and he pulled the trigger, and a can flew away from the fence. Charles hadn't even seen him pull the hammer back.

It wasn't quite as fast as Dusty. Charles supposed no one was, not even Mister McCabe himself. But damn, it was smooth. He meant, *darn* it was smooth.

"Okay," Carter said. "You got a Peacemaker there."

"Yes, sir."

"Five shots loaded?"

Charles nodded.

"Load a sixth. I'm gonna show you how to do what I just did. School's about to begin."

50

Harlan stood in front of the door of his little farm house and took a look around. It was dark. The breeze that touched his face was cool and with a trace of balsam. The moon rode high in a clear sky. There was a wall of darkness out beyond the farm, and he knew it was actually the ridge that lined this side of the valley.

Everything was at peace.

The family had a dog, though Harlan hadn't named it because he figured what was the point of naming it when it couldn't talk or understand what you said? He figured to the dog, the words spoken by a man sounded like gibberish. But his wife and Nina insisted on calling it Scout, for whatever reason. It was a mix of German Shepherd and something else. Harlan had no idea what.

But the dog was reliable. You could depend on him to tell you when something was wrong. When there was something out in the night that shouldn't be there.

Scout paced about in front of him, sniffing the air, then sat down and looked out at the darkness alongside Harlan. If Scout thought everything was all right, then that was good enough for Harlan.

Harlan went to the door and stepped in, then held the door and looked to the dog. The dog came scooting in. Harlan shut the door.

He didn't bother to bolt it. Anyone coming into this house unannounced at night—well, it would be their funeral.

The stove was still warm so he heated some water and washed up. Working on a farm can sure raise a man's sweat. Then he climbed into bed.

Harlan thought Emily was asleep, so he climbed into bed easily, but once he was settled on the pillow, she rolled over to face him and said, "Harlan, is it really necessary? Teaching that boy?"

He said, "I thought you was asleep."

"I never sleep well unless you're here beside me. You know that."

This man smiled seldom, but he allowed himself a grin. He reached over and stroked the side the side of her face. "I do know that."

She said, "So, answer my question."

"Because he needs to know."

"As simple as that?"

He shook his head. "It's never as simple as that."

She nodded. She understood.

She said, "Couldn't it wait until the McCabe men are back from their trail drive? Couldn't Johnny teach him? Or one of the boys?"

Carter shook his head. "Can't wait for that. The gunman at the house, he was looking for Charles. He was willin' to kill all the women there if it came to it. More are gonna come gunnin' for him."

"Have you asked him why?"

Carter shook his head again. "He don't know. But he's a good boy. Got a good heart. Every bit as good as Jack and his brothers. He's got the wrong kind of men gunning for him. I suppose it don't really matter the reason. He has to be able to stand against them."

She looked at him sadly. "It isn't easy being you, is it? Being the kind of man you are? The kind of man the McCabes call a gunhawk. The kind of man Ginny Brackston calls *a knight with a gun.*"

He chuckled. "I don't know that I'd call me a knight. Considering the kind of stuff I done."

"Whatever you were before I met you, I never knew that man. I only know the man here with me now. And you are so incredibly a knight."

He chuckled again. "No, I guess it ain't easy bein' me. But you make it much easier than it could have been."

51

Charles unloaded his gun on the cans at the fence. Not aiming, but just pointing, like Harlan Carter had been teaching him. Just letting the weapon become a part of him.

Charles was getting good at this. Generally, his bullets found their targets. But not this morning. He fired six shots, and when the smoke cleared, two cans were still standing.

Carter said, "You're off your game, boy."

Charles nodded. He flipped open the loading gate and dropped the empties to the ground and reloaded.

Carter said, "When someone's shootin' at you, you can't afford to be off your game. You're having a bad day, it can get you killed. Johnny McCabe can't afford to have a bad day. And neither could I, back in the day."

Charles slid the gun back into his holster and faced the fence. There were twelve more cans still standing. He drew, bringing his arm out to full extension and cocking the pistol as he did so, and began firing. Hauling the hammer back and pulling the trigger, again and again. Trying to concentrate. Trying to let the gun just be an extension of himself.

He got four of the six cans again.

"All right, boy," Carter said. "Talk."

Charles flipped the loading gate open and dropped more empties. He would have to ride into town soon for a couple more boxes of ammunition. It's a good thing room and board were part of the deal at the McCabe ranch, or he would be going broke paying for cartridges.

He said, "This thing about a man trying to kill me. A man I never seen before. Have you ever had a man want to kill you, but you didn't know why?"

Carter hesitated a moment, like he was searching his memories. Is struck Charles as a little amusing and yet unsettling that Carter had to think about it before he could give an answer.

Carter said, "Nope. As I remember, everyone wanted to kill me, I knew why. Couldn't blame most of 'em."

"Well, I've got to know why. Because if I don't, then how do I know someone else won't be coming to finish the job?"

Carter nodded. "Good point. All right, think about it. Do you have any enemies?"

"None that I know of. Except for Aloysius Randall."

"Just about everyone around here could call him an enemy. But if he was gonna start hiring men to kill people, I don't think you'd be his first target. Probably Johnny McCabe, then Dusty or Josh, or both of 'em. And Victor Falcone. Maybe that preacher in town, Matt's son. Get him out of the way, too."

"Then, it has to be someone else."

Carter nodded again. "That's the way my line of thinkin' would go. Where you from, boy?"

Bree knew, but she was about the only one. He said, "New York."

Carter gave him a curious look. "Really?"

Charles nodded. "Brought up in the heart of Manhatten."

"You sure don't sound it. And you don't act like no city feller I ever met. I figured you was from Virginia or some such place."

"Well, I've been out west a long time."

"All right. Anyone back there in New York want to kill you?"

Charles shrugged. "I can't imagine who. I never caused trouble."

"Think about it. Somewhere out there is someone who wants you dead. Who would benefit from your death?"

And then it occurred to him, but the thought gave

him a chill that ran all the way to his bones. Could it be possible?

Carter was looking at him. He saw the look that came over Charles. Carter said, "Who?"

Charles looked at him. "My brother."

52

Granny Tate spent three nights at the McCabe ranch, tending to Fred. She had expected him to die within hours, but he didn't. His breathing was shallow and his heart beat was fast and weak. But he continued to breathe, and his heart continued to beat.

The next day, he seemed to be holding his ground. Haley said, "Is that a good sign?"

Granny Tate shrugged. "It ain't a bad one, child."

Granny went downstairs, taking each step one at a time, using her cane and holding onto the railing with one hand. Then she joined Ginny in the kitchen.

"If I may be so bold," Granny said, "I could surely use a cup of tea."

"You may indeed be so bold," Ginny said with a smile. "I was just fixing one, myself."

Ginny fixed two cups of Earl Gray, while Granny sat at the table.

"My land, but that's good tea," Granny said.

"I have an unopened box of it. I would be pleased if you took it home with you."

"Oh, I couldn't."

Ginny nodded. "Yes, Granny, you could. You never accept payment. At least let us do something for you, once in a while. It would mean a lot to me."

Granny looked at her through spectacles with lenses that reminded Ginny of magnifying glasses. The old woman squinted and Ginny wasn't sure just what she saw. And yet, Granny seemed to miss nothing.

Granny said, "Well, if you insist."

Ginny smiled. "I insist."

Granny Tate took another sip of tea. "That young man upstairs is still hanging onto life."

Young man, Ginny thought with a smile. Fred was past fifty. But to Granny, probably everyone around here seemed young.

Ginny said, "This reminds me of when Johnny was shot. All we could do is sit and wait."

"Fred took only one bullet, and Johnny took two, but in a way, Fred is hurt a lot worse. He lost a lot more blood. And he was layin' outside for a long time. Even though the boys treated him for infection with corn whiskey, it might not be enough. His wound is deep and dirt can get inside. Dirt can cause infection, even in a wound that's been cleaned good."

Granny stayed on for another day. Fred's breathing began to grow more even, and his heart rate became stronger.

On day three, he opened his eyes.

He said, "I've been shot."

Granny was smiling. "That you have, child. Shot real good, too. Thought you weren't gonna make it."

"I feel weak as a kitten." His voice was light and whispery.

She nodded. "It's gonna be a while before you're back to full strength. Maybe a long while. That bullet tore you up real bad inside. But I think you're through the woods, now."

Granny headed home that afternoon. Ginny drove her in her buggy.

As they rode along, Granny said, "You keep an eye on him. He might be through the woods, but he ain't all the way through. I'll be out to check on him every day. But you watch out for fever. Any sign of it, you send someone for me right away."

Ginny nodded. "I won't hesitate."

When Ginny got back, she found Haley standing in the bedroom doorway.

Haley said, "Fred's sleeping again. Do you think Granny's right? He's really going to make it?"

Ginny said, "I would put Granny Tate's medical knowledge up against any doctor I have ever met."

"She's really old."

Ginny nodded. "Yes, that she is."

"Have you ever thought about what we'll do when she's gone?"

Ginny had to admit, she never had. Granny Tate was one of these people who seemed to be so implanted in the lives of those around her that it was difficult to imagine life without her.

Haley said, "I want her to teach me."

53

In the morning, Aunt Ginny asked Charles to hitch a team to the buggy for her.

She had said, "I'll be going into town to check on Hunter, then I'll pick up Granny Tate and bring her out so she can have a look at Fred."

Charles said, "You want me to come along?"

Ginny shook her head. "Thank you, but no. I won't be alone. Haley's coming along."

Charles was in jeans and a white shirt, and his pistol was at his belt, but now worn toward the front of his left side and turned for a cross-draw. Something Mister Carter had said some men did. Charles found this method of drawing a gun was working fine for him.

Bree was outside with him, holding a cup of coffee in one hand. She was in an ankle-length skirt, but her pistol was buckled about her hips. Charles doubted she would be comfortable going without it for a while, after being held hostage by that man Moody.

Charles had never seen Bree look afraid until that day. The memory stayed with him, and maybe it was what drove him strongest in his sessions with Harlan Carter.

As he worked on hitching the team, he said, "I wonder how long it'll be before Fred can take over wrangling duties."

Bree shrugged. "He's lucky to be alive at all. Granny Tate said she's seen men shot not nearly as bad, but who died. He's worse-off even than Pa was, after that raid three summers ago."

Once the rig was ready, Aunt Ginny and Haley climbed in. Aunt Ginny had a hat pinned to her hair and a shawl about her shoulders.

Charles said, "You sure you don't want me to come along? I could saddle a horse right quick. It would be no trouble at all."

Aunt Ginny said, "Charles, that man is dead. He's no more danger to us. We'll be fine."

Haley took the reins. She gave them a snap and made a clucking sound with her mouth, and the team started forward.

Charles and Bree stood and watched the buggy make its way down the trail toward the wooden bridge.

"I wish you would tell me what's going on at the Carter house," Bree said. "You've been there almost every morning for a week."

Charles said, "I could go for a cup of coffee."

He started for the kitchen door.

Bree said, "Now you hold on, Charles Cole. You're not getting away that easy. I asked you a simple question."

Charles climbed the back steps and was into the kitchen. Temperance was cutting up some chicken that had been killed that morning. She was going to watch Jonathan while Haley was off with Aunt Ginny. The boy was on the kitchen floor, in the wicker playpen Johnny had made.

Temperance said, "I'm gonna bake up some chicken for dinner. That all right with you two?"

Bree was right behind Charles and said nothing, but Charles said, "That'd be right fine."

"Charles," Bree said.

She reached up to grab his shoulder. She had to really reach up to do this.

She said, "I know you're doing something that involves guns. You come back smelling like gun smoke. And I see you wearing you're gun different now."

He said, "Bree. I don't really want to talk about it."

"Why are you here this morning?"

"With Fred shot, there's one less man here to do the work. I have to do the work I had been planning on doing, and the wrangler work, too."

"So you're not going over to the Carter house today?"

"No, ma'am." Then he said a little more quietly, "Mister Carter's comin' over here this afternoon."

"Fine," Bree said, in the way a woman does that lets a man know it's really not fine. "You don't want to talk about it."

"No, I don't. I guess I just ain't ready, yet."

"Then let's talk about that man who was here, holding us prisoner and wanting to shoot you."

Temperance visibly shuddered. She said, "That's something I never want to think about again."

Charles had been putting some thought into who might have sent that men. Who could possibly want him dead. Then one name occurred to him, and the thought chilled him. He had talked to Carter about it, but to no one else.

But now Bree was asking. He didn't want to lie to her about anything at all. He believed marriage was in the future for them, and he wanted to build the kind of marriage Mister McCabe and Miss Jessica seemed to have. A marriage like they had was rooted in honesty.

He figured he could say he didn't know who sent the man, because he didn't really know for fact. But in reality, he knew he could get away with this kind of thing for only so long, and by the way Bree was looking at him, he thought maybe he wasn't going to get away with it much longer.

She said, "Charles, I see how nervous you are about any of us going to town. Whatever it was that man was here for, you know fully well what he wanted, and you know it's not over."

Bree slid a kitchen chair out for him, and pulled out another chair for herself.

He sighed with resignation. He wasn't getting out of this. He went to the stove and poured himself a cup of coffee, and then took the chair.

Temperance was at the counter, working a knife through the chicken on a stone cutting board Johnny had made years ago. She looked over her shoulder at them and said, "Maybe you two would be more comfortable in the parlor. Have some privacy."

Charles shook his head. "No. We're all family here. Maybe it's high time I told you all."

Bree sat and waited. And it was all Temperance could do not to abandon the chicken and scurry over to the table and grab a chair.

Charles said, "You all know I'm from New York."

Bree nodded.

But Temperance said, "I didn't know that. You don't talk alike anyone I ever met from New York."

He glanced over his shoulder at her. "Well, I've been in the West a long time. Spent a lot of time with drovers from Texas, at one time. But I originally come from New York."

"Where about?"

"The city itself." He looked at Bree. "And I told you how my father was mean and more than willing to take the back of his hand to my brother and me."

Bree nodded.

"There's a lot more to my background than that."

Charles took a long sip of coffee and then he began talking about his life in New York, and why he had left it behind. And how when he left it behind, he had left behind enough money to buy the entire town of Jubilee two or three times over.

Bree's mouth was hanging open. So was Temperance's.

"Why didn't you tell me any of this before?" Bree said.

"I told you about my father."

"But you didn't tell us about the money. How rich you are."

"*Was*. How rich I *was*. And the reason I didn't was

because look at the two of you. You don't see me as the same. I'm still the same man I was, but you're looking at me like I'm someone totally different."

"No," Bree said, embarrassed at herself. "I don't mean to, at least. It's just that..."

Temperance said, "It's not every day you meet someone who's rich. You must make Aloysius Randall look like a beggar."

"You don't understand," Charles said. "When I walked away from that life, I left behind the money, too. None of it's mine. I don't want it. All I have is the money in my pocket that's left over from the last payday. I want to make it in this world by the sweat of my brow and the strength in my back."

Bree said, "You mentioned that man in town who was looking for you told you your parents had died."

Temperance said, "How does any of this tie into the man who tried to kill you?"

"Legally, the money belongs to both my brother and me. This man Wellington—he's the family attorney, apparently. I told him I was willing to sign it all over to my brother, but Wellington said there was nothing I could sign that could prevent me from showing up years later and trying to claim it. The only way my brother could have full, clear, undisputable claim to the entire family fortune would be if he was the only heir."

Bree sat for a moment, looking at him. Digesting all of this. Then she said, "Do you mean you think your brother is trying have you killed?"

He shrugged. "It would solve a lot of problems for him."

Temperance said, "But he's your brother. You grew up with him. Could he really be capable of that?"

Charles looked at her, and said, "My brother? Considering the family I come from? I would say, yes."

54

Carter said to Charles, "You ever know why I didn't want Nina marrying Jack?"

Charles had no idea Carter had ever been against Nina's marriage to Jack. But he said nothing.

Carter said, "It weren't that I didn't think he was a good man. I think he thought that, at least for a while, but it wasn't true. It was that I wanted her marrying a man who was just a farmer. A man who worked hard sun-up to sundown and could be a good husband to her and a good father to their children. I didn't want her marrying a man who knew how to kill five different ways with his bare hands. Someone who was too good with his gun. I didn't want her marrying someone like me. I could see it in his eyes, the first time I met him. You ain't like that. You're just a regular man. I wish I could have been like you. But when I'm done with you, you'll be like me. Like Jack."

They were leaning against the rail fence. They had just got done shooting a line of cans from it, then standing up more cans on it and reloading and doing it again. And again. Charles could still smell gunsmoke in the air.

Charles said, "Was I wrong in asking this of you?"

Carter shook his head. "That man who was holding the McCabe women hostage—he was a killer. And he was looking to kill you. More are gonna come, especially if you're right about your brother. You have to be ready."

Charles nodded.

"Break time's over. Reload."

Charles began thumbing cartridges into his pistol. He said, "Do you really know five different ways to kill a man with your bare hands?"

Carter gave a little chuckle. "Well, maybe only two or three."

55

They needed to take some time off from training. Carter had work waiting for him at the farm, and Charles was now not only the acting ramrod of the ranch, but now he was also the wrangler. Carter also wanted to go into town and check on Tom McCabe. Turned out Falcone had taken a bullet the Saturday before, and Tom was wearing the marshal's badge while Falcone recovered.

Tom McCabe was a man who puzzled Charles a little. He was pastor of the Methodist church, and yet he often wore a gun, and he wore it like he knew how to use it. Low and tied down. And the look in his eye was the same look he saw in the eyes of Josh and Dusty. The look of a gunhawk. And Carter spoke of him as an equal, the way he did Marshal Falcone or Johnny McCabe.

"I'm sure Tom can handle things," Carter said. "But I'm gonna go in and make sure he's all right, anyway."

They had a thunderstorm one night, the kind that can descend on you from out of the mountains as though with the holy wrath of God himself. Rain pounding the house like it wanted to break in the roof. Wind that rattled the windows. At one point, hail started falling.

Aunt Ginny invited Charles to sleep on the sofa in the parlor, that night. He was the only occupant of the bunkhouse at the moment, until the rest of the men came back from the trail drive, and the bunkhouse roof was in need of repair. The following morning, Charles found some rotted timbers had given way and part of the bunkhouse roof had caved in. The hail had also cracked some wooden shingles on the roof of the main house. He had some work to do.

A sawmill was now set up at the edge of town, so

he took the buckboard in and got two-by-fours and two-by-sixes, and some bundles of shingles. He had it all added to the ranch's tab. It would be paid back once Mister McCabe and the boys were back from the trail drive with the money the herd was sure to fetch in Cheyenne. He rebuilt the bunkhouse roof and then reshingled part of the roof of the main house.

The sun was riding low in the western sky as he was climbing down the ladder he had braced against the side of the house. He heard a rider coming, and looked off toward the trail, and he brought his hand to his gun as he did so.

Before the incident with the man Harlan Carter had killed, Charles wouldn't have worn his gun when working on a roof. Now it was with him constantly.

He saw it was Carter riding up.

Carter said, "They keepin' you busy enough?"

Charles nodded with a tired grin. "And then some."

"Come on out to the house tomorrow morning. It's time to learn scrappin'."

Charles stepped down from the ladder to the grass. "You gonna show me them two or three ways we talked about?"

Carter shook his head. "I'm passable good with my fists, but I'm not the best there is around here. I tell Jack that he only beat me because I was drunk, but between you and me, he would've beat me anyway. I need someone better'n me to teach you. He'll be at the ranch tomorrow."

"All right. I have some morning chores to do here, then I'll be right out."

Carter nodded and turned his horse back toward his farm.

The sun was peeking over the ridge to the east when Charles rode onto the Carter farm. He swung out of the saddle. Scout was barking, not the angry warning bark he used to give when Charles showed up, but a happy welcoming bark. His tail was wagging, and Charles reached down to scratch the dog's head.

Harlan Carter stepped out of the house. "Easy on the dog," he said. "I don't want anyone makin' him soft. It's bad enough the way Emily and Nina coddle him."

"So," Charles said. "That man you mentioned. Is he here?"

Carter nodded. "He's in the kitchen. The most dangerous man I know. Come on inside."

At the table with a cup of tea in front of him was the old Chinese man, Chen. The swamper at the Second Chance.

"Mister Chen," Charles said, a little surprised. Charles knew the old man was a little clever at wrestling, but what could he possibly know about actual hand-to-hand combat that Carter didn't?

"Morning, Charles," Chen said.

Mrs. Carter was at the kitchen counter. "Charles, have you eaten?"

Charles pulled off his hat. "Yes'm. But thanks for asking."

"Would you like some coffee?"

He couldn't turn that down. Emily poured him a cup, then excused herself to go outside. Today was laundry day.

When she was gone, Carter said, "The real reason she went outside was to give us room to talk. She don't like this business. What I'm teachin' you. She understands it has to be done, but it don't mean she likes it."

Charles nodded. He understood.

Chen glanced at Charles, then looked at Carter. "You want him to try and push me down?"

Carter shook his head. "I want you teach him how to kill a man."

That was when Charles saw it. A look in Chen's eye. He had the same look Carter did. He had never noticed it before. Often Chen seemed like nothing more than a jolly old man. Quick with a smile. But as he was looking at Carter, Charles saw the look of the gunhawk in his eye.

Chen said, "We start as soon as I finish my tea."

56

Chen worked Charles hard. How to position his feet, how to keep his weight centered. The importance of keeping his elbows close to the body.

Chen said, "You let your arms swing out like chicken wings, and this can happen."

He snapped an open finger to the side of Charles' ribs. Charles was surprised by how much it hurt.

"Ow," he said.

"See? Don't flap your arms like chicken wings. Keep elbows in and tight."

Harlan grinned, as close as he ever came to laughing. He was leaning against a fence rail, a cup of coffee in one hand.

Charles was taking a stance the way Chen showed him. Or at least, as close as he could get to the way Chen showed him. One foot forward, the other a little ways back. Weight evenly balanced between them. Facing an imaginary opponent at a three-quarter angle.

Charles shot out a jab. Then another.

"No," Chen said. "You not doing what I said."

Charles was getting a little exasperated. "I'm doing exactly what you said."

Chen shook his head. "You leaning into the punch. Must hold weight even, and turn body into punch. Lean into punch, and you too easy to take down."

Charles looked at Carter, who just shook his head.

"All right," Chen said. "You take jab at me."

Chen stood in front of Charles. Charles took a half-hearted jab with his fist, and Chen swatted it aside.

"No," Chen said. "Take real punch."

"I can't do that," Charles said. "You're old enough to be my great-grandfather. I can't just punch you in the face."

"Not that you can't. That you *won't*."

Charles looked at Carter again.

Carter said, "Go ahead. Try to knock him down."

This was getting Charles' dander up a little. Maybe he wasn't an expert at boxing or wrestling, but he had been in a scrap or two since he had come west, and he had held his own.

All right, he thought. If this old man wants to get knocked down, then Charles was going to oblige.

He took the stance. What Chen was calling a *fifty-fifty* stance. Charles shot out a jab, and Chen sidestepped it, grabbed him by the wrist and elbow with hands that were impossibly fast, and turned and threw Charles over his back. Charles landed hard on the dirt.

He lay there, gasping for air. After a couple of moments, he said, "How'd you do that?"

Chen said, "You did that. I just helped you along."

Carter took a sip of coffee. He was still leaning against the fence. He said, "The way you lean your weight into your punches, all Chen had to do was grab your arm and give you a little pull. Your own weight and strength worked against you."

Chen gave his hands a good hard clap. "Exactly! I'm glad someone paying attention. You threw yourself to the ground. I just helped."

Charles rolled over slowly, making sure nothing was broken, and sat up. He said, "How can I get all my strength into a punch if I don't lean into it?"

"You don't put all strength into punch. You just put most. Not all. You keep in fifty-fifty stance, and turn body for more power. Better to put most but not all into a punch, than put all in punch and end up on ground."

Charles nodded. It was making sense.

He said, "How will I ever get as good as you?"

"Take years and years."

"I don't have years and years. There are men trying to kill me. I have to learn now."

"Can't teach you all I know. But maybe I can teach you enough so you can keep them from killing you."

Charles nodded, and started to get to his feet, but then staggered and went down again. He had hit the ground hard.

Chen looked at Carter. "Maybe I should have shown him how to fall first."

57

Fred's recovery was coming along slowly. Every day there was progress, but not much. After two weeks, he was able to sit up, but if he tried to stand, he blanched and had to sit back down.

He said to Aunt Ginny, "I guess I have to face it. It may be a long time until I can get back to my wrangler duties."

Ginny said, "You let it take time. You're not just the wrangler, here. You're family. Charles is handling the wrangler duties, and once Johnny and the boys are back, they'll figure out what to do until you're back on your feet."

He shook his head. He had a plaid robe tied about him, and he was sitting in a wooden upright chair by the bed. He hadn't been downstairs since before he was shot. He struck Ginny as looking ten years older.

He said, "I might never be back to my duties. It's been over three weeks, and I still can't stand up for more than a few seconds. I can't take a full breath."

"That's because Granny Tate said the bullet broke your breast bone, and snapped some ribs."

He nodded. "That's what she said. I'm starting to wonder if I'll ever be able to get back fully to where I was. I'm not a young man."

"Fred, you have to be optimistic."

"With all due respect, Aunt Ginny, I have to be realistic, too."

He was silent a minute.

She said, "What are you thinking?"

"I have a son, Jeff. He has a small ranch a day's ride south of San Francisco. Has a wife and kids."

She nodded. He had talked about Jeff more than once. She said, "I sent him a letter, a couple of weeks ago, to let him know what happened.'

"Maybe I'd be better off there. Maybe it's time I got

to know my grandchildren a little better. Maybe this is God's way of arranging things so I can spend some time with them."

Fred drew a shallow breath. It hurt to breathe.

He said, "I didn't spend the time with Jeff when he was growing up that I would have liked to. His mother died when he was young. I was a cowhand, then. The only life I knew. Couldn't raise a boy like that. He went east to stay with my wife's sister and her husband."

Ginny nodded. She knew the story.

He said, "Maybe now I have the chance to spend some time with him. I have a small savings account, thanks to you and Johnny. This ranch has paid me real well over the years."

Ginny smiled. She couldn't imagine this ranch without Fred. She felt a tear forming, but wiped it away before it could begin trailing down her face.

"We'll miss you, Fred. But we understand. And I hope you know, you'll always have a home here."

He nodded. "Means a lot to me. This place has been a home to me for fifteen years. The only home I ever had since I was a kid. If it would be no bother, I'd like to write a letter to Jeff. Ask him if he'd like his father underfoot for a little while."

"I'll get you a pen and paper."

58

It was night. Dinner was done, and Charles and Bree were standing on the back porch. Aunt Ginny had offered Bree a glass of wine, and she had accepted. They had eaten pork, and Ginny considered this a meal that called for a white wine.

"It is often debated," she had said over dinner, "whether pork should be served with white wine or red. I've always leaned toward the white-wine side of that argument. But then, I've never been much for red wine."

Even though Charles was a hired hand, and the hands took their meals in the bunkhouse, Charles had been eating with the family in recent weeks. Partly because of his relationship with Bree, and partly because Aunt Ginny felt he shouldn't be eating his meals alone.

As he ate and Aunt Ginny talked, he was only half-listening. There was tension between him and Bree and he didn't like it, but he thought he was right in the matter and was not going to back down.

Once dinner was done, Charles and Bree found themselves on the back porch. Bree held in her hand a glass that was now half-filled with wine. Aunt Ginny had offered him some of Johnny's scotch, and he had accepted.

They stood on the porch saying nothing. The moon wasn't yet up, and stars were scattered across the night sky. Frogs were chirping from the stream off beyond the house.

Charles said, "I'd like to do something to thank Mister Carter. I've been training with him for weeks now. Maybe we could have him and Mrs. Carter here for dinner some night."

She said, "Right now, I don't want that man in this house. I'm grateful for what he did, helping us against that man. But I don't like him training you."

"I can't just be a cowhand, anymore."

"I love you, Charles. But I liked it better when you were just a cowhand. When you weren't wearing that gun like you're ready to use it."

"Why's it so wrong for me? Your Pa and brothers all wear their guns like they know how to use 'em."

"But they were always that way. I don't like seeing you become like that."

"Well, I can't be just a cowhand. Not anymore. Not after what almost happened to you and the other ladies here."

She turned to look at him, though he could hardly see her in the darkness.

She said, "It takes more than being able to kill to be a man. I thought you understood that."

"All I know is if Mister Carter hadn't been here that day, we might all be dead."

He took the rest of his scotch in one gulp. Shouldn't have done that, he realized. It burned all the way down and he suddenly couldn't breathe. But he refused to let her know. She would laugh, and he was tired of being laughed at.

He had always been the charming, clumsy Fat Cole. Loveable, and a man they respected, but not one they took seriously. He hadn't minded, even when Bree fell in love with him. If he was looking in her eyes and then tripped over his own feet and she laughed, he didn't mind. But all of that ended with the man Carter had to kill. A battle that Charles felt belonged to himself, but another man had to fight for him.

Once the burning of the whiskey had passed and he was sure he could speak again, he said, "I'm going in for a refill."

He left her on the porch, and went to the bottle of scotch that was standing on the desk in the parlor.

Aunt Ginny was in her rocker by the fire. "Please, Charles. Have another."

He had been about to take it, and then realized how poor his manners were to even consider it without asking.

"Thank you, ma'am," he said, and poured another.

She said, "Would you join me by the fire?"

As much as he loved Bree, he didn't really want to go back out onto the porch at the moment. She was even more mule-headed than Josh. Everyone seemed to cave in to her demands, like calling him *Charles* when he really didn't mind Fat, but he was not going to budge. If he and Bree were to have a relationship, then he believed problems had to be worked out by a sharing of ideas. Not by out-stubborning each other. But she didn't seem ready to share ideas at the moment.

"I'd be glad to, ma'am." He walked around the back of the sofa and sat at the end of it with his glass of scotch in hand.

Bree stood looking off at the dark expanse that she knew to be the valley. Once the moon was up, then the valley floor would come alive in a shade of dull gray. In the winter, when the land was covered with snow, a full moon could reflect off the snow and bring the whole night alive in a magical show of sparkles and bluish light. She loved winter nights.

She stood now and listened to the frogs chirp, and took a sip of wine.

She didn't realize Jessica was standing at the foot of the porch until Jessica said, "I really didn't mean to eavesdrop, but I couldn't help but hearing."

"That's all right. Not much to hear, anyway."

Aunt Ginny said to Charles, "I understand you've been training with Mister Carter. Learning to shoot and to fight."

Charles nodded. "Yes'm. From Mister Chen, too."

She raised a brow. "There's a lot more to that man than is readily apparent."

"Yes'm. He dropped me on the ground a few times. One time hard enough to knock the wind out of me."

"I just want you to know, I understand. The men in this family, well..,"

He said, "They're gunhawks, ma'am."

"Indeed they are. That's the name Johnny gives to them. And do you know what that fully means when he says it?"

He said, "It means they take care of their own. And they don't like injustice."

"Quite right. But it goes even beyond that. You'll notice, they never allow the weak to be bullied. They stand against evil."

She chuckled, "Oh, Johnny will say I'm reading a lot more into it than is necessary, but there's something noble in the ways of the McCabes. I sometimes call them latter-day knights. Knights in buckskin, if you will, and carrying guns instead of swords. But the effect is the same."

She took a sip of tea. "Now, what's growing between you and Bree will grow in its own time. But presuming you are to be part of this family long-term, you'll find a man can't be around McCabe men long without becoming one of them. I suppose what I'm saying is the training you are receiving from Mister Carter and Mister Chen was inevitable."

"I don't see why Bree can't understand that."

"Oh, I think she does, Charles. It's just that sometimes being married to a gunhawk can be a little maddening. It means watching the man you love being put into danger. Sometimes it seems almost as if he goes out looking for it. Bree has seen the worry Johnny has brought me, and I'm just his late wife's aunt. I think Bree was hoping for maybe a simpler life, married to a rancher who was simply a rancher, not a knight in buckskin, on a personal crusade to defend the weak. Whether or not he wants to admit he's on a crusade."

Bree said to Jessica, "Why can't he just be satisfied with being who he is? Why can't he just be a rancher. Why can't we just get married one day and have a small ranch? I don't want him swaggering about with a gun and looking for trouble. Do you know how many gunfights my father and brothers have been in, in just the past three or four years?"

Jessica shook her head. She was standing on the porch beside Bree, now, and Bree could see her in the dim orange light thrown out from the hearth inside.

Bree said, "I couldn't really count. I'd have to stop and think about it."

"I'm new to the family, but I've heard about a gun battle in town a couple of summers ago. Jack was home from college and had been hired as the local marshal. Back before the town was what it is now. Some outlaws were coming in to free a member of their gang who Jack had in his jail."

"That's right. It was a bloody fight, too. Mister Carter got shot and almost lost his leg."

"It seems I've heard that you rode in to take part in it."

"Well, I couldn't let Jack handle it alone. Josh and Dusty were off with the herd. And I'm hell-on-wheels with a rifle."

"In fact, I've heard that you were actually the one who arrested the member of their gang, after putting a beating on him."

She chuckled. "Yeah. Try to mess with me, and you live to regret it."

"It seems to me it's not just the McCabe men who are gunhawks. Latter-day-knights, as Aunt Ginny calls them. It seems that you fit that definition, too."

Bree stood looking at her for a moment. "I never

thought about myself that way."

"Last summer, when Aloysius Randall tried to force himself on you, what'd you do?"

"I beat him to a bloody pulp."

"It seems to me Charles tried to defend you, but was outmatched by Randall. You had to give Randall a beating not only to save yourself, but to save Charles."

"Are you saying I was wrong to have done that? There was no other choice."

"No, I'm not saying that. I'm just saying, put yourself in Charles's place. A man wants to protect the woman he loves. It might sound a little barbaric to the suffragists back East, but it's part of human nature. Maybe life out here on the frontier brings this sort of thing more to the surface. I don't know. But he wanted to protect you, and couldn't. And again, just a few weeks ago, you were in danger again. We all were. And it was Mister Carter who had to protect us. Do you think Charles could have stood up to that man?"

Bree shook her head. "He would have gotten himself killed."

"I think Charles wants to be a man who can ride alongside you. Who can protect you in times of trouble. A man who can stand alongside your brothers."

"But I don't need him to be. I love him regardless."

"Maybe *he* needs to be. Sometimes loving a man is about letting him be the man he needs to be, even though he might worry you to death."

Bree let that sort of settle on her for a moment. She said, "Do you worry about Pa?"

Jessica said, "All the time. But he's the man he needs to be. It's part of loving him."

Ginny said to Charles, "You need to be the man you need to be. But what's important in all of this is that you don't evaluate your sense of self-worth based on Josh or Dusty or anyone else. You have to be your own man. And, as Mister Carter and Mister Chen show you what they know, remember not to lose yourself. Don't lose the redeeming qualities that make you the good man you are."

He finished the whiskey and thanked her for the conversation, and headed back out to the porch. He passed Jessica on the way out, as she was stepping back into the house.

He stood on the porch facing Bree. They were silent a moment, then he said, "I think I understand."

She said, "So do I."

And they pulled each other in for a long hug.

59

They stood out behind the farmhouse, Charles Cole and Harlan Carter. Cole was facing a line of cans that were standing on a fence rail. They were running low on empty cans, so some of the cans already had bullet holes in them, and had been warped or bent from being shot already.

"Turn around," Carter said.

Charles looked at him.

"I'm serious. Turn around. Put your back to the fence."

Charles did.

"Now, turn and drop and take out six of those cans."

Charles spun, grabbing his gun as he did, and twisted down to a kneeling position and began unloading his gun on the cans. A cloud of gunsmoke grew around him, and cans went flying away.

When he was done, six cans were on the ground. It had taken him seven seconds.

He rose to his feet and flipped open the loading gate on his revolver to drop out the empty cartridges.

"Not bad at all," Carter said.

"I'm not as fast as Dusty."

Carter snorted a chuckle. "Ain't seen anyone who is. Not even the old man, himself."

"I don't think I'm as fast as Josh, either."

"Maybe not. But it don't matter how fast you are. What matters is how good you are."

"I've seen Dusty do a trick where he holds the pistol with the trigger squeezed tight, and shoots by swiping at the hammer with his other hand."

"That's called fanning. It's a trick shot."

"I saw him do it and get three out of six cans, but he got off those shots fast."

"That's the problem with it. Ain't very accurate. I

could never do it and hit any cans at all."

The most recent box of ammunition Charles had bought was now empty. He reached to the cartridge loops on his belt to find more to feed into his pistol.

Carter said, "I think we're finished. I've done taught you all I can. You've learned a lot in the past five weeks. You're better with a gun than I ever was."

Charles looked at him with a little surprise. "We're done?"

Carter nodded. "The last part of it, I can't teach you. No one can. It's the ability to keep calm and steady when the bullets start comin' at you. Most men find their hands shake. Fear hits 'em. But to hold calm and just shoot back with your hand steady- -that's the secret. Don't matter how fast you are. What matters is how calm and steady you are."

"How do I learn this?"

Carter shrugged and shook his head. "You can't. You either have it or you don't."

"Dusty. Josh. Mister McCabe. They have it."

"Bree does, too. Seems to be inherited."

"So I still may not be good enough."

"Ain't about being good enough. Your ability to stay calm and shoot steady in a gun battle ain't what makes you a man. It's integrity. Courage. Honesty. You were already a real man, Charles, before we even began these training sessions."

It felt good to hear that. Charles couldn't help but smile.

Charles said, "I'm beholden to you."

He reached out his hand and Carter shook it.

"Weren't nothin'," Carter said.

It was only ten in the morning, so Charles rode back to the ranch. There was some work to do. Mostly firewood to split, so he grabbed an axe and went to work. In a few days, he thought he might take

another ride out to the line cabin. Check on the boys there. See what the condition of the range was. The work on a ranch was never done.

He ate a light lunch. Roast beef sandwiches, and biscuits oozing with butter. Just the way he liked them. Afterward, he sat on the porch in an upright chair. His shirt had a streak of sweat running down the back from his work on the woodpile, and he had some trail dust on him from the ride out to Carter's farm and back. He didn't want to go inside the house in this condition.

Bree came out and sat with him.

"So," he said, feeling like he was in a mood to playfully needle her. The tension that had been between them was now long forgotten. "These sandwiches are mighty good. Did you make them?"

He knew the answer. Bree was practically an authority on horseflesh and knew a lot about cattle. She could track a deer and was a good shot with a revolver, and was the best shot around with a rifle. But she was as out of place in a kitchen as you could be.

She sighed with what he took to be a little mixture of exasperation and embarrassment. "No. Temperance did."

He nodded. "Well, I was thinkin'. If I asked you to marry me, and we started our own ranch, who would do the cookin'?"

"Oh? Are you thinking on asking me to marry you?"

He shrugged. "Well, I thought about it, but I'm afraid we might starve to death."

She gave him a shove and he fell out of his chair, and sat there on the porch floor. He was laughing and so was she.

She stood up and reached a hand down to him, to help him up. He took her hand and pulled her down to him. She landed on top of him.

They kissed, then she pulled back a bit and

looked at him. Her hair was back in a bun, but some strands had come loose and were hanging across her face. He reached up and moved them aside.

She said, "Maybe you better ask me to marry you soon, mister. I don't know how much longer I can trust myself."

60

Once lunch was done, he saddled up. He was going to head into town and grab some more ammunition. Not for target practicing. There would be no more of that, except maybe for fun once Dusty and Josh were back. He felt Mister Carter was probably right. The rest of his journey toward being a gunhawk would be based on what was inside him. His nerve. How steady he could be in a gunfight.

He had to admit, he hoped he wouldn't have to find out. He respected life. He surely didn't want to die, but he didn't want to have to kill anyone, either. That one Comanche he had killed on a trail drive years ago left him feeling a little shaken. He didn't want that feeling again. But he hoped if Bree should ever be in danger again, he would be able to defend her.

He was down to five rounds in his gun and eight more in his belt. He would remedy that with a visit to Franklin's. And then maybe stop at the Second Chance and grab a cold beer, and thank Mister Chen again.

He told Bree he would be back before nightfall, and headed out. He took the back trail that would come out behind the Second Chance. A mile or so of trail that wound through a small heavily wooded pass. After the pass but still a short ways before the town, the land widened out a bit. Rocks and short pines at either side of the trail.

He was riding out of the pass and into the more open stretch of land and was thinking about a cold beer, when a gun was fired from ahead and off to the right and the bullet took his hat off.

His horse reared and he knew what was happening. The shot had not been an accident. Someone was shooting at him.

He let himself fall backward off the rearing horse, hoping his feet wouldn't stick into the stirrups. They didn't. He fell cleanly to the ground, rolling to break his fall.

He got to his feet, drawing his gun as he did so.

A bullet whizzed by his ear, and he could see the man standing halfway in view from behind a rock a couple hundred feet ahead and to the right.

Charles should have been afraid. His knees should have been shaking. But they weren't. He felt strangely calm. He didn't aim but just pointed his gun like Mister Carter had taught him and got off a shot. He missed, but the bullet ricocheted off the rock not a foot from the man's head, and the man ducked back.

Another shot came at Charles from behind a rock and off to his left. This one nicked his left shoulder.

He turned and ran, cutting to his left and back and away from the shooters. The land formed a natural trench here. Gravel that had been washed away by spring run-offs over the years. He jumped into it. He landed in a sitting position and came to a sliding stop on the gravelly slope.

He checked his arm. It was bleeding, but not much. He figured it wasn't anything more than a deep scratch. If he lived through this, he would have Granny Tate take a look at it.

He had four shots left in his pistol. He flipped open the loading gate and dropped out the empty, then reached to his cartridge belt for two more. This filled his gun to the limit with six shots, but was left with only six more in his belt.

He decided to risk a peek above the edge of the trench, but when he did, a bullet kicked up dust inches from his face. He pulled back.

He had to think fast. He had twelve shots left. There were at least two men out there, and they probably each had more bullets than he did. He would have to out-think them.

He asked himself, *What would Johnny McCabe do*

in a situation like this?

He figured his answer immediately. Mister McCabe wouldn't have let himself get into this situation. He would have been watching the trail ahead, and not thinking about a cold beer. He would have been watching for anything that seemed amiss. Anything out of place.

So, I've learned my lesson, he thought. *Now let's hope I live long enough to do things different.*

He realized he wasn't going to get out of this by out-shooting these two. They had him pinned down. He thought by the sound of the shots that they were using rifles, too. Much more accurate.

He decided if he was to come out of this alive, he was going to have to do it by outthinking them.

An idea occurred to him. He had always been good at small-stakes poker. He played some in the bunkhouse and once in a while at the Second Chance. He liked Five Card Draw the best because it relied a lot on reading your opponents and outthinking them. He decided he was going to take the poker approach to this. And the approach he was going to use was one he had used on Josh a couple of months before Josh left for the trail drive. Charles had been holding a pair of threes, and he could tell by the way Josh was betting that Josh had a good hand. Charles just kept pouring money into the pot until Josh decided enough was enough and folded. Josh had three kings, but lost to a pair of threes. Dusty had laughed so hard he almost fell out of his chair.

Charles decided these men had to know one of their shots had hit him. They could tell by the way he flinched to one side when the bullet skimmed his shoulder. What they wouldn't know was how badly he was wounded. He was going to let these men think he was hurt a lot worse than he was.

With his gun fully loaded, he scrambled down to

the base of the trench. There, he lay down on the ground on his stomach. Eventually, the two gunmen would come out from cover to check on him. See if he was hit. See why he wasn't trying to return fire.

He hauled back the hammer of his revolver, his body muffling the click of the gun being cocked.

He was going to have to shoot fast, he knew. Any window of opportunity would be brief, and it wouldn't come again.

The sun was hot, baking down on him. There was no shade in this trench.

Then he heard a sound. Like gravel scraping on a boot sole. Then he heard the voice. It was coming from above, and he figured it was one of the men standing at the edge of the trench.

The man said, "He looks dead."

There was a second voice. "Go down and see."

"Why should I have to go down?"

"All right. We'll both go."

Charles heard more sounds of boots scuffing, and men huffing for breath as they half-walked, half-slid down the side of the trench.

Charles took a deep breath and held it. He didn't want these men to see him breathing. They had to think he was dead or at least unconscious, if his plan was going to work.

They walked over.

One of them said, "Give him a kick."

He had to time this perfectly.

He rolled over and snapped off a shot, catching the one closest to him in the forehead.

The second one was ten feet away and holding a rifle in both hands, aiming at Charles from the hip.

Charles snapped a shot at him and missed. He then fanned two more quick shots at him while the man's rifle went off. The rifle bullet caught Charles by the right sleeve near his elbow. Both of his bullets caught the man in the chest, and he staggered back.

He kept his balance for a moment, and looked at Charles with surprise. He dropped to his knees in the gravel, and then fell face-forward.

He rose to his feet and with his gun ready and still holding four shots, he checked first one man and then the other for any signs of life. There were none.

He nodded to himself. He had now killed three men in his life. Not a good feeling. And yet he couldn't help but feel a little smile trying to rise to the surface at the thought of telling Mister Carter how he had used a trick-shooting method like fanning his gun to save his own life.

Charles rode out from the trail, emerging behind the Second Chance. He was leading two horses, and each horse had a body tied to the saddle.

A boy was crossing the street. A boy who was the son of a man opening a general store that would compete with Franklin's. A boy with a wild mop of dark hair and freckles. He was in coveralls and a barefeet, and he stopped to look with his mouth hanging open at the two bodies draped across the horses Charles was leading.

"Billy," Charles said. "Run and fetch the marshal, will you?"

Billy nodded and took off running toward Falcone's office.

Charles had a bandana tied around his left arm just below the shoulder. When Charles finally had the chance to look at the wound, he saw it was a little deeper than a scratch, and had bled some. Once he had dropped these two men at the marshal's office, he would take a ride out and see Granny Tate. See if she could clean the wound.

Hopefully it'll leave a good scar, he thought with a smile.

61

Granny Tate said to Fred, "Now let's see you stand up."

Fred was sitting in a rocker, and he was dressed in jeans and a range shirt. His boots were on his feet.

He placed both hands on the arms of the chair and gave it a try. Rising to his feet was slow and painful. When he was finally standing, he had to take a moment to catch his breath.

"Can you walk?"

Fred said, "Not by myself. I get dizzy. Charles helped me downstairs a couple of times. But getting back upstairs, you'd think I was climbing a mountain."

Haley was there, on hand to assist Granny.

He sat back down and said, "I'd like to go to California and see my son. I sent him a letter and I'm waiting for a response."

Granny said, "Well, waiting won't hurt you none. You're not ready for travel yet, anyway."

Fred had a book Aunt Ginny had picked up for him at Franklin's. *Frankenstein; or the Modern Prometheus.* There was also a copy of *Robinson Crusoe* that was Aunt Ginny's, and she had loaned it to him.

Fred said, "I've taken to reading. Never had much time for it, before. But the days are long up here with nothing to do but stare at the walls. The people in this book, they got troubles that make mine look mild."

Granny and Haley headed down to the parlor. Granny was having a good day and her knees weren't creaking too badly, but even still she held firmly to the railing and Haley held her by her other elbow.

"Granny," Haley said. "Can I talk to you?"

"Well, sure, child."

They sat by the hearth. The day was warm, and the hearth was blackened with soot and devoid of fire.

Haley said, "Would you teach me? I want to be

your student. I want to learn everything you know about healing."

Granny chuckled. "Well, everything I know has required a lifetime of learning."

Granny thought for a moment. "You know, I'm not getting any younger. It would be good to have someone I can pass on my knowledge to. Them city doctors, they're good for what they're good for. Jack showed me how he could repair a blood vessel. Saved Harlan Carter's leg doing that. But there are things a city doctor just plain can't do. Or can't do well enough. Child-birthin' is one of 'em."

She nodded her head with a sense of authority. "A community needs a granny doctor."

Haley said, "I've given this a lot of thought. I'd like to be a granny doctor."

"Then, child, you shall be. We can start tomorrow morning."

62

Charles was in the barn. A horse was in a stall, and Charles had a brush in his hand and was giving him a good brushing down. Some appaloosa heritage had led to some dappling along the horse's rump and Bree had given him the name Spot.

It had been a few days since Charles's run-in with the two gunmen on the trail to town, and the wound on his arm was healing nicely. Granny Tate had assured him it would leave a scar, though.

He had told Aunt Ginny and Bree and the others all about it. He didn't want to worry them, and yet he wasn't one who believed in withholding truth. These women had been held at gunpoint by a man aiming to gun Charles down, and he figured they had a right to know. Especially Bree.

She had hugged him long, her head against his chest. She wasn't quite tall enough to reach his shoulder.

Then she said, "I didn't want this for you. This is the life Pa leads. This is the way he was the whole time I was growing up. Then when Josh was old enough, he started following Pa's trail. And Dusty is like this. Even Jack. He might be a scholar, but he's every bit the gunfighter the rest of them are. I so didn't want this for you. I wanted us to have a life on a horse ranch. That's what I want to do. I want us to build a little cabin up in the ridges, and to go mustanging and break them the Shoshone way, and sell them to ranches and the Army and whoever. I don't want the gunhawk life for us."

"But you live that lifestyle, too. Almost as much as your brothers."

She nodded. "I guess I do. I guess I was hoping if you were just a rancher, maybe I could be just a rancher, too."

He reached a hand up and stroked her hair.

"Bree, I don't think anyone is just anything. I think everyone of us is all sorts of things."

She nodded silently. His shirt felt a little wet. He thought maybe she was crying.

He said, "Here's a way to think about it. Those men were sent to kill me by someone. Could be my brother—I don't know. I hope not. But they're being sent by someone, and it has nothing to do with the training Mister Carter gave me. But his training saved my life. If they had come gunnin' for me a couple months ago, I'd be dead right now."

She looked up at him. "I hadn't thought of it that way."

He let his fingers trace down the side of her face. He said, "If you want that cabin up in the ridges, then that's what we'll have. We'll have us a little horse ranch. But I have to ask you to marry me."

"Well, go ahead."

He shook his head. "I have to ask you proper."

As he brushed down Spot in the barn, he thought about his talk with Bree and wanting to marry her. He thought about a place to put a cabin and a barn and a corral. He thought he might know the spot. A little grassy shelf a half mile or so north of the valley, just beyond Zack Johnson's ranch. Not far from the canyon where Mister McCabe wanted to build a home for himself, Miss Jessica and Cora.

His thoughts were interrupted by the sound of horse shoes and steel rims clattering on the covered bridge, down by the stream.

He hung the brush on a nail on the wall, and started for the barn door. He looked down to the gun at his left side and pulled it with his right. He quickly checked the loads, and then thumbed in a sixth cartridge. He was going to be prepared this time.

He stepped out of the barn and saw Bree skipping down the porch steps, her hair tied into a long, dark pony tail that swung back and forth as she moved. She was wearing a skirt and riding boots, and her pistol was belted about her hips.

"We got company," she said.

He nodded. "Could be nothing, but let's be ready."

They saw a buggy working its way up the trail that led to the house from the bridge. A man had the reins in his hands. He was a little heavy set, and was in a tie and jacket and wearing a short-brimmed bowler.

"It's Mister Wellington," Charles said. "The man from town who was looking for me a few weeks back."

Wellington gave the reins a tug and the buggy came to a stop in front of the porch.

"Howdy," Charles said. "Didn't expect to see you again."

Wellington said, "Neither did I. I just came in on the noon stage and rented a buggy to come out here. I'm glad I caught you. I have news to tell you and it isn't good."

Wellington sat at the kitchen table with a hot cup of coffee in front of him. Fred was downstairs and sitting across the table from him. Today was the first time Fred had attempted the stairs and he had managed them better than he had expected. Though Charles was fresh from the barn, he also took a seat at the table and Bree was beside him.

"It's your brother," Wellington said. "I've come to warn you. I resigned as his lawyer, and I'm legally bound by attorney-client privilege, but I decided to throw that all to the wind. You need to be warned. Your brother's dangerous, and he wants you dead."

"Why?" Bree said.

"Because as long as Jehosaphat is alive, then the entire family fortune will never be entirely Adolphus's."

Wellington looked at Charles. "Like I said to you in town, you can never fully sign away your rights to an inheritance. Not one of that size. If you chose to challenge it years down the road, there would always be a lawyer willing to represent you. And judges willing to listen. He will never have one-hundred-percent claim on that money as long as you live."

Charles sat back in the chair. He had suspected this, but to have it confirmed made him feel a little defeated.

He said, "I remember growing up with Dolph. He was always a little harsh. Willing to win regardless of the cost. He would cheat at card games. Father saw nothing wrong with it, because he said life isn't about playing the game, it's about winning. But I never thought he would be capable of murder."

Wellington took a sip of coffee. "You've been gone a long time. He's grown up, and he's changed. Or maybe qualities in him have become more pronounced. Dark qualities. He's staying in St. Louis right now. He said he wants to be closer to the action. He sent the two who shot at you a few days ago. I last saw him the day before yesterday, and he was waiting for them to come back. He was going to give them another week and then look into hiring someone else."

"Why'd you quit on him?" Fred said.

"I'll be honest, Mister Mitchum. I'm a corporate attorney, and I'm willing to bend the law sometimes. I worked for their father for a lot of years. But I just can't be involved in any more of this. I resigned yesterday and was heading back to New York, but then I thought I should talk with Charles first. So I hopped a train to Cheyenne, then a stage coach north from there."

"What hotel is he staying at?" Charles said.

Bree looked at Charles. He could tell this question concerned her a little.

Wellington said, "The Missouri."

Charles nodded. He said nothing more.

When the coffee was done, Wellington went back

out to his buggy. He was going to get a room at the hotel in town. The stage came through Jubilee daily now, so he was going to grab tomorrow's and head back to Cheyenne.

"Then I'm grabbing the first train to New York, and I don't plan to be this far west, ever again. Some people might find comfort in these remote areas, but I want cobblestones underfoot and gaslights on the streets."

Charles extended his hand. "I want you to know I'm beholden to you for coming all the way out here to warn me."

Bree and Charles watched Wellington drive the buggy down the trail and across the wooden bridge.

Bree said to him, "You're planning on going to St. Louis, aren't you?"

He nodded. "It's something I have to do."

She wanted to tell him he was wrong. He didn't have to go confront his brother. But she knew he had to. So she said nothing more and just took his hand and they stood silently watching Wellington ride away.

63

Charles threw a loop around an appaloosa named Chance, and led it to the barn. He didn't bring it into the barn because he knew these horses, and he knew Chance didn't like to be indoors. When Fred was doing the wrangling duties, he brushed Chance down outside. Chance had been a wild one Charles and Josh and Dusty had caught a year ago, and they had broken him Shoshone style.

"Problem with breaking a horse this way," Mister McCabe had said, "a horse is never truly broken. They only get used to you. I say it's a problem, but I think it's actually a good thing. A horse is a creature of God and has a spirit, just like anything else. A creature's spirit should never be broken."

He slipped a bridle over Chance's head, and then gave the rein a couple of turns around the iron ring of a hitching post outside the barn. He then went into the tack room to grab his saddle. It had an empty scabbard, and it would remain empty. Charles owned the pistol he wore, but had no rifle. He had been intending to go into town and see if Franklin had any for an affordable price, but now it would have to wait. He needed to get to St. Louis before his brother gave it up and headed back to New York. Charles wanted to confront Dolph, to hear Dolph admit he was actually hiring men to kill him, but Charles had no intention of riding all the way to New York.

Once Chance was saddled, he went to the bunkhouse to grab his bedroll and a canteen. When he came back out, Chance was waiting for him and so was Bree. She had a Winchester carbine in her hands.

"You'll need this," she said. "You have a long ride ahead of you, and you'll need a rifle."

He was reluctant to take it. "It's bad enough I'm borrowing a horse that belongs to the ranch. But to take a rifle from your father's rifle rack..."

"Nonsense. You're family." She handed him the rifle.

It was a .44-40, just like his pistol. It would take the same cartridges. He slid it into the scabbard.

"You all should be safe," Charles said. "I've talked to Mister Carter, and he'll be checking on you regularly. And I've talked to Hunter and Mister Chen. And your father and brothers should be back in a few days."

The long project of stringing telegraph wires from Bozeman to Jubilee had been finished, and Josh had wired them a day ago. They were in Cheyenne and would be leaving for home soon.

Bree said, "You'll probably meet them on the trail down to Cheyenne."

He shook his head. "I won't be following the trail. I'm going to go overland, cutting my own path southeast. I'll pick up the main trail that goes east somewhere east of Cheyenne."

"Going overland. Not taking a trail. I'm thinking you're more and more like Pa all the time."

"That's a comparison I never thought anyone would make."

"I don't want you to go. But I know you have to."

He took her in his arms. They fell into a long kiss.

She said, "Come back to me. Come back safe."

He nodded. "I will."

He pushed his foot into the stirrup and swung into the saddle.

He turned Chance toward the edge of the woods, and the trail that would come out behind the Second Chance.

Bree stood and watched him ride away, and then once he disappeared into the line of trees, she turned back toward the house. She had to reach up and wipe away a tear.

Aunt Ginny and Jessica were both standing on the porch watching. Bree hadn't been aware they were there.

Aunt Ginny said, "Are you all right?"

Bree nodded. "I will be."

She climbed the stairs and stood there with them, looking off toward the trees where Charles had disappeared.

"It's hard," Aunt Ginny said. "Watching them ride off like that."

Jessica said, "When you belong to this family, apparently there's a lot of waiting."

"Indeed. Waiting and hoping for their safe return."

Bree said, "What happens when someday, one of them doesn't return?"

"We'll deal with that when it happens."

64

Charles was no stranger to nights alone, out in the wild.

Before he had gone west, his life had been cobble stone streets illuminated with gas lights by night, and tall buildings that blocked out much of the sky. His introduction to the west had been driving a freight wagon along the Santa Fe trail, and he had become accustomed to the emptiness, and to the dark nights where there were no gaslights. Only the stars overhead.

At first he had found nights out here a little frightening. Then he learned to find a certain peace in a western night. By the time he reached Texas, he found the darkness and the lack of gaslights comforting. He found wonder in the way there were no buildings to block out the sky. He would stand and look off at the long stretches of prairie, with rocks and scrub brush, and the sky that seemed to reach all the way down to touch the earth.

He had now been out here eight years. New York seemed like another lifetime, and he supposed it was. A lifetime he had left behind. He was now comfortable in the grasslands and the mountains, as though he had been born here. He could track a deer and clean a carcass and roast it over a campfire. He knew how to find water where to the untrained eye, there would appear to be none about. He had never sat in a saddle before he had come west, but now he rode along on Chance as though riding were second nature to him. He moved with the horse, not bouncing along in the saddle as he had when he was first learning to ride.

He left Jubilee and turned Chance southeast. By noon, they were out of the ridges, and surrounded by grassy hills dotted with junipers and short pines. By evening, he was in longer, flattened-out hills that were mostly grass with occasional outcroppings of bedrock.

He found a low hill that cut off sharply on one side, and it was beside this hill that he made his camp. Before he had left the ridges, he had broken up some dead pine branches and tied them in a bundle, and tied the bundle to the back of his saddle. He now used them to build a small fire and heat a can of beans.

He rolled up in his blankets while the fire burned low. The fire would soon be out but he knew he would be safe. Chance was picketed within a small stone's throw, and a horse was as good as a watch dog at night.

When the sun began to peek above the eastern horizon, Charles and Chance had been on the move for half an hour.

He reached main trail east of Cheyenne after three long days of riding. The very same trail wagon trains had used a generation earlier, crossing from Missouri to Oregon or California. Some still called it the Oregon Trail.

Three days, he thought. He was making good time.

He stopped at a farmhouse late in the afternoon, split up some firewood in exchange for a meal, and slept in a barn. The next night, he found a small creek off the side of the trail and slept near it.

The trail picked up the Platte River after a while. Not really what he thought of as a river. It was more like God had taken a lake and spilled it across the land. It was made up of sluices and streams that crisscrossed their way across the land. A couple feet deep in some places, and no more than inches deep in others.

As he rode along, he saw a rabbit burst into a run off to his right. He brought Chance to a stop and pulled his rifle and jacked in a cartridge. The rabbit had come to a stop and was standing still, facing sideways to Charles, about two hundred feet off. Charles brought the rifle to his shoulder and sighted in on the rabbit and fired, and the rabbit ran off.

Charles shook his head and couldn't help but laugh at himself. Bree would have made that shot.

He continued on. About a mile later, he saw another rabbit. This one was off to his left, between the trail and the river, and was about the same distance as the first one had been. It took off, running in a zig-zagging path through the grass, but Charles knew the ways of rabbits, and knew it would run at a dead sprint for a short ways and then stop. The rabbit did as expected. Charles brought the rifle to his shoulder, and this time he didn't miss. He would be roasting rabbit for supper tonight.

Charles had heard Mister McCabe saying once that you couldn't drink the water from this river. It was drinkable only if you boiled it for coffee water. Charles remembered the chuck wagon cook on one of the trail drives from Texas saying the same thing. There were little islands that were wooded, islands the water spilled around, so he rode Chance through the water to one of these islands and he used a small hatchet in his saddle bags to cut wood for a fire. He boiled river water for coffee and roasted his rabbit, and he and Chance stayed there for the night.

From what Charles had heard, it took wagons a good two months to make it from the Missouri River to where the town of Cheyenne now was. But wagons traveled slowly, at walking speed. The settlers had their wagons packed full of supplies, and the wagons were pulled by teams of oxen or mules, and the settlers walked along beside them. Walking speed, all the way from Missouri to Cheyenne. Fifteen miles was a good day. Any mishaps along the way would limit them to only five or six miles. A man on a horse could cover a lot more ground, and in ten days, Charles found himself sitting in the saddle looking off at the skyline of St. Louis.

Calling it a skyline made him chuckle a little. Nothing like what you saw in Manhattan.

No sense to put this off, he thought as he sat in the saddle and looked off at the rooftops. He was here to attend to business. Might as well get to it.

He gave Chance a nudge and they started in toward the city.

65

St. Louis was a city unlike any Charles had ever seen. Part full-fledged urban, and part frontier town. The street he rode along was paved with cobblestones, and along one sidewalk, a man in a tie and jacket and with a bowler on his head walked along arm-in-arm with a woman in a long dress with a lacey neckline and a hat that looked like it was out of a Parisian catalogue. But riding along the same street and passing Charles was a man in buckskins, with hair to his shoulders and a beard that fell to his chest, and a floppy wide-brimmed hat that looked like it had seen a lot of sun and rain.

Charles reined up in front of the Missouri. A three-floor building of brick, with a green awning that stretched out and over the front door and the sidewalk, all the way to the street.

A boy of maybe twenty stood in front of the door. He was in a military-style green jacket with gold braid on the shoulders and a green felt cap. A porter.

Charles swung out of the saddle and walked up to the porter. Charles knew how things worked in the city, and he reached into his vest pocket and pulled out a dollar bill.

He said, "I need to know if an Adolphus Cole is still staying at this hotel."

The boy looked at him curiously for a moment. Charles supposed he did look a little ragged. Over two weeks on the trail, in the same clothes. The only bath he had received was when he and Chance were hit with a downpour a couple of days ago. Charles now had thin, young-man whiskers that were maybe a quarter inch long, and his hat and vest were decorated with a layer of dust and his shirt was rumpled. He was sure the porter could smell him before he even got off the horse.

The boy finally said, "Sorry, mister. The hotel

doesn't give out the names of its guests."

Dang. This was going to cost him more cash than he had hoped it would. He had eight dollars remaining from his last pay. He pulled out five and handed it to the porter.

The porter said, "I think I just might remember someone here by that name, but let me go check the registry."

Charles waited under the awning. He watched a couple cowhands go riding by. Texans, he figured. Wide, Boss of the Plains hats and thick mustaches. They each wore their shirts buttoned up to the neck. They were in the city, after all. They each wore a vest, and one of them had the vest buttoned tightly. One wore a revolver high on his hip, and the other like Charles, at his left and turned backward for a crossdraw. They wore spurs with big rowels.

The porter returned. "Yes, sir. If you need to know the room, it'll cost you a sight more."

Charles didn't have a sight more.

Charles said, "Do you happen to know how long he's registered for?"

"Seems to be indefinitely."

"Much obliged."

Charles needed to be able to move about the city, but couldn't do it looking like a saddle tramp.

He headed for a bath house, and spent two dollars more of his hard-earned money soaking in a tub, with a mug of beer in one hand.

By sunset, he emerged from the bath feeling more civilized. He was clean-shaven, and in a white broadcloth shirt that he had brought along in his saddle bags. He had brushed the dust from his vest and hat as much as he could. His pistol was in place at his side— no need to be too civilized.

He had left Chance at a livery, so he walked down the street. His boots were now also dust free, and his spurs jingled a little as he stepped along. He was walking toward the Missouri, but there was no need to hurry. A man hurrying draws attention.

Two women walked along toward him, maybe a little older than he was but not much. One in a blue checkered dress and another in gray. They also wore hats that, after eight years of living on the frontier, struck Charles as a little much. Each had a parasol.

He touched the brim of his hat, and they nodded politely and continued on without a word.

It had been late afternoon when he rode into the city and was fully dark by the time he got to the Missouri. This was the high-end part of town, and gaslights had been installed, and the street was illuminated with a pale light.

Charles stepped into the Missouri and walked through the lobby, stepping as though with a purpose, and into the small restaurant all high quality hotels had attached to them.

He removed his hat and glanced about, and immediately saw who he was looking for. Dolph was sitting at a table, a drink in front of him. Dolph looked more than just eight years older. Charles thought he looked like maybe twenty years had passed. His face had filled out and his hairline had pulled back a couple of inches, but it was still Dolph.

Charles hadn't expected to find him so quickly. After all, St. Louis had a lot of restaurants, some providing dining as fine as anything you would find in New York or Paris. Dolph could have gone to any one of them. Charles had been expecting to have to order a meal and wait a few hours and hope to find Dolph on his way in or out of the hotel. But here he was.

Dolph was sitting at the table with his eyes fixed straight ahead but not really seeing what was there. He looked like a man with a heavy weight on his mind. Charles remembered their father sitting like that a lot.

Not only the weight of responsibility, but the weight of guilt for all of the betrayals he had committed along the way to grow and maintain the family fortune. All of the men he had ruined. If Dolph was truly capable of hiring his own brother killed, Charles had to wonder what his father had been capable of.

The room was filled to maybe half capacity, and the sound of a couple dozen men engaged in various conversations filled the air, making a sound as though they were all saying *wa-wa-wa* with occasional laughter thrown in. Some were businessmen. There were a couple of men sitting with women. A few men were in wider-brimmed hats and looked like cattlemen.

There was a host at a stand that looked like a lecturn. He was in a tuxedo, and said, "Dining for one? Or will someone be joining you?"

"Actually, I'm here to join a man who's already seated," Charles said.

He strode across the floor, the heels of his riding boots tapping on the wooden floorboards and his spurs giving a little jingle. He approached Dolph's table, and if Dolph had seen the motion out of the corner of his eye, he didn't react.

Dolph took a sip of whiskey and set the glass down. Charles reached for the glass and took a sip himself. This got a reaction from Dolph, who gave him a look of surprise and indignance. Dolph said, "Now, see here!"

"Single malt," Charles said. "Your tastes haven't changed any."

Dolph sat looking at him. It took him a moment, then he said, "Jehosaphat?"

"The one and only," Charles said. "Except everyone calls me Charles, these days."

Dolph stared for a moment. Then he said, "You've changed a little. But you're still one of the tallest men I've ever met."

Charles didn't wait to be invited. He slid out a chair and lowered himself to it. He set the glass back in front of Dolph.

Two men at the bar began over, but Dolph held out a hand to them in a stopping gesture. They nodded and went back to the bar but kept a careful eye on the table.

"Body guards?" Charles said.

"I would be foolish to travel without them. A man of my stature and importance. I own nearly half of New York, now. Of course, you would know that, had you not run off."

Charles nodded. "I suppose I would."

"And now you're back. I suppose you want your portion of the inheritance."

"I'm glad to see you too, Dolph. How have you been? Are you well? I'm fine, not that you've asked."

Dolph didn't seem to appreciate the sarcasm. He said, "Well, is that why you're here?"

Charles shook his head. "I'm here because I want to hear it with my own ears. That you have hired a man to kill me."

Dolph said nothing.

Charles said, "Three men in recent weeks have been sent to kill me. One worked alone, and a friend of mine killed him. Two of them rode together, and I handled them myself."

"Well, I'm sorry for your misfortunes, but there is nothing to tie any of that to me."

Charles didn't want to indicate that Wellington had seen him. After all, Wellington lived and practiced law in New York, and if Dolph was the man Wellington claimed he was, then Dolph could easily afford to ruin him. Maybe even have him killed.

What Charles said was, "Maybe one of the gunmen you hired talked before he died."

"Why should you be entitled to any of the money?

You walked away from it all. But Father left your name in the will. I'll never understand why."

"Guilt, maybe. A man like he was had a lot to feel guilty about. How about you, Dolph? Are you a man like our father?"

"Maybe it's time for you to leave."

"I want you to understand something, Dolph. I don't want any of your money. Not one red cent. I have a life now, and people I care about. If you send anyone gunning for me again, I'll come after you. And you won't find me the same boy I was, back in New York. Your last two gunmen—I took them both out by myself. Tw o men, two bullets. And I didn't work up a whole lot of sweat doing it."

Not entirely true, but Charles was trying to make a point.

Dolph gave him a look that reminded Charles of a wild cat eyeing its prey. A look that reminded him of Father.

Dolph said, "Are you threatening me?"

Charles said, "Yep."

Dolph looked over to the bar and nodded, and the two men started over. They were large men, though not as tall as Charles. They were each in a tie and jacket, and Charles was sure they were armed. Probably short-barreled revolvers somewhere under the jackets.

Charles got to his feet. "Tell your men to back off."

Dolph ignored him. He looked to his men. "Throw him out of here. And make sure you hurt him a little. I want him to learn a lesson about whom he is dealing with."

One of the men grabbed Charles by the shoulder, and Charles snatched the man's wrist and stepped back, pulling him with him, and dug one thumb into a tender spot just north of the man's hand. The way Mister Chen had shown him. The man gasped in sudden, unexpected pain and dropped to one knee.

The other man reached for a gun, but Charles was able to maintain his grip on the first man with his left hand, and with his right, he grabbed his own gun and beat Dolph's thug to the draw.

"Drop it," Charles said, "or I'll give you a new eye socket in your forehead."

Charles then heard guns cocking behind him. Four of them.

Dolph chuckled. "Really, Jehosaphat. Do you think I would travel this far from home with only two men?"

66

They then heard two more guns being cocked from further behind. Charles glanced back, and saw two men he hadn't expected to see. Dusty was there, in his buckskin shirt and his long hair. He wore a layer of dust, and in one hand was his revolver. Josh was beside him, equally covered in dust. His gun was also cocked and ready to fire.

Patrons at tables all about them were jumping to their feet and scampering away. One woman screamed, and chairs were knocked over as some people ran to the far walls or ducked behind the bar, and others ran out the door.

Charles said, "I would suggest your men drop their guns. They're outnumbered."

Dolph looked at him like he thought he had lost his mind. "There are only two of them."

"Do you know who these two are?"

"It doesn't matter who they are," Dolph said. He looked at one of them. "Take them all."

Charles saw the intent in the gunman nearest him. The man's pistol was aimed at him, and he saw the look in his eyes. He was going to fire. Charles fired first, and the man's gun went off and Charles felt the bullet slam into his shoulder. Then guns were going off behind him.

Dusty fanned two shots, and caught two men. Josh held his gun in one hand and fired, taking one man. A second man fired at him, but Josh was already ducking to one side, cocking his pistol as he moved and fired from the hip. The second man went down.

A cloud of gun smoke swelled out around them like a fog, dissipating slowly in the still air of the room.

As the smoke cleared a little, Charles was standing with his gun cocked. Josh and Dusty were doing the same. All five of Dolph's gunmen were down on the floor. The one who had first grabbed Charles by the shoulder was still on one knee, holding onto his injured wrist. It was all that had saved him from being the sixth man down.

Men ran into the room. Four of them, and they were in dark blue uniforms and each with a badge pinned to the front of his shirt. Each held a scattergun.

"Don't move, boys," one of them said. "Drop them guns and put your hands in the air."

Four hours later, at the police station, the sergeant was giving them their guns back.

"You're free to go, boys," he said. "Enough witnesses testified it was in self-defense. The DA says there's no need for an inquest."

The sergeant was man of maybe fifty, with a few extra pounds filling out the front of his uniform. He had a bushy mustache that hid his upper lip.

Dusty slid his revolver back into its holster. "Inquests. A DA. Things are so much more civilized here in the city."

"It's the way of the world, boys. Civilization is working its way west."

Josh said, "Let's hope it doesn't work its way too fast."

The bullet that hit Charles' shoulder hadn't done much damage. It was more a deep graze than anything. With five stitches and a bandage tied around it, he was free to go. He didn't need a sling.

"Well," he said. "That's two bullet scars I'll have."

They hadn't found any time to talk, so as they stepped out onto the boardwalk, Charles said, "Not that I don't appreciate you boys being here, but I'm kind of surprised to see you."

Josh said, "We got home just a couple days after you left. They told us all about what had happened while we were gone, so we lit out after you."

Dusty nodded. "We tried to catch you, but you can make good time when you want to. We were about an hour behind you when you rode down into the city."

Charles saw the porter from the Missouri crossing the street toward them. "I wonder what he wants."

The porter said, "Mister Cole. I have a note for you."

Charles opened it. Written in a flourishing hand was,

Please meet me in my room at the Missouri. Room 202. I'll be waiting.

It was signed, *Dolph.*

"Well, boys," Charles said, "doesn't look like it's over yet."

They found Dolph in his room. There was one other man with him. He was smallish and thin, with white hair and a white mustache, and spectacles were perched on his nose.

"No bodyguards?" Charles said.

Dolph shook his head. "I don't have any left. Besides, I don't think they'd do any good against you boys."

Dolph introduced the older man. "Mister Hollingsworth, my attorney."

It didn't take long to replace Wellington, Charles thought.

Dolph said, "I want to know where we proceed from here."

"I don't want your money. Simple as that. Leave me alone, and I'll leave you alone."

The attorney said, "There's nothing that can be signed that would hold up under extreme scrutiny in court. With the right lawyer, you could materialize years from now and tie up my clients holdings in court for years."

"Where I live now," Charles said, "a man's word is

as binding as any contract."

Dolph chuckled and shook his head. "Well, I don't live in any such fantasy land. But signing a contract will be binding only until it's challenged. If it's challenged successfully, then it's only as good as the paper it's written on."

Hollingsworth nodded sadly.

Charles said, "Here's the deal. I'm going to make it verbally. You can accept it or not. You stay away from me, and you'll never hear from me again. But if you send any gunmen after me again, and if they hurt anyone I care about, I'll find you even if you're all the way back in New York. I'll throw you out a third floor window. You won't be safe from me. Violence seems to be the only language Father understood, and apparently you're a chip off the old block."

"That's it?" Dolph said. "I agree to this, and you'll never come for the money?"

"That's it."

Dolph looked to Hollingsworth.

The old man said to Dolph, "The problem would be if you pass on untimely, while your brother is still alive. But as long as he doesn't challenge the estate in probate, then your heirs will inherit it all."

Charles said, "I won't make any challenge."

Dolph shifted his feet, and rubbed his chin with one hand. "You have to understand, I've never done business this way."

"There's a first time for everything."

Dolph said, "So, you just ride back to your little backwater town in the West, and I return to New York, and that's the end of it?"

Charles nodded. "That's the end of it. Except..."

Charles was thinking fast. He said, "I want a thousand dollars. In cash. Right now. And then that'll be the end of it."

Dolph said, "The estate is worth many, many

more times that."

"A thousand is all I want. I just realized I do have use for that amount of money."

Dusty and Josh were looking at Charles with a question in their eyes.

Dolph said, "I don't see as how I have much choice. All right, Jehosaphat, I agree."

He reached to a pocket inside his jacket and came out with his wallet, and pulled out some bills. He counted them off to Charles. Twenties and hundreds.

Charles was a little startled. He had lived in the West so long, where cowhands were lucky to make fifteen dollars a month, he had forgotten how the extremely rich lived. To Dolph, a thousand dollars was pocket money.

Charles folded the bills and put them in a vest pocket.

"Now you leave," Dolph said. "And I'll never hear from you again."

Charles nodded. "I expect it to be mutual."

Dolph looked at him long and hard. Charles returned the gaze. Then he turned and he and Dusty and Josh left the room.

They stepped back out onto the sidewalk. St. Louis traffic was moving past them. A carriage pulled by a fine team of horses. A couple of riders who looked like trail hands. Another carriage, this one more of a coach with an enclosed back seat. The driver was in a top hat and tails.

Charles said, "Not the family you boys have, is it?"

Josh shook his head. "I can't imagine wanting to kill one of my own brothers."

"My family was family in name only."

Dusty let that one sink in for a moment. Then he said, "I rode a thousand miles to find my family, three summers ago. I can't imagine a family like yours."

Charles started walking along the boardwalk.

Josh and Dusty fell into place beside him.

"If you don't mind my saying," Josh said. "You don't seem anything like that. We've all seen how well you treat Bree."

Dusty said, "You seem to know what family is all about."

Charles nodded. "I used to have some friends, sons of laborers. Irishmen in New York back then were considered second class citizens. Probably still are. But I was friends with a number of them. I ate at their tables more than once. This horrified my father and Dolph, but I wouldn't be the man I am today if not for them. It was among those families that I learned what family was all about. I saw in them what was missing in my own. And I see that in your family."

"A family you're part of," Josh said, and slapped a hand to Charles's back. "I hope you know we consider you family."

Dusty said, "I had to ride all the way to Montana to find my family. Looks like you did, too."

Charles nodded. "You'll never know how much that means to me."

Dusty grinned. "Yeah, I think I do."

"So," Josh said. "You ready to saddle up and get out of here? I've had about enough of civilized life as I can take for a while."

"Got a little shopping to do, first. That thousand I got from Dolph? I wasn't gonna ask for any money at all, but then I thought of something. Bree is a girl who's more happy riding through the mountains with a pistol at her side than she ever would be with all the finery and lace some of these rich St. Louis girls have. But a girl should have at least one piece of finery in her life. Even a mountain girl. I plan to ask her to marry me, and I want to give her a ring that would be fit for a princess."

Epilogue

Josh and Dusty headed for town. A cold beer at the Second Chance sounded good. Life since returning from St. Louis had been almost as hard as the trail drive. Fred had gone to live with his son, so Dusty was handling the wrangler duties. Josh and Charles spent time at the line cabin, and with the help of Kennedy and Taggart they moved the brood stock and the calves to fresher grazing. They were also helping Pa with the building of his new cabin.

They would have asked Charles to join them for the cold beer today, but Charles had already asked Bree to join him on a picnic lunch out in the mountains. There was a little grassy area at the edge of a ridge that overlooked the valley, and he had said that was where he wanted to present her with the ring. He would have done so at the fine-dining restaurant in town, but he knew she was happier in the mountains.

Josh and Dusty were riding along the trail that came out behind the Second Chance.

Josh glanced at a pine-covered ridge that rode up to their right. He said, "You know, that grassy area Chuck was talking about is up at the side of this ridge. Wouldn't take us long to get there."

"We couldn't do that. Wouldn't be right."

Josh shook his head. "Wouldn't be."

"A dollar says he chickens out of asking her."

Josh shook his head. "I might have taken that bet at one time, but since we've been gone, he's different."

"He went through a lot while we were gone."

Josh glanced at that ridge again. "Wouldn't take us twenty minutes to reach a little cliff that would give us a view of that grassy spot."

"Wouldn't be right."

"Nope."

They both turned their horses off the trail and up the ridge.

They reined up at the cliff that looked down toward the grassy area. A blanket was spread out and Bree and Charles were sitting there. This grassy area was at the edge of a small shelf, and a view of the valley opened up below them.

Josh said, "Kind of glad we didn't catch 'em doing anything too personal. Might have made me blush."

"I do so hate it when you blush."

They watched while Bree and Charles got to their feet and looked off to the valley below. They could see Bree and Charles were talking, as they would move their heads a little or shift their feet, the way people do when they're talking.

Then Charles reached into a jacket pocket and pulled out the ring box. He opened it and dropped to one knee. Bree covered her mouth with her hands.

Josh said, "Even kneeling down, he's still almost as tall as she is."

"Long drink of water, that's for sure."

She nodded and he placed the ring on her finger and then he rose to his feet and she jumped up and at him and they took each other in a long hug and a deep kiss.

"Well," Dusty said. "We've seen enough."

"Yep. That personal stuff is gonna start up. I don't want to blush."

"I do so hate it when you blush."

They turned their horses and started down the side of the ridge, and on to the Second Chance.

Josh and Dusty found Aunt Ginny in the barroom. Now that she was a part owner, she spent most of her days there. She was sitting at a table with a blueprint spread out in front of her. The place was going to be expanded, which would double its size. One half was going to be the saloon and the other half a restaurant. The framework for the restaurant part was already up. Aunt Ginny hoped to have the restaurant open by August.

Hunter was there, too. He went down to the root cellar and came back with three mugs of cold beer.

He said to Josh and Dusty, "I wouldn't have you drink alone."

The three joined Ginny at a table and they talked about the farms that were going to be built at the center of the valley. Two thousand acres of grassy bottomland that had been sold to a land prospector, who in turn broke it up into four sections and was selling to farmers.

The buyer was from California, a vice-president of a land outfit called *The Singleton Group*. He had arrived in town not long after the boys had been back from the trail. His name was Edward Singleton, and he proudly talked about how his father had started their company back in '49, during the big gold rush.

When the boys left, Hunter said, "Do you think they'll ever find out?"

"I hope not. Johnny is a man of pride, and if he were to find out, that pride would be wounded. It was a lot for him to accept my funding of Jack's education."

What Johnny and the boys didn't know, and in fact only Ginny and Hunter knew, was that Brackston Shipping owned forty-nine percent of the Singleton Group and was a silent partner. Since Ginny was the sole owner of Brackston Shipping, this meant she essentially owned almost half of Singleton. So it was partly Brackston money used to buy the acreage in the valley.

She knew how much the ranch meant to Johnny and the children. She wanted to make sure they got top dollar for the sale of the acreage. The only way to ensure this was to buy it herself, but she had to do so in a way that wouldn't hurt Johnny's pride.

Hunter said, "For years, you were always there to take care of us. To pull bullets out of us when got ourselves shot up and to set broken bones, in those years before Granny Tate moved in. You helped Johnny raise the children and you provide all of us with meals. You've done so much for us over the years. You bought half of this saloon so you could have a seat on the Town Council and keep us all safe from Aloysius Randall, and you also did it to help me out. Don't think I don't know that."

"Well, Hunter, you're family too."

"Johnny is the heart of the family, but you've always been the rock. And in a way, you just pulled a bullet out of Johnny again."

Bertram Reed knocked on a hotel door in Bozeman. Room Seventeen.

The door opened. Aloysius Randall stood there. "Reed. Do come in."

He stepped aside and Reed walked into the room.

Randall had removed his jacket and tie and unbuttoned his vest. He had a cigar smoldering away in one hand, and a bottle of whiskey and a glass were on a small table.

Randall said, "Would you like a drink?"

"Thank you, but no. I have to report some unpleasant news. I failed, Mister Randall. The herd arrived in Cheyenne. Not all of it. In fact, not even half of it. There won't be enough for them to make the sale they needed, and I estimated they would have to sell off some land to avoid bankruptcy."

"Well, then we'll just buy the land they're selling. That is at least one step closer to our goal."

Reed shook his head. "We can't even do that. A buyer swooped in from California and gave them more than I ever would have offered. The sale was completed before I even knew it was happening. There won't be any way to force them to sell their ranch."

Randall took a puff off of his cigar. "What happened with the herd?"

Reed shrugged. "Sometimes plans just don't work out, I supposed. My man Chandler was found dead out on the range the McCabes use. I have to presume they were the ones who killed him, but I can't know for sure. The doctor in town said it looked like a knife wound in his chest. The other two men I hired, Jenkins and Lawson, are nowhere to be found. For all I know, they took the salary and rode off. If not for a hard storm that hit and scattered the herd, then my effort would have been an entire failure. I'm so incredibly sorry."

Randall nodded. "All right. We'll just have to try again. I hate to resort to this, but their ranch house is made of wood. A judiciously placed match could change the game entirely."

"Arson?"

"I am not fond of the idea. I had plans of living in that house. But now I'm forced to more drastic measures."

Reed held his hands up in a stopping motion. "Mister Randall, I can't."

Randall looked at him with a mixture of curiosity and annoyance. "What do you mean you can't?"

"I mean, I can't be a part of this anymore. That's also what I came up here to tell you. Chandler was killed. Who knows—I could be next. Those people are rough. It feels like I'm playing with dynamite when dealing with them. I came here to tell you I'm resigning. I'm catching the first stage to Cheyenne, and then I'm going back to Chicago."

Randall nodded. He was silent a moment like he was letting it all toss itself around in his mind. "I suppose there's nothing I can say to talk you out of it?"

Reed shook his head. "I'm afraid not."

Reed stood waiting for Randall to offer his hand

and to say something like, *You're a good man. I'm going to miss you.* Or, *You're going to be a hard man to replace.* The normal things you expect your employer to say when you are resigning. But Randall just stood silently, looking at him. His cigar was smoldering in one hand.

"Well, then," Reed said. "I'd best be going."

He turned toward the door, and Randall sprang into motion, stepping up behind him and at the same time pulling a small derringer from his vest pocket. He cocked it and while Reed was beginning to turn back to him, realizing Randall was scampering up behind him and hearing the gun cock, Randall shot him.

Reed's mouth opened as though he had been punched in the stomach. He took a staggering step backward and then fell to his knees.

Randall said, "No one quits on me, Bertram. That's something I thought you knew. You work for me until I dismiss you. This is a lesson I have to teach Victor Falcone, too. His day will come. But your day is here, right now."

The derringer was a Remington over-under, meaning it had two barrels one on top of the other, and held two shots. Randall had one bullet left, and he aimed the gun at Reed's forehead and squeezed the trigger, and then he had no bullets left.

A man came running in. He was a hard-muscled man and was in a white shirt, and a string tie that was a little crooked. He was wearing a holster tied down low on his right leg and a revolver was in his hand.

"Pennock," Randall said. "Took you long enough."

"Sorry. I was down stairs."

"No matter. Get this man out of here."

Reed was lying on his back, his eyes staring toward the ceiling. A bullet hole was in his forehead.

Randall said, "Dump him in an alley."

"Yes, sir," Pennock said, and slid his gun into his holster and knelt down to grab the body of Bertram

Reed under the shoulders and begin dragging it.

Randall said, "Make it look like a robbery. Take the wallet. You can keep any money in there."

Pennock nodded and said, "Thank you, sir."

A lumber mill had been set up in Jubilee and buying milled boards from them would have been convenient, but Johnny had decided it might be best to run up as little debt as possible with the merchants in town. He and Josh had paid off the men from the sale of the herd but had little money left over. Aunt Ginny had gone to Bozeman and she sent a wire to a land speculator she knew in California, and he purchased two thousand acres of McCabe land in the valley, which allowed Johnny and Josh to pay the ranch's debts, and there was a small cash reserve left over. But rebuilding the herd would take at least two years, so money was going to be scarce for a while.

Johnny decided he would be building his and Jessica's new cabin the old-fashioned way. Felling the trees himself, splitting them and forming them into timbers.

This was the way he had built the main house, and it was still standing strong.

He was working every day on the new cabin. Josh and Dusty and Charles helped out when they could.

Johnny and the boys had been back from the trail drive for six weeks, and the framework for the new cabin was now up. Johnny was putting the floor in, which meant laying hand-cut boards down across the joists and then drilling holes and pounding in hand-cut wooden pegs.

He stood up to rest his back. He found his back hurt as much as a full day in the saddle, just in different areas. He had pulled off his shirt, and his undershirt was streaked with sweat.

His gunbelt was nearby, but the fact that he

didn't need it belted on was a sign that he was making progress. Even though he had been shot at on the trail drive, he was still able to sleep with the gunbelt slung over the edge of the bed. When he and Jessica were at the ranch house, he was able to leave his gun upstairs.

He twisted his back first one way and then the other, snapping out a couple of kinks. He saw Jessica standing off by the edge of the floor he was building, and he figured it might be a good time for a break, so he stepped out of the framework and walked over to her.

She looked up at him with a smile. He didn't think he would ever grow tired of looking at her.

He wasn't going to actually touch her because he was covered with dirt and sweat. It was now the middle of summer and the days were hot, even at this altitude. But she sort of snuggled into him, so he put his arm around her anyway.

He said, "I should have the floor finished today. If one of the boys can help me, we'll have the roof done in a day or two. Then I'll start on the chimney. I'll build it like the one at the house. Out of stones. There's plenty of 'em right down there on the canyon floor."

From where they were standing, they had an open view of the canyon floor. Thunder was down there, running about like it felt good to be alive.

She said, "I think Thunder missed you while you were gone."

"I sure missed him. More'n once I wished I had him with us."

Old Blue was down there, too. He stood lazily chewing some grass. When Johnny and the boys had been riding back from Cheyenne, they found Blue standing on the grassy summit of a long low hill, about twenty miles from where the twisters had struck. He was standing there like he was waiting for them, so they brought him home. They found twelve additional steers with their brands on them, so they brought them home as well.

She said, "I think Old Blue's enjoying his retirement."

"He's earned it."

She was smiling. "You know, this little canyon already feels like home."

"At this rate, we'll be moved in before winter."

She said, "We'll raise Cora here. And other children, too."

He looked at her. "Other children?"

"Well, at least one more."

"Are you trying to tell me something?"

She gave a broad, beaming smile. "Well, when you came back from the trail drive, I remember I welcomed you home right proper. Such things tend to have consequences."

Johnny found himself smiling. At his age, he hadn't thought he would become a father again.

He pulled her in for long tight hug.

He said, "There's no one I would rather build a life with."

She nodded, her face rubbing against his shoulder. "And we'll build that life right here. In our little canyon. Our own little corner of the world."

Made in the USA
Monee, IL
06 June 2021